HE THOUGHT HE COULD POSSESS THEM BOTH, UNTIL DESTINY FORCED HIM TO CHOOSE. . . .

DAVID—A successful writer, a respected university professor, he toyed with memory, love—and fire—trying to recapture the past and the beautiful woman he had never truly known. . . .

FRONY—She was older, wiser, his teacher in the art of love. She would haunt his days and nights. David thought he could never rest until he held her in his arms again. . . .

GRACE—Lascivious, abandoned, she was the wanton youthful image of her mother, the forbidden fruit he couldn't resist, that he had to reach out and taste. . . .

They were bound to one another by blood, by passions of the past, and the menacing shadows that lingered from childhood . . . shadows that watched . . . waited . . . threatening them all from the . . .

WIDOW'S WALK

WIDOW'S WALK

William Tucker

A DELL BOOK

Published by
Dell Publishing Co., Inc.
1 Dag Hammarskjold Plaza
New York, New York 10017

Dell ® TM 681510, Dell Publishing Co., Inc.

ISBN 0-440-19500-4

Printed in the United States of America

First printing—November 1983

My thanks to
A.C.J. Brickel, Jr., M.D., F.A.A.N.,
for providing my story
with medical believability.

To Betty Lee

Chapter One

David stepped back a few paces from the front porch steps and looked up through the balustrade that marched around the square of the widow's walk. Grace leaned over the railing and looked down at him for a moment and then raised her head to stare toward the river again. She stood exactly the way her mother would stand, he thought—relaxed, with her forearms crossed on the railing and her legs crossed at the ankles. Well, why not? Frony and Grace were more alike than any two people David had ever known.

"Why did you buy this old barn?" she shouted from thirty feet above. "It's sixty miles from the ocean and five hundred yards from the river." She leaned farther over the rail, projecting her voice down at him to make her point. "You can't even see the goddamn river, just a few slivers of it through the trees."

"You can see the river when the trees are bare in the fall," David said a little defensively.

"Are you looking up my dress?" She had straightened and was standing with her legs slightly apart. Her thighs curved into the darkness of her skirt.

"Yes."

"Do you want me to take it off? I don't have anything on underneath."

"For God's sake, Grace!" he said and walked into the house.

He could have answered her easily—the question about why he had bought the house over a year ago. He could have said,

"Because I've always wanted it." But he didn't feel like explaining even that much.

She was right about the house—it was something of a phony, an architectural bastard, standing on this hill so far inland. It would have been more legitimate if it were on the shore of some ocean or on the bank of some broad and navigable river. And with its widow's walk and rococo latticework around the porches, it had pretensions to more age than it could claim, although it was over a hundred years old. David was sure Alfred Parsons, the old academic grandee from the university a half mile to the east, had built it to suit himself; he hadn't cared that it was out of place and out of time.

David didn't care, either. He had wanted to live in it for almost thirty years, since the first time he'd sat in the grass on the university's south campus and stared at it while his parents spread the picnic food on the old tablecloth.

In those days, before the central Virginia town grew up around the university, the south campus was far enough away from David's neighborhood to qualify as an excursion. A few families in town used it as a picnic ground because it was such a beautiful place, five hundred acres of rolling greensward with a few maple trees randomly scattered to provide shade. The university buildings were a mile away, clustered on the north side of the school's property, and the students rarely used the south campus.

During those summer excursions David would sit out there in the grass and look at *his* house, the white clapboards of its southern front shining brilliantly in the summer sunlight, and he would imagine himself standing on the widow's walk with a telescope pressed to a searching eye. Maybe, he thought, from up there he'd be able to see all the way to the coast, or miles up and down the river. His feeling for the house must have been strong to have lasted through all the years, until the time came when he could have it.

One thing that still astonished him was that the house never diminished from his boyhood vision of it. Everything else had grown smaller as he grew larger. When he came home from college the first time, his parents' house had shrunk and the distances in his neighborhood had grown shorter. His father was not quite so tall, and his mother was almost fragile standing beside a son who had outstripped her by six inches. But this house never changed when he drove out to College Road and stood looking up at it.

Over the years the house and property had come to be known as Parsons, an abbreviation of "the old Parsons place." Because of its size and isolation and the reclusiveness of generation after generation of occupants, the house had taken on an air of mystery. Although no murders or legends of crazed and violent wives or sisters locked in attic rooms could be credited to Parsons, there was something sinister about the place, some implied threat to a stranger who would dare to venture close.

This was fine with David. He loved the austere privacy of the place, with still no obvious encroachment from the houses that kept creeping closer to the property's borders as the town expanded. Except for a few small parcels of land to the west, sold off by one of Parsons's previous owners, the estate was still intact—thirty acres of near wilderness, except for the hilltop plot where the house stood. The land rolled gently from the riverbank to the front of the property where the hill began, rising steeply for several hundred yards to a flat plain two hundred feet above the level of the south campus to the southeast. Parsons was situated close to the front of this surprisingly level plateau, which continued three hundred feet to the north to form a deep field back of the house. At the property's north boundary a fringe of maples edged an escarpment that fell vertically for over a hundred feet to the river's tributary. To the west the land was heavily wooded and fell away from the house more gently than did the southern slope, and, to the east, the maple fringe continued to the cut made on that side of the hill when College Road had been built fifty years before.

Perhaps the one thing that always appealed to David about Parsons was its protectedness from the intrusion of the outside world. It sat on its hill in almost arrogant inaccessibility from all sides. The backyard, as big as a football field and wooded on three sides, was his joyous discovery. He hadn't even guessed it would be such a glorious pool of green, with just the number of maple and tulip trees spaced about to give it the comfortable, unmanicured appearance of a highland meadow. This yard became his private domain, unseen from any view except from the house itself, so remote and isolated that he deluded himself into thinking no uninvited eye could penetrate it.

None of the dimensions of Parsons was modest. The house was a large square with a broad gallery running its front length. Deep and elaborate moldings bordered the high ceilings of the enormous rooms. Heavy sliding doors opened from the center hall to the drawing room on the right and library on the left. The dining room could easily accommodate a table for two dozen, and the kitchen was too large for a single person to work in conveniently. An informal parlor larger than most modern living rooms overlooked the field from the house's northeast corner.

On the second floor there were six bedrooms, four baths, and a sitting room. Dormers cut into the roof's slope gave light to the three bedrooms, bath, and small sitting room on the third floor. A back staircase led from these third-floor servants' quarters to the kitchen, and an outside stairway led from a small railed platform at the third-floor level up to the widow's walk.

The house was complex and interesting and much too big for David. But he loved it; he wandered its sparsely furnished rooms and gloried in its bigness. He sat on the front gallery like a baron, regretting all the years he hadn't lived there, hadn't been able to look down the front slope toward the river.

David Fleming had done many things during those twenty-plus years between the dream and the actuality of his possession of Parsons. He had grown up in the same neighborhood with Frony Campbell and had loved her until she left him—a shattered fifteen-year-old boy—to marry D—Dwight Bennett. He had hated her after that for being three years older than he was and for giving birth to Grace when she was only nineteen years old instead of waiting for him to grow up and father her child. Sometime during the growing up he started to love Frony again and he never stopped, though he didn't see her again for years. He loved her when he was with other girls in high school and college. He loved her while he was in New York working on the newspaper and then the magazine, and he even loved her during the two miserable years he was married to Helen Connelly. But he loved her most while he was writing his book, because it was about her. Although she didn't know it, Frony had drawn him back to this town when he discovered, six months after his book was published, that he could soon afford to leave the strangling magazine job that had once so intoxicated him and the crushing city that had once put the fever of excitement in his blood. The money from the book (more than he had ever imagined he would have) and the fame gave him the freedom to come home and sit on the university's journalism faculty. At the time, he didn't even know he could buy Parsons; he was just coming back home, back to where he and Frony had begun.

Of course, the money also allowed him to come back and complicate his life with the two women—Frony, who had moved back to town four years ago and who was responsible for most of his life's joy and despair, and her daughter, Grace, who was her unbelievable replica, with the same fair skin and raven hair and unusual height. One day nine months ago Grace had walked off the university campus onto David's front porch and into his life with no more introduction than "Hi, I'm Grace Bennett, Frony's daughter. Madelyn Walker said I should come over and say hello." Madelyn was an old friend of David and Frony's and a friend of Grace's now as well. Because David had been in town a few months, he was surprised he and Grace hadn't already crossed paths, either on campus or in Frony's company. But Grace had been busy with her classes and friends and he with his, and evidently she had been asserting her independence from her mother, because Frony said she spent little time at home these days.

It had all been so innocent in the beginning, Grace being encouraged to come over and say hello to an old friend of her mother's. But the innocence stopped when Grace fell deeply in love with David. It stopped when David admitted to himself that Grace was more than a five-foot ten-inch package of energy and spontaneity and excitement. The innocence ended on the couch in David's study six months after Grace first stepped onto Parsons's front porch.

That's when the guilt and the sense of betrayal began, because of Frony, because she didn't know. David was totally confused, no longer sure how he felt about Frony. He had seen her fairly often during the past year, and he knew he still loved her, but he was baffled by the fact that she would not let him make love to her, would not resume the intimacy they had once shared. When he had moved back to town they had started over almost like strangers— she widowed, he divorced—being polite and proper, and they still hadn't really relaxed with each other. She seemed to ignore their past emotional and physical connections, which were so unforgettable to David. Without actually lying to anyone, though, David let his friends—including Grace—assume he and Frony were sleeping together.

Grace didn't see herself as a competitor to her mother. She just wanted David, complete, with no sharing and no compromise. She wanted him to stop seeing Frony, to *do* something that would solve the problems their relationship caused. But David didn't know what to do.

"I don't have any more classes today," Grace said from the door of the study where David was sitting at his paper-strewn desk, thinking. He hadn't heard her come down the stairs, and started at the sound of her voice.

He frowned because he knew what she was thinking. "Neither do I. But I guess you know that."

"Do you want me to stay and fix us something to eat later?" David hesitated, and a little sharpness came into her voice when she asked, "Are you expecting Mother to come up here?"

"No, I don't expect her."

"David, do you want me to stay?"

Before answering, he sat for a few moments thinking what a fool he was. "Yes, Grace. I want you to stay."

Her smile indicated the small victory that she knew had never really been in doubt, and she started forward, then paused, undecided whether to come into the study. On other occasions he had asked her not to bother him when he was working.

"How long will you be?" she asked.

"An hour, maybe less. Go on out back, and take a beach towel for me. Do you want something to read?"

"I brought something. I'm doing a paper. Maybe you would look at what I've done when you come out." She grinned, and David smiled in spite of himself. Again, he knew what she was thinking. They would never get around to it.

"Stay in the shade, Grace," he called as she walked down the hall toward the back of the house.

Grace couldn't take the sun. Her skin was like Frony's, unbelievably smooth and white with the slight translucence that makes some brunettes so incredibly beautiful. This comparison of the two women brought David's thoughts back to where they had been before Grace interrupted them. But the thoughts came in fragments, moving from Frony and Grace to his new book, which was going badly—the novel of epic proportions that would assure his place in the literary sun. It was impossible for him to work with Grace so close, lying out in the field on a beach towel.

David looked around the study as he had done countless times before, with the same feeling of possessiveness. It was a scholar's room, paneled in dark oak with bookshelves on three walls from wainscoting to ceiling. There was only one window, heavily draped, and it bisected the bookshelves on the south wall. The north wall was similarly divided by a broad unmanteled fireplace. David hadn't properly furnished the room; his desk looked pitifully small against the west wall, which was an unbroken thirty-foot expanse of almost empty bookshelves. Even the light from his desk lamp seemed sallow in the huge room, so diffuse that it picked up only occasional umber gleams from the dark woodwork. His library, so carefully collected over the years, filled only a third of the shelves, and the empty spaces gave the room an appearance of vacancy and disuse. An ear-ringing hollowness that caused David to shudder and look apprehensively over his shoulder would sometimes drive him to a more cheerful part of the house.

Still, this was his favorite room. All he needed was time to furnish it and fill the shelves with books he wanted, selected one by one. David had made a feeble beginning with the leather couch in front of the fireplace. That and a dictionary stand were the only other furnishings besides his desk and chair.

On top of the desk were a pile of papers he dreaded grading and a three-quarter-inch stack of pages from the manuscript of the book he knew he should be working on. He looked distastefully from one to the other. The book was going badly because he couldn't concentrate on it; he hadn't written a usable line in over a month, and he didn't know why. His plot was solid and his research was good and his characters were alive because he knew every one of them. They were composites of the people he had known in that amoral world of journalism, and he was writing a moral novel about them. David riffled through the student papers from his creative-writing class. They would be passionate and terrible, just as all the ones before had been. He hadn't detected an ounce of talent in any of the twenty-six students—all of whom wanted, with varying degrees of desperation, to become writers.

"Get down to it, Fleming," David admonished himself aloud in his great empty study. "Grace can wait."

Thirty minutes later he threw down the red grading pen and stood up. He had graded only four papers and each had seemed worse than the one before. David realized that he was taking out his frustration on his students, who weren't supposed to be able to write—they were paying their tuition to learn. With this realization came a sense of guilt, to add to the guilt he had come to feel in the last several months since he and Grace had first seduced each other. He sighed and walked out of the house into the field.

Chapter Two

Grace was lying on her stomach in the sun, propped up on her elbows with a notebook in front of her, and as David approached, she closed the notebook and turned to lie on her back. She was completely nude and lay in a posture of childlike immodesty with her legs slightly spread. He had seen her like this before, and as he stood looking down at her, it registered as it always did that she was the most beautiful woman he had ever seen. The rough surface of the towel had embossed her thighs and stomach, but her breasts were smooth and, though large like Frony's, stood remarkably erect, tipped with the conical pink buds of her nipples. A light dew of perspiration had formed at her hairline, and moisture also glistened in the dark pubic triangle. Grace's hair was jet-black and she wore it short and parted in the center, falling in deep waves on either side of her face. With one hand she shaded her eyes as she looked up at David and with the other patted the beach towel she had spread out beside hers.

"Come down here," she invited.

"You're getting pink," he observed, ignoring the invitation. "Why don't you lie in the shade?"

She sat up and examined herself, craning to look at her shoulder. Her breasts jutted marvelously as she twisted from side to side. There wasn't a wrinkle in her flat belly. "I'm just about right, from what I can see," she judged. "What about my back?" She turned for him to see. "Am I even all over?"

David paused long enough to give weight to his appraisal. The slanting rays of the late afternoon sun had brought a rosy glow to her skin.

"You're about thirty minutes overdone all over. I don't like sunburned women."

"I'm not sunburned. This is the beginning of a great tan," Grace said with conviction.

"I don't like tanned women," David said, which was true. "I like women with white skin. I liked you much better an hour ago."

"I think you like me enough right now," she opined as her eyes slipped down to the front of his pants. A thin line of white teeth showed between her lips as she smiled knowingly up at him. Abruptly she turned and picked up her dress, which was lying in the grass beside her towel. For a moment David thought she was going to put it on, but she was only looking for her wristwatch, which was under it. He noticed that there were no other clothes, no brassiere or panties, and realized that she had sat in her classes all morning with nothing on but that pale-blue nylon jersey dress. It was an arousing thought.

Grace consulted the watch.

"I think you're especially ready today," she said as she looked thoughtfully at him and then down at the watch again. "I'll give you ten minutes."

David walked over to the tree and sat down in the shady grass, leaning against the trunk. He was relatively fair-skinned himself, with that complexion that frequently accompanies auburn hair. "Courtesans always had white skin, avoided the sun," he pronounced. "Even the first-class whores today have milky white bodies."

"Bullshit."

"No, it's true. Somerset Maugham said so."

"Somerset Maugham's an old fart."

"Courtesans didn't say 'bullshit' and 'fart.'"

"Did they say 'fuck'?"

"No. Only lower-class whores with suntans and smart-assed young girls said 'fuck.'"

Before he could get up she crossed the ten feet that separated them and was on top of him, her fingers digging into his ribs, tickling, and her mouth fastened on the side of his throat. He writhed in the grass, struggling to get her tormenting fingers out of his ribs and to dislodge her sucking mouth. Convulsions of laughter made his attempts feeble. Grace locked his leg between hers and they rolled over and over until, defeated by his ticklishness, David lay helplessly on his back, alternately whooping and giggling. Sensing her victory, Grace relaxed her fingers and massaged his burning throat with her tongue until the spasms died from his nerves. Confident now that he wouldn't resist, she released his leg from between hers and came up to straddle him at the waist. David's shirt had opened and he could feel the warm wetness of her sex on his belly. She was aroused and knew that he could feel her slickness as she moved to widen herself on him. Her breasts bobbed tantalizingly over him, but as he reached to cup them in his hands she grasped his wrists and forced his arms down on his chest. She leaned over until their faces were about six inches apart.

"Say, 'Grace and I are going to fuck in the grass under the tulip tree.' "

Without waiting for David's repetition, she leaned down and ran her tongue over his lips. Before he could take it into his mouth, she unstraddled him, turned, and began unbuckling his belt.

"Wait, I'll do it," he said and kicked the loafers from his sockless feet as he stood up.

"Take everything off. Hurry!" Her voice was urgent. He shucked his shirt and danced out of his pants and shorts.

She came and pressed herself against him, and because she was only several inches shorter than his six feet, he hardly had to bend to kiss her. She gave him her tongue and flattened her breasts against his chest. Their thighs searched between each other's legs, and their hands explored up and down each other's back. David's hands settled on her buttocks and pulled her into him.

The kiss was long, but the other urgency parted them. As they drew apart, Grace said, "You lie down."

Again she straddled him, more carefully this time, lowering herself, gasping as he entered her. Before she started her motion she leaned forward for him to take her breast into his mouth. And when she began to move, rocking slowly at first, then faster and faster, he realized they had waited too long; it would be quick for both of them. After a minute, maybe two, the rolling nerve thunder began with the wail in her throat. Her nipple popped from his sucking mouth as she threw herself upright to get more purchase from her thighs—jolting straight down on him, holding her own breasts. He lifted to meet her thrusts. The panting breath from her open mouth was in the same rhythm, as though he were pumping it out of her from below. When his spasm started, he felt her first shudder of climax and watched her wildly rolling eyes until she cried out, "Now! Now!" and battered him into the earth, plunged down on him with the full slap of her buttocks on his open thighs, mindlessly taking from him and giving herself to him in that final dilation of her insides to accept his gorge—until she collapsed on his chest.

The exhaustion of their lovemaking flattened them side by side on the ground, momentarily too spent even to speak. David stared into the branches of the tulip tree, thinking once again about his inability to come to terms with his feelings for this girl and her mother.

Then he knew Grace was going to begin talking about it; she had to, because lately she had been less willing to leave the subject alone.

"Is it like that with her?"

David didn't answer.

"She's three years older than you are."

"We've been through this before, Grace."

"Well, she is. She'll be forty on her next birthday."

"And I'll be thirty-seven and you'll be twenty-one," he said somewhat impatiently. "Try your arithmetic on my being sixteen years older than you are."

"We've been through that, too."

"That's right. So what's the use of digging this up every time we're together?"

"We've got to talk about it. Do you love her?"

David sat up so abruptly that it startled her. She looked at him in mild alarm, afraid he would leave.

"I'm sorry I asked that again," she apologized.

His impulse had been to get up and walk away to somehow avoid the frustration of trying to cope with her questions. He had done that in the past, but the questions still remained to be asked over and over again. They might as well talk it out now. But he was hesitant to put into words these feelings he didn't understand himself, and he was also very conscious that anything he said could change the status of his relationship with Grace—or with Frony.

For a while he sat sorting out in his mind what he should say, and then he lay back down, propping his head in the palm of his hand so he could look into her face.

"Grace, I want to explain how I feel, and I don't want you to say anything until I finish. If you still have any questions after I'm through, I'll try to answer them as honestly as I can. Okay?"

She paused only briefly before she said, "Okay." It was evident in her eyes that while she might wish she had never persisted with her questions, she was determined to hear what he had to say.

"I've loved Frony since I was a little kid, seven or eight years old; it's been so long I can't remember. We grew up together, and I believe I know more about her than any man alive does, even though there were long times over the years when I didn't see much of her. I wasn't around her when she was your age, so maybe I'm trying to make up with you what I missed with her." A frown flickered on her face when he said this, but Grace made no effort to speak.

"I don't mean you're a substitute for Frony—I don't fantasize when you and I are together—but I don't think any love is separate and apart from everything else. I think a part of why I love you is that you're a part of her, and I can't completely separate you from what I've felt for so long. After she married D and went away with him, I didn't see her again for sixteen years, not until a year after D died, but I followed her in my mind during all that time as we both grew older. I pictured what she would look like, how she would change. So, when I saw her again she was thirty-four and she looked exactly as I thought she would. I had also pictured her in my mind when she was your age, and Grace, *you* are exactly as I conjured her then. That first time I saw you through the screen door, standing on my front porch the way she stands, I thought I was experiencing déjà vu, because I had seen you years before, in my mind's eye." Here he paused, until the image of that first jolting discovery of Grace had faded enough to allow him to go on. His hesitation didn't prompt her to speak; instead she turned on her side and forced him to lie flat so that her head rested on his shoulder, her arm across his chest, and her leg crooked across his thighs.

"Sometimes when we're together I get the feeling I'm reliving something from a different time in my life, as if I'm getting a second chance, and some of the things that were empty and painful can be erased and replaced with what I wanted them to be. You've done that for me, Grace, and I love you for it—it's not gratitude, and it's not the same thing I feel for Frony. I just love you, and I can't explain it any better than I have."

How else could he say it? Without Frony, Grace would be enough, and the sixteen years that separated them wouldn't matter. The unsettling thought came to him that without having loved Frony *he* wouldn't be enough, but the thought was too complex to pursue.

He could feel Grace's mouth move on his shoulder.

"Am I just a reflection of my mother to you?" she asked without any petulance in her voice.

"I hoped it wouldn't come out like that, Grace. That's not what I meant about déjà vu."

"Would you love me if you had never known her?" She seemed to be reading David's mind.

"Desperately." He couldn't resist going on with the other part of the thought that had disturbed him. "Would *you* love *me* if we were starting from scratch, just you and me?"

This question brought her head up off his shoulder so she could look down into his face. She was so quick to understand, that there was anger in her intelligent eyes. "David, do you think I'm competing with her? Do you think that's all there is to it?"

"I've wondered, Grace," he admitted. "I can't help wondering what would have happened if we had come across each other under different circumstances, with different backgrounds in a different town."

"It would be the same. I don't love you because of anything to do with my mother, and I don't keep asking you if you love her because I want to take you away from her. I just want to be sure you're not in love with something you've created out of twenty years of memories, something that doesn't really exist after all this time. Maybe it never existed, not the way you think it did."

David had thought about that himself. Maybe he had edited and rearranged his memories of what he and Frony had been to each other to take out most of the pain. Maybe his resulting conclusions were in fact inaccurate. The remoteness in his relationship with Frony now was certainly not consistent with the depth of his feelings for her. He was amazed at how much Grace seemed to understand.

"We haven't solved our problem, have we?" he asked.

"No. But I understand what you said, David, about you and Mother and what she's meant to you over the years. Still, I just believe that it's you and me now. I can wait until you accept it. Just don't make it too long."

Her head was still propped in her hand as she smiled down on David. She leaned down to kiss him and their tongues explored each other's mouth as they strained their bodies together. When they broke apart he was erect again.

"Do you want to do it now?" She had felt him against her.

"No, not now, I . . ."

"Is what we've done so terrible?" She seemed to sense that once they really talked about it, things would change, would become more complicated than just sex.

"It is if Frony gets hurt by what we've done."

"Does she know anything about us?" she asked in sudden alarm. "Has she said anything?"

"No, she doesn't know."

"Doesn't she suspect something? She knows I come over here sometimes after class."

"Curiosity, Grace. She believes you just come over to poke your fingers through the cage of the eccentric old novelist."

"Is this our last day together, David?" she asked him. "Do you want me to come over here anymore?"

"Maybe we'd better cool off for a while, Grace. Leave it alone for a week or so. This is the first time we've really talked about what we feel for each other and what it means, and I want both of us to think about how to handle it."

Grace's face was solemn as she considered what he had said.

"Will you let me spend the night, David?" she finally asked.

"Grace, I . . ."

"I'll get up early and go back to the dorm to change," she reasoned.

They had never slept together, not really slept after all the passion was gone and most of the hours of the night were left to lie together without any urgency to disturb their rest.

"Umm," David deliberated. Up until now some peculiar sense of propriety had kept Grace from staying all night at Parsons, but the idea did appeal to him.

"I know you want to."

"Umm . . . well, I . . ."

"Then, it's settled," she pronounced, sitting up cross-legged by his side. "Listen to me, David. I thought it all out while you were making up your mind. Let's don't put our clothes back on at all until I leave in the morning." She paused, the wantonness of the idea captivating her. "You lie out here and take a nap, and I'll go in and fix us something to eat. I'll bring it out here, and we can eat, and then . . ."

"Grace, I've got work to do."

"You don't have to grade those papers today, and you haven't written anything in a month. Please, David, not tonight. Let's just do what we want to do until I leave in the morning."

She was right. He didn't really have to grade the papers or worry about the book in the next twelve hours.

"All right. What else have you got planned?"

"There's a full moon tonight—it'll be up in another hour or so—and I want to sit out there"—she pointed to the middle of the field—"mother naked and eat in the moonlight."

She looked at him expectantly, her excited eyes darting over his face, waiting for him to react to what she considered an outrageous proposal.

"Well, I must confess I've never sat over there in the moonlight mother naked and eaten dinner with an equally naked nymphomaniac."

"That brings up the other thing I want to do in the moonlight," she said with as much of a leer as she could manage.

"Why, what's that, Grace?" he asked innocently.

"I want to fuck in the moonlight," she said and bounded to her feet. He slapped her behind as she ran past him toward the house.

It was past eleven o'clock. They had done everything Grace had wanted to do and lay on the picnic blanket passing a cigarette back and forth. David took the last drag and flipped it away. It made a glowing arc against the dark shadow of the trees.

"Maybe you'd better help the old man to bed," he said as he sat up. He felt a slight giddiness from lying so long looking into the comparative brightness of the moonlit sky. The trees that lined the west side of the field formed a jagged black monolith, absorbing the soft moonlight. As he looked into them, adjusting his eyes to their dark fringe against the sky, a pale spot seemed to move within their shadows a hundred feet away. Squinting, he leaned forward. Grace caught the tenseness and sat up by his side.

"What is it, David?" she asked and followed his straining stare with hers.

But the dim lantern of a face, hovering six feet above the ground, was gone, had receded as he stared into the dark umbra of the woods.

"Nothing." He stood and reached for Grace's hand to help her up. "Let's go in."

She walked ahead of him and several times he turned his head to look back into the trees. A face! Had it been a face? Someone lurking in the woods watching them make love, still there even an hour after they had finished? Or had it been a moon spot that remained on his eye to be transposed onto that darker background? He shook his head in an effort to clear the apparition from his mind.

Just as he was drifting into sleep Grace whispered her question in the dark. "What was it you saw, David?"

He didn't follow her; he was too close to the edge of sleep. "What?" he asked.

"What was it in the woods? Was it someone watching us?"

"What did you see, Grace?"

"This spot. Maybe a face. I couldn't tell—it was so dim, so far away."

"You saw it, too."

"Yes, I saw it. I can't believe anybody would be out there in those woods."

David felt her slight shudder.

"I can't either, sweetheart. Go to sleep so you can get up in the morning without making a lot of noise."

David dreamt of another time when he and another girl had made love on the edge of another wood.

Chapter Three

David and Frony grew up in the same neighborhood of their medium-sized city sixty miles from the Virginia coast. There were nine kids in a two-block length of Seneca Street, and they were all within four years of the same age.

David lived on one corner of the two-block stretch and the Hammond boy, whom everybody called Simple Son, lived directly across the street. If Simple Son were included in the group, the number of neighborhood kids would have been ten. But he wasn't included because he was five years older than any of them and because he was feebleminded. Dwight Bennett, whom everyone called D, lived next to the Hammonds, and Gilbert Thomas lived several houses down on the same side of the street. Madelyn Phillips, Glenn Walker, the McKenna twins, Dick and Howard, all lived in the next block.

Frony, whose real name was Margaret Louise Campbell, lived four houses from David with two old-maid cousins, Hazel and Mary Henderson, both over twenty years older than she, and with her aunt—her father's sister—and her aunt's husband. Frony's mother was dead and her father was a phantomlike character who seemed to show up every couple of years to check on her, only to disappear after a few days, leaving not so much as the mention of his name in his wake.

Hazel and Mary Henderson were both good-natured women in their late thirties, not at all embittered by spinsterhood, and although he didn't really know, David suspected the name Frony was their invention. Some of David's earliest and most pleasant recollections involved the Henderson women and their friendship with his parents. Almost every warm summer evening the wicker-seated rocking chairs would be carried from the front porches and arranged in someone's front yard for the endless after-supper conversations. Sometimes the gathering would be at the Bennetts' or the Thomases', but most often it was in David's front yard or the Hendersons', and the most constant of the nighttime talkers were his parents and Hazel and Mary Henderson. Hazel's sharp hoots of laughter and Mary's soft chuckle were always there in the murmuring summer sounds that rose and fell in the constant rhythms of David's memory.

They were like part of his family, more like aunts than the real ones he never saw, and Frony was the authentic cousin. So looking back it was understandable that Frony and David should be so close when he was fourteen. Harder to understand was why she abandoned him for D.

D was older than any of them, except Simple Son, whose age didn't count because he was too simple to play any of their games with them. Then came Frony, a year younger than D, and after her, grouped at one-year intervals, were Glenn and Gilbert, then Madelyn, Dick, and Howard. David was the youngest of all and didn't compete much with the others, especially not with D or Frony, who ruled them all from the beginning.

David's separation from Frony was gradual, but nonetheless unalterable, especially during the three years before she entered high school. To him the ignominy of still being in grade school was almost unbearable; he was still a little boy and she was a magnificently formed girl of fifteen who had grown smoothly, with no period of teen-age gawkiness to give him comfort. She was D's girl, and David was wildly in love with her, and therefore he was miserable.

Fortunately, there were distractions along the way. When David was ten, Simple Son was taken away for killing his mother. Although he didn't understand at the time exactly what had happened, David learned the story through overheard whisperings of his parents and neighbors.

"Strangled her," he heard them say. "Must have thought she was a ghost the way she looked in that white nightgown. I never could understand why she let Simple Son listen to the kids tell those spooky stories. He must have woken up and seen her standing there in that white nightgown. Scared the bejesus out of him. I bet that's why he did it." David experienced a strange pang of loss—which would later change to guilt—when Simple Son, a hulking man-boy of nineteen, was taken from the house across the street, by two men who had come down from Whitfield, the state sanitarium.

Of course, he didn't understand either of his losses—his gradual separation from Frony or the abrupt departure of Simple Son. But his young mind didn't dwell on such anxiety—instead, David lapsed into prolonged states of happiness that were disturbed only by jealousy at the sight of Frony and D walking hand in hand.

A few months after David's twelfth birthday his pubescence was upon him, and he achieved a precocious erection thinking about Frony's breasts and the considerable probability that D had felt them, had possibly even seen them. Standing on his desk chair, David examined this throbbing marvel from all angles in the mirror over his clothes chest. (It would be another year before Gilbert Thomas and Glenn Walker showed him how to masturbate under the bleachers of the high school football stadium.)

His first tight-lipped kisses came from girls he hardly knew, at Halloween and birthday parties, where he played girl-invented kissing games. These embarrassing public embraces were the precursors of more private fumblings with Dorothy Ann Fagan. They kissed with softer lips but with closed mouths as they pressed together in the darkness of her front porch, so dreadfully frightened of each other that their hands fluttered in the helpless ignorance of what could be touched. David was terrified that some forbidden caress would bring so strong a rebuke that the kissing would stop. So they held each other's arms and ground their genitals together.

David was grateful to Dorothy Ann for the year and a half of relief she gave him from his Frony mania. She allowed herself to be his first adolescent sweetheart. Although he shared her time and affection with the McKenna twins and a few other boys from out of the neighborhood, she allowed David a possessiveness, gave him a certain preferential position over all the rest. She helped him get to be fourteen and a half without playing the melancholy fool that he would have played otherwise, then delivered him to Frony in a state of reasonably good emotional health.

The week after D graduated from high school he left town. Several times David saw Frony walk past his house alone, looking across the street at the Bennetts' place as if she expected D to come out and join her. She would walk slowly past David's front yard, then quicken her pace until she reached her house four doors down the street. One day in late June, David was sitting on the front porch drinking iced tea and thinking about going to the movies when Frony ran diagonally across his lawn, jumped the two steps to the porch, and plopped into the wicker-bottom chair next to him. She was barefoot and had on a pair of shorts and a halter top. The hair around her face was wet with sweat so that it matted at her temples. She was breathing heavily as though she had been running for quite a while.

"Where've you been, David? I haven't seen much of you lately." She was still a little out of breath, and her chest heaved as she talked.

His first instinct was to be petulant. He had been right here—she just hadn't noticed. That was the thing that bothered him the most. During the years he spent being absolutely insanely in love with her, he had been to her house a hundred times. They had talked to each other, and he had sat around talking to Hazel and Mary and to Mr. and Mrs. Henderson. He was almost part of the family. For God's sake! Where had he been? He's been dying in Dorothy Ann's arms.

"You been running? You're all sweaty."

Frony ran a flattened forefinger down the side of her face and collected a fingerful of sweat. She flipped her finger and the moisture made a pattern of dark spots on the porch floor. It was a masculine gesture, but for some reason it didn't make her appear unfeminine. Her sex was so completely obvious in the way she was dressed. David watched a little pool of sweat collect in the depression at the bottom of her throat, overflow, and trickle down between her breasts.

"I raced a kid on a bicycle for a couple of blocks. Got any more of that iced tea?"

"Yeah. Wait a minute." David went inside, fixed the tea, and came back with it. When he handed her the glass she didn't take it. She was staring across the street at the Bennetts' house. He thrust the glass in front of her face. "Here," he said.

She was startled and almost knocked the glass from his hand when she reached for it. "Thanks, David." She thirstily drank half the liquid before removing the glass from her lips. With a satisfied sigh she slouched in the chair with her legs straight out in front of her. "Boy, I was thirsty."

"Where's D, Frony?" David was almost afraid to ask, afraid to bring up D's name, but he had to know. D lived directly across the street and David didn't even know where he was, just that he hadn't seen him in over three weeks.

She hesitated only briefly before she answered. "He's in Norfolk. He enlisted in the Navy."

Well, I'll be damned! David thought. So that's it, enlisted. And the Navy, all the way over in Norfolk. He'd be gone all summer, at least.

Frony was looking across the street again, so he leaned forward in his chair to try to get her attention.

"Why'd he do that?" he asked.

"He wants to be a pilot. That's all he talked about for the last six months."

"But I thought he was going to college. He was supposed to go to medical school." David had heard the Bennetts talk about *that* enough. D's father was Dr. Bennett, David's doctor, and just about everybody else's on the street. He had planned for his son to go to medical school since the time he was born. "I'll bet Dr. Bennett had a fit over him going off to the Navy."

"Yeah, he did," Frony said with a little giggle. "He wanted D to go to the university in the worst kind of way."

"Didn't Dr. Bennett try to stop him?" David couldn't believe that D could just decide he wasn't going to do what his father had wanted him to do for so long. He thought about how disappointed Dr. Bennett must be, about how disappointed his own father would be if he didn't go to college. There had been a lot of talk about *that*, already. "My dad wouldn't let me just decide not to go to college."

"You're not even fifteen yet, David. D's eighteen, almost nineteen," she said a little defiantly.

David couldn't understand what difference those extra years made in terms of the freedom to decide about something as important as college. But he was afraid Frony would say something more about his age that would put her out of reach— something his mother would say, like "Wait till you're a little older, David. Then you'll understand." So he dissembled. "He won't be nineteen until December, the week before Christmas. The Bennetts always have trouble with presents because—"

Frony jumped up and put her hands on the arms of his rocking chair. She rocked him back and forth so violently that he almost pitched out on the floor. He could see all of her breasts except the nipples as she leaned over and her halter fell away from her shoulders.

"Let's don't talk about D anymore," she said as she let go of the chair and stood up to look at him. He wondered if she had noticed him looking inside her halter. "I've got to do some ironing for Hazel. Want to come down to the house for a while? You could talk to me and help me fold the stuff up."

"I was thinking about going to the movies," David said stupidly, not really knowing why he said it. He didn't care about the movies. All he wanted was to be with her, now that D was gone, wanted desperately for just the two of them to talk while she ironed Hazel's clothes and he folded the things she'd let him handle. But he knew that Hazel would sit with them and do most of the talking, just as she had all the other times, and he didn't want to go back to that.

"What's on?" she asked.

"A Buck Jones movie is on at the Strand."

Frony wrinkled her nose in disapproval. "Horse opera. What

about at the State?" The Strand and the State were the only movie houses within walking distance.

"Another horse opera. This is Saturday, Frony."

"Okay. We'll go to the Strand. Want to take me with you?"

Did he! Boy, did he! She matched his grin when she saw how her proposal pleased him.

"Sure, I just got my allowance. I've got enough for both of us."

"I didn't mean for you to pay. I meant just go together. I'll have to do the ironing first."

Hazel talked and laughed at her own comments for the full hour it took Frony to iron. David sat and watched Frony's breasts wobble back and forth with the stroke of the iron. Hazel must have been watching, too, because she told Frony to go put on a brassiere and blouse before they left for the movie. She also told her to wear a pair of sandals.

If Frony hadn't been in such a good mood, she might have thought David was crazy during the ten-block walk, or run, to the Strand. He jumped around like a young goat and ran across front yards, vaulting hedges and hiding behind trees, until she caught his fever and outdid his zaniness. Once, when he had lost her, she sprang from behind an oleander bush and tackled him. They rolled in the grass of someone's front lawn until she straddled him, pressing him back into the earth, pinning his arms over his head with her strong hands.

"Give up?" she asked, panting down into his face.

David rolled from side to side, trying to dislodge her. He whooped and laughed convulsively until, with one last gasp, he surrendered. "Yes. Yes, I give up." As he looked up at her triumphant face, framed by a tangle of black hair, she leaned forward and kissed him hard on the mouth. The kiss was dry, just a hard pressing together of lips.

"That's for not saying anything else about D," she said and rolled over to lie beside him as they both caught their breath. That was the first time Frony had kissed him and he almost died from the thrill of it.

They were exhausted, so they walked the last two blocks. David couldn't have gotten back into his previous mood, anyway. He was still remembering the kiss. He didn't think of anything else, didn't even notice they had passed the shops that came before the Strand and were finally standing in front of the ticket booth.

The movie house was so dark that David stumbled as Frony, holding his hand, led him up the stairs to the balcony. Some unwritten rule had kept him from ever sitting in the balcony before. Some silent arrangement had reserved it for the kids in high school, and any younger intruder was made so uncomfortable that he could endure no more than the comedy or the serial before he skulked back downstairs to join his own kind. But now David let Frony pull him along up the stepped aisle until they reached the last row against the wall of the projection booth. She selected middle seats, and as his eyes gradually adjusted to the gloom, he could see that only a few other seats, down toward the balcony front, were occupied. They were virtually alone in darkness relieved only by the flicker of the projection beam over their heads.

Frony still held his hand, and as they settled in their seats, she took it and pressed it to the warm moist inner part of her thigh, close to her crotch, his little finger under the hem of her shorts. He felt the edge-band of her underpants. He was frightened and could hardly breathe. Inside his pants his sex had come alive and he had an enormous erection that was painfully misaligned in his undershorts, but he was afraid to adjust it, afraid of any movement. After fifteen minutes he lost the feel of Frony's flesh. Except for the trickle of sweat that ran between his fingers, he could feel nothing at all. He tried to restore the feeling in his mind by thinking about the incredible position of his hand, under the cuff of her shorts, next to the source of her heat, but he was aware of only the sweaty slipperiness under his hand. When he moved his fingers, squeezing her thigh softly, she exerted more pressure on his hand with hers, a signal to be still, to remain as they were. She shifted in her seat occasionally but always kept his hand clasped to the same burning spot. David's erection melted as his hand became numb. Frony appeared to be engrossed in the movie, but he couldn't follow it at all. He thought of Frony with her breasts bare and tried to think of her with no clothes on at all. He had never seen a completely naked woman. Then he started wondering. What had Frony and D done in the last row of the balcony? Where had D's hands been? Which of her juices had flowed over *his* fingers? David's heart alternately sang with excitement and raged with jealousy during the two hours it took for his arm to become paralyzed to the shoulder. When the movie was over he could hardly get out of his seat.

Chapter Four

That was the beginning of their summer together, when the difference in ages didn't seem to matter in anything they did. Frony could be as juvenile as David wanted her to be, and he matured in strange and subtle ways. He became infinitely more patient than was natural at such an impatient time in a young boy's life. He waited for her for hours, idling away the time until she was ready for whatever they were to do together.

Frony and David spent a lot of time at the river that summer. They were usually alone, because everybody else who had swum there in past years now went to the new town pool. The river was twice as far to walk, but after they crossed the fifty yards of deep water they could swim in the shallows and lie in the shade on a small crescent of sandy beach on the west bank. Most of the time they swam the river, starting upstream and letting the current carry them to the small strip of sand on the other side. Occasionally they would paddle across in a flat-bottomed boat that seemed to have been abandoned by some fisherman, left tied to a tree near a path that led off into the woods.

One day they just drifted downriver, sitting next to each other on the floor of the boat, trailing their hands in the water. Not until they passed Huntington, a preserved colonial plantation house, did they realize how far they had come. More than once during the struggle back upstream, fighting the current with the hand-blistering boards used for paddles, they thought of leaving the boat behind. When they got back it was almost dark and they lay exhausted on the sand. They had been under the sun in the near nakedness of their bathing suits all afternoon, and Frony was so sunburned she groaned at the touch of the sand on her back. They dreaded even the short trip back across the river, but they had left their clothes hanging from tree branches on the beach side. After a rest they paddled over to retrieve them.

Frony didn't go back into the woods to dress the way she usually did. She stripped off her bathing suit and stood naked before David for that instant it required for her to stretch and pick up her clothes. In the murk of dusk he could see the dark line of sunburn above her white breasts. He stared in fascination at the black patch between her thighs. The front of his bathing suit bulged and he turned his back so she wouldn't see when he dropped his trunks and pulled his pants on without even bothering with the undershorts. David saw those swinging breasts and the dark pubic triangle on the back of his eyelids for hours before he could go to sleep that night.

They went to the movies twice a week, always in the afternoon, and they always sat in the last row of the balcony. Frony would place David's hand on her thigh, and, after that first time, she allowed him to move it when he had lost the feel of her. Never closer to the steaming wet entrance, but within a prescribed space that suited her, he could explore her flesh with a gentle massage that caused her to slide forward in her seat and match the rhythm of his hand with a slight pulse of pressure from her own.

They hadn't kissed again since the day she had thanked him for not talking about D. To David it seemed strange that they hadn't. He wanted them to kiss but it just didn't seem to occur to Frony. It was mid-August when she announced that he was taller than she and celebrated the discovery with an open-mouthed kiss that made him bring his hand up to cup her breast. A week later David was fifteen and Frony celebrated his birthday by going to the movies without any underpants on. She was wearing a dress this time and she guided his hand under her skirt as she spread her legs. David recoiled with surprise when he felt her wetness, but her hand was insistent as she pressed his fingers up inside her and started the motion that would make her shudder for five minutes. Then she stiffened and he felt the spasm of her orgasm and heard her short-breathed gasps in time with the contractions of his fingers. The feature hadn't even started when they got up and left the movie house.

"We'll take a picnic to the river," Frony said when they got outside. There was excitement in her voice and David was still too stupefied by what had happened to say anything at all. She was planning as they walked along. "We won't go till about seven. We can picnic on the beach and then swim after it gets dark." David kept his hand with its sticky fingers in his pocket all the way home.

When he left her in front of her house, she asked, "Can you bring a blanket?" He must have considered the question for too long because she said, "I'll bring one. Come by at seven."

For three hours David thought unbrokenly of fingerfucking Frony in the movies. He wanted desperately to lock himself in the bathroom and masturbate, to use the same hand that still smelled of her dried juices, but he couldn't. Both his parents were home and he felt his guilt too heavily. What he had done had to show in his face, and a locked-door session in the bathroom would be a dead giveaway. So he sat and suffered and fantasized and looked at his birthday wristwatch fifty times and almost came in his pants without touching himself.

They both went into the woods together and Frony undressed in front of him. There was no modesty, no attempt to cover up. When she stepped out of her pants and was completely naked she stood easily, almost casually, and let David look at her. There was no darkness this time, no shadow of nighttime. She was exquisitely beautiful.

"Take your clothes off, David. I want to see."

He was ragingly erect and his face burned with embarrassment when his great stiffness sprung from his lowered shorts.

Frony was pleased with him, or with herself for the excitement she had caused in him. She seemed surprised that his fifteen-year-old penis was so large and so rigid. Her eyes widened as she looked, and a smile parted her lips.

"My goodness, David!"

They were ten feet apart, and as David started toward her, she turned to walk out of the woods.

"Let's go swimming like this," she said over her shoulder. "It will be dark soon enough, and nobody can see us."

Who cared? David thought wildly. At that moment he could have gone swimming with her as naked as a jaybird in the pool in town at high noon.

Not even the cold river water softened him, probably because they didn't swim. They played. She jumped on his back, trying to push him under, and he could feel her hard nipples pressed against his shoulder blades. She straddled him at the waist, pressing her opened sex against his stomach, burying his face in the hollow between her breasts. They toppled over together in a tangle of arms and legs and felt each other with wild hands while they fought back to the surface of the water. David tried to subdue her, to be better at this game, but he couldn't. Frony was as strong, as intent on winning, as he was. In that cold river he could feel her heat. It grew as the frenzied contact of their bodies became so intense that they both knew they would have to stop this to go on to something else.

They did. She led him onto the beach and lay down on the blanket without even using a towel on her hair. Little rivulets of water ran from her body and formed pools on the blanket. "No, not yet," she said as David knelt in front of her. "You stand up and look at me. I want you to look at me." So he stood and watched as she spread her legs, as she pulled her knees up and widened herself, used her hands to open herself for him to see. They stared in fascination at each other's sex. When she started her motion, lifting her hips to their common pulse, he began to tremble. She held out her arms to him. "Now. Do it now, David."

But it was too late. He came when he touched her, while he was fumbling to get inside her with her frantic hands trying to guide him. His mortification was such that he hardly felt his orgasm. As he lay beside her he turned away, hazel eyes glistening with tears of frustration and shame. Frony put her arms around him. She pulled him to her until his head was on her breast.

"I'm sorry, David. I made you wait too long." She squirmed down on the blanket until their faces were together. David could see the teary brightness in her own eyes. "I wanted you to be excited. I wanted your first time to be so good you'd always remember." She parted his lips with her tongue and panted into his mouth as they kissed. The motion of her hips began again as they strained against each other. Her passion was burning his skin and he felt a reawakening between his legs. Frony broke off the kiss and, getting to her knees, trailed her tongue down his chest and belly. When she took David's penis in her mouth he jerked his head up to look at her in disbelief. Propped on his elbows he watched until he grew enormous in her mouth and she suddenly pulled her head away and rolled over on her back. David was in control of himself this time when she spread her legs and guided him into her.

"Go slow, David," she directed. "Not all the way out. Just follow me."

She showed him how and he stroked slowly, gently. He held himself away from her on stiff arms so that he could see her face and breasts and could watch himself sliding in and out of her. As her pace quickened, he matched it. When she began to buck wildly and lift her hips off the blanket, he felt the gathering in his groin, the beginning throb that nothing could stop until it was over.

"Now, David. Harder," she commanded.

David did as he was told.

When Frony relaxed and David collapsed on top of her, she took his face between her hands and kissed him softly. After a while he slipped out of her and she shifted under him until they came to lie on their sides, facing each other.

"I love you, Frony," he said hoarsely.

"I know you do, David." She nuzzled against his shoulder, kissed him lightly on the throat, sighed comfortably. They lay this way for a few minutes before she propped herself up on her elbows and looked down into his face. "Remember me, David. Remember what we did. Nobody else can ever be first with you. Not for anything."

They sat naked and cross-legged on the blanket and ate the picnic food Frony had brought. It had never really gotten dark because the moon was up. Frony's body shone in the moonlight, and David was getting excited again. She must have sensed it. She began to gather the sandwich wrappings and soft-drink bottles strewn on the blanket.

"We'd better go," she said. "It must be ten o'clock."

David was facing the woods, and as he knelt to help her he thought he saw a movement among the trees, some passing darker shadow, a rustling not quite heard but felt along his spine, and he paused and looked intently into the gloom. There! There it was again! A denser darkness moving back farther into the woods, moving slightly, just a flickering change of light and pattern, like a wisp of cloud blown across the moon.

David shook his head and leaned forward on rigid arms, straining to see. Frony sat back on her heels and examined his face.

"What's the matter?" she asked.

"I thought I saw something in the woods."

Alarm widened her eyes and she jumped to her feet to turn and stare into the darkness.

"Was somebody watching us? Do you think somebody was in the woods watching us, David?" Frony held her arm across her breasts, placed a hand between her legs.

"I don't know. I didn't really see anybody. I just thought I saw something move."

"Go get our clothes. I'm afraid to go in there."

So was he, but he had to go, without hesitation, to show his bravery. David marched into the woods with the chill of fear running down his stiff back into his quivering legs. If anything, anyone, had been there, he wouldn't have known it; he didn't search for the chimera his mind was conjuring. His eyes avoided the place among the trees where he thought he had seen the movement, not looking to either side or over his shoulder. He just snatched the clothes from the tree branches and hurried back to the beach.

Frony was already in the boat and they dressed as they crossed the river. When they reached the opposite bank, she threw the picnic hamper up the steep incline and clambered up after it. She was running before David finished tying up the boat, and he didn't catch up with her until they fell, gasping for breath, into the grass in her front yard. They lay on their backs with their arms and legs flung out and laughed uncontrollably.

They went to the river a few more times, and while they agreed there probably hadn't been anyone in the woods, they never again stayed after dark and always swam with their bathing suits on.

Frony was eighteen on September twelfth, about a week after school started. After supper David walked down to her house to present her with a heart-shaped locket that had required most of his allowance money since midsummer. Hazel, Mary, and Mr. and Mrs. Henderson were leaving to go sit in David's front yard and talk away one of the few remaining evenings before the cool weather forced everyone back inside. Hazel had hand-cranked a freezer of homemade ice cream for Frony's birthday, and as David sat eating a huge portion out of a soupbowl, he pushed the gift-wrapped locket across the kitchen table.

"Is that for me, David?" Frony asked innocently. Her gray eyes smiled at him and she was already opening the package when he answered.

"Happy birthday, Frony. I hope you like it."

She held the ornate gold locket in the palm of her hand and ran her fingers over the embossment of roses on the front cover.

"Oh, David, it's beautiful!" she exclaimed as she slipped her fingernail between the two halves to snap it open. When she read the inscription—it had taken a great deal of courage for David to have the jeweler inscribe *I love you* inside—and looked up at him, the smile faded and her face softened into misty-eyed seriousness. She jumped up and ran around the table to kiss him, her tongue tasting the ice cream that was still in his mouth.

"Oh, I love it! I just love it!" she said as she broke the kiss. "You wait here a minute, David." Clutching the locket, she ran out of the kitchen. He sat alone for five minutes before he heard her call, "Come back here, David. I'm in my room."

All she had on was the locket. It glistened between her breasts in the light of the bedside lamp. She was sitting on the edge of the bed and beckoned him to come stand in front of her. Before she started to undress him she put her arms around his waist and squeezed him to her, pressing her head against his stomach. She took his clothes off slowly, deliberately, as though she were thinking through each unbuttoning. Her hands were cool against his skin. When she was through, when he was naked, she pulled him down to kneel between her legs. She clasped his sides with her knees and alternately pushed each breast into his mouth. Then the pressure of her hands on his shoulders told him to stop, to go farther down, to her navel and farther still until his face was between her legs.

"There, David. There. Use your tongue. That's right." Her hands were on the back of his head pressing him into her, teaching him the one thing she hadn't taught him before.

Three weeks later D came home on leave, and two weeks after that D and Frony were both gone. David couldn't believe it. He had still seen Frony while D was home—not very often and not in the same way, but a few times after school. "I can't see very much of you while D's here," she had said. She wouldn't let David kiss her or hold her breasts the one or two times they were alone together, and he tried not to think about what she was doing with D. Two weeks seemed like an eternity, but he could wait. After that D would be gone.

They left Saturday night, and Hazel came to David's house the next morning and told his parents about it. "Frony and D went over to Stillman and got married yesterday afternoon. Justice of the peace married 'em. They left for Norfolk on the eight-ten last night."

David and his parents were having a late breakfast, and Hazel was sitting at the table with them, drinking a cup of coffee. David's mother looked at him and saw the shock on his face, and from the look in her eyes he could tell she knew how he felt about Frony, knew about everything but the sex. Maybe she even suspected that.

He went to his room and cried like a little kid, lying in bed shuddering, sobbing his heartbreak into his pillow. His mother waited an hour before she came in and sat on the edge of the bed.

"Don't grieve for Frony, Dave. You would have had to give her up sometime. It's better now than later. I thought you realized D would come back for her."

But David did grieve, for over twenty years.

Grace was born eleven months after Frony and D married. When David learned from Hazel that Frony was pregnant, he thought, hoped, it had been from the night of her eighteenth birthday. He despised her enough then to want to be the father, the fifteen-year-old stud that had knocked her up. But he wasn't. Later, when he counted the months and realized it couldn't have been him, he was relieved.

During the three summers that were left of his youth, before he went off to college and never really came back home, David took other girls to the river. He taught the ones who didn't already know, the things Frony had taught him, but he never told any of them that he loved them. Because he didn't. And because Frony had never told him that. She'd never told David she loved him.

Chapter Five

Grace was gone when David woke up. She had left a note on her pillow. "I made coffee. Call me after you get your strength back." He made himself a big breakfast, ate it, and sat with a cigarette and a third cup of coffee trying to separate the dreams of the past night from the realities of his life. In sleep he had revisited the beach on the other side of the river, but Grace and Frony kept replacing each other, and the scene had shifted to the field in back of the house. Over and over he saw the dark shadow move in the woods, saw the look of alarm on Frony's face while she covered her breasts with her arm. But the voice that said, "What is it, David?" was Grace's, and the pale spot in the woods on the fringe of the field was transported to the riverside. "I saw it, too, David" was repeated again and again in the dreams. Had he dreamt that? He couldn't remember. Shaking his head to clear away the mental cobwebs, he got up to finish dressing. He hadn't prepared for his eleven o'clock lecture, and it was almost ten.

It took him fifteen minutes to walk across the campus to his office. It was the end of May and very warm, so he didn't wear a suit jacket. His shirt was sticking to the middle of his back, and he was a little out of breath from climbing the steps to his second-floor office, when he saw his best friend, Glenn Walker, coming toward him. Glenn, tall and blond, was as neat and cool and relaxed as always. David couldn't recall ever seeing him sweat, even when they were kids together on Seneca Street.

"You look like you ran all the way," Glenn observed as David turned to unlock his office door. "What's your hurry?"

"I've got about twenty minutes to put together some lecture notes. I goofed off last night."

"Frony?"

"No. Not that kind of goofing off," David lied. Not about Frony, because it was true that he hadn't been with her. He just knew Glenn assumed that any divorced man and widowed woman who had been seeing each other that long were sleeping together. Part of the reason David never denied it was because it bugged him so much that it wasn't true. He let Glenn think he was sleeping with Frony because he wished he was. Also, he wasn't ready yet to let Glenn know he was actually sleeping with Frony's daughter.

"You want some lunch?" Glenn asked.

"I can't go to the faculty dining room. I didn't bring a jacket. What have you got this afternoon?" After almost a year he should have remembered Glenn's schedule, but he didn't.

"Nothing until three. Want to go to Cicero's?"

"Yeah. I'll buy you a beer," David said just before he closed the door to his office. Glenn understood that he wasn't being shut out. Only fifteen minutes to scribble some lecture notes, without really knowing what he wanted to talk about—Glenn had been that route himself, many times, during his fifteen years of teaching.

David's lecture stank, smelled up the classroom. He lost them in the first fifteen minutes and didn't know how to get them back. He spent the rest of the class period hating the sound of his own voice.

"God, I'm glad I didn't have to listen to that lecture," he said loud enough to be overheard as he walked past Glenn's open office door. Out of the corner of his eye he saw Glenn look up and smile, so he shot a question back over his shoulder. "Do full professors with twelve-year-old English lit doctorates ever give shitty lectures?"

"Never," Glenn said as solemnly as he could manage, still smiling. He got up from his desk and followed David down the hallway to his office.

"Come in and take a load off," David invited.

Glenn sat down in the only other chair in the office besides David's desk chair. Compared to Glenn's, this office, with its sparse furnishings, was almost clinical. It had two chairs, a desk, a file cabinet, a small bookcase, two windows, painted beige walls, and a tile floor. As a tenured professor next in line for department head, Glenn had paneled bookcase walls, a huge mahogany desk, two leather easy chairs with a matching sofa, four windows, and a carpeted floor. They usually sat in Glenn's office.

"I never listen to my own lectures," Glenn said as he sat down. "Too boring. I thought you could always get 'em with stories about your journalistic triumphs in the big city." He wasn't being sarcastic. David had once jokingly told him that was what he used for course material instead of the dry stuff in the textbooks. It wasn't that much of a joke. David realized how pitifully little he had learned from the droning lectures he had sat through in college classrooms. He sure hadn't learned how to write a feature story out of a textbook. He had learned it from the years he had spent on the street, from the despair and terror and love and hope in people's eyes, from mean-bastard editors who cut his stories to ribbons with merciless blue pencils. He had learned the rest, the terrible discipline of writing for his daily bread, by working every desk on a half-dozen newspapers for over ten years, by pushing himself up to the executive editorship of a magazine with four million circulation, by being the meanest-bastard editor of them all. And he had learned from the loneliness of writing for himself. That blank-paper, blank-mind torture had produced the only part of his work he really valued—the thirty short stories and the best-selling novel that had allowed him to come home again. He didn't know what he had proved, except that he knew something about his craft—not everything—but a hell of a lot.

"Not today. No big-city romance, just cold turkey out of the book. That's why it was so dull. I can't remember anything I said, and they won't either. Let's eat."

They headed to Cicero's Tavern, a respectable café five blocks off campus, which served the best submarine sandwiches in the west end of town. On the walk over the conversation was disjointed and sporadic. David's troubles were very much with him—Frony, Grace, an inadequate classroom performance, a going-nowhere novel—and he was responsible for the lapses into uncomfortable silence. Glenn looked at him speculatively after they had sat down and ordered their beers. "You seem to be in some sort of a funk, Dave. Any particular disenchantment you can tell me about?"

David temporarily avoided answering his question by thinking that Glenn was the only one besides his mother who called him Dave. Well, why not? They had been friends since their dirty-shirttail days on Seneca Street.

"No disenchantment in particular. Take your pick."

"How's the book coming?"

"Horseshit."

Glenn smiled broadly. "You know, Dave, I just figured out why you're a writer while I write those tiresome essays about what writers write. You said more in one word—I guess 'horseshit' is one word—than I say in a paragraph."

"You're just out of touch with modern idiom."

"Mm. I'm not sure that's idiom—or modern, either, for that matter. Every generation thinks it invents all the vulgarisms. Actually, they've been around for a long time—"

"Glenn," David interrupted, "you're starting to lecture me. After what I just did to my class, I ain't in the mood."

"Okay. Let's have a sandwich."

They went to the sandwich counter, pointed to the ingredients they wanted, and Cicero's wife manufactured the submarines to their exact specifications. They each got another beer and carried the food and drink back to the table. Both ate in silence and not until they had munched through half their sandwiches did Glenn lean back, drink thirstily, and speak. "I don't think stalling out on your book is what's eating you, my friend," he said seriously. "I think you have another disenchantment."

Glenn was regarding him with sober and compassionate eyes, and in that instant David finally accepted what he had really known all along: Neither Glenn nor his wife, Madelyn, had been deceived about his relationship with Frony. They had known him too long, had been too close to him, to miss seeing the remoteness that persisted between him and Frony. So he supposed he might feel better if he went ahead and talked about it. He had to wonder now what they knew or suspected about him and Grace.

"I think I know what you're going to say and, frankly, I'm surprised you waited this long. I'll bet Madelyn's been working on you lately." Glenn started to speak, but David held up his hand to stop him. "Look, let's finish lunch and get out of here. I've got a feeling this is going to take a little time."

Glenn nodded. As they ate in silence, it occurred to David that it had been a long time since anybody but his parents cared enough about what was happening in his life to worry about him. Glenn and Madelyn were concerned, and he was sentimental enough to be pleased that they were. Old friends from his childhood, they had played with him and with all the other kids in the neighborhood, had grown up, got married, remained childless for whatever reason, and were now adopting him and his troubles. A few strains of *Little Genius* ran through David's head as he pictured Madelyn and Dorothy Ann struggling through the two-step with him and one of the McKenna twins. By the time they left, David was in such a wallow of sentimentality, he knew he was going to spill his guts.

They sat in wrought-iron chairs on a little patio in back of the library. Few students or teachers ever used the place, and Glenn never could understand why, since it was one of the most pleasant spots on the campus. Bordered on three sides by enormous azalea bushes and on the fourth by the brick wall of the library, the patio was a twenty-foot square of privacy and peacefulness.

Once they had slouched comfortably into the chairs and propped their feet on the low wrought-iron table, Glenn began. "Dave, I think Frony has problems. Or, rather, I think you and Frony have some problems."

"Okay, Glenn," David said. "I knew this would have to do with me and Frony, but before you go on, answer one question for me." He paused until Glenn nodded. "Is this your observation or Madelyn's?"

"Mine all the way; Madelyn just agrees with me. And it goes back twenty years. For God's sake, Dave! Did you think nobody was watching the two of you that whole summer?"

A thought flashed through David's mind. "You weren't hiding in the woods down by the river that summer, were you? You didn't follow us down there and watch us from the woods?'' From the look on his face it was obvious Glenn didn't know what David was talking about.

"What woods?'' he asked in complete bewilderment.

"Oh, nothing. Forget it, just a random thought.''

"That was one hell of a non sequitur.''

"I know. Go on with what you have to say.'' David was ready to hear him talk about it now, and didn't want to pursue the man-in-the-woods question.

"It's just more than idle concern. I don't give a damn what you say, you didn't come back here just because you wanted to buy Parsons and live in baronial splendor on top of a hill. You could have bought a house on top of any of a hundred other hills—in other towns.'' He paused, expecting a rebuttal. When he didn't get one, he went on. "You didn't come back because your roots are here, because of family—your folks moved to Atlanta almost ten years ago—or for old friendships; you've been away too long for that. You came back because Frony had moved back here. She wouldn't come to you in New York, so you came back to her.''

"You're wrong about Parsons. I've always wanted it. But for the most part you're right about the rest. What's the point? I don't deny I came back because of Frony.''

"D's been dead for six years. You've been back for over a year.'' Glenn seemed to be having trouble working out what he wanted to say, and he seemed impatient with David, for not understanding something.

"I know that, Glenn. What do you expect from us? We're not a couple of kids who want to run off to the JP like Frony and D did when he thought he was going to go get his ass shot off in the war. I guess that was why they got married in such a hurry. I've spent twenty years trying to figure the whole goddamn thing out.''

"Hasn't she ever told you about it? For God's sake! What do you talk about when you're together?'' Glenn was agitated, still hesitating over something he wanted to say, something he thought David should know.

"Told me about what? You're trying to get something out, so get it out. You'll tell me eventually. It might as well be now.'' Both men pulled their feet from the table at the same time and leaned closer together as Glenn began to speak.

"Dave, I would have brought this up months ago if I'd known Frony wasn't telling you. Let me back up just a little bit. There were a number of years, while you and Frony were gone—you were off pursuing journalistic fame and Frony was in Germany with D—when Madelyn and I never really thought about what had gone on between the two of you the summer before she married D. It was just something that had happened in the past. We were all grown up enough then for it to be more than just some kid thing, still, it didn't seem that important. Except that Madelyn and I remembered how that summer had changed you. You seemed to have suddenly grown older, more serious, as if you had shucked off your adolescence almost overnght. And there was the smack of cynicism in some of the things you would say; we remembered that.

"Of course, Madelyn and I would amuse ourselves from time to time speculating about what had happened between good old Dave and Frony way back there on the edge of childhood. Well, Dave, we stopped speculating five years ago. Frony told us all about it. She came back here to get Grace after the two of you went to Europe together. Grace was only fifteen and we had been keeping her. Anyway, all we ever really knew about that trip is what you told us—that Frony had shown up at your apartment in New York about a year after D's death and you went off to Europe together, no questions asked. Well, Frony hardly ever talked about that when she came back."

"Okay, Glenn." David sat back in his chair, repositioning himself. The wrought iron had become hard and uncomfortable. "Frony didn't tell you what went on in Europe, but even if you knew all the details they wouldn't bother you. It was the best month of my life. So she came back to get Grace and told you about the more distant past, including my teen-age sex education." Harsh cynicism filled David's voice. "Did she tell you how crazy in love with her I was, even without the sex, and how she fucked me into thinking I was something important to her before she went off and married D?"

"Frony married D to get away from you," Glenn said solemnly and rushed on to keep David from interrupting. "She was in love with a fifteen-year-old kid and it was driving her crazy." The stunned look on David's face made Glenn pause, but when he saw that David couldn't speak, he continued. "She was three years older than you, Dave. That's a hell of a lot at that age. Hell! You were just a freshman in high school and she had been a woman since she was fourteen. She had the biggest guilt complex you can imagine. Frony knew what she had done to you, and she didn't see any way she could do anything about it. She couldn't wait for you—it would have been years!—so she married D to get away. That was the biggest mistake she ever made, because she didn't love him and he was a mean son of a bitch, and semi-impotent. Oh, not at first. He could get it up okay in the beginning, Frony said, but whatever was wrong with him was progressive. It wasn't physical—it was something inside his head." Glenn stopped abruptly. He had dropped his head to stare at the ground as he talked. Now he looked up into David's face, which had stiffened in disbelief. "Dave, you didn't know any of this?"

He didn't. Not one goddamn bit of it.

"No, and I don't understand any of it. Why would she tell you and not me?"

"She didn't tell me. She told Madelyn. There's more. Do you want to hear it?"

"I want to hear it all, Glenn." David leaned forward with his elbows on his knees. He rubbed his face until some of the stiffness was gone.

"You didn't hear from Frony for a long time after you two came back from Europe, did you? She left you in New York and just dropped out of sight for a while, right?"

"Right. I didn't know where she was going. She wouldn't tell me."

"She was with us. For over six months. When she came back to get Grace, Madelyn talked her into staying a few days before she moved into the house she'd bought with some of the money Dr. Bennett had left her and D. She was in a hell of a state, Dave. I've never seen anybody as emotionally tight as she was then. Of course, I didn't have any idea why, and neither did Madelyn. And we didn't know it had anything to do with you. From the minute she walked into the house, we felt like she was ready to blow. That's why Madelyn asked her to stay for a while. The next day she came unglued, unloaded everything on Madelyn. I guess she was pretty far out of her gourd, and at first Madelyn couldn't make any sense out of most of the stuff she said. But Frony kept saying that she was responsible for your divorce from Helen.''

"Holy jumping Jesus!" David exploded and jumped up from his chair to stand glowering down at Glenn. "I can't absorb one single goddamn thing you've said. What is this about her causing my divorce? Helen and I had been separated for a long time when Frony showed up like a ghost from the past at my apartment door. I told her all about it, so there's no way Frony didn't know it was all over between me and that juiceless woman. Helen had only been a substitute—an inadequate substitute—for three miserable years, and I told Frony that.''

"She didn't talk about D at all while you were together?" Glenn asked, as if he already knew the answer.

"She never mentioned his name, and I was glad she didn't. Why should she? We were starting over again. I swear to God it was just like it had been during that summer before she—before she went away with Đ. We romped around Europe like a couple of kids on a month-long picnic. There wasn't any guilt in her then. She didn't need to talk about D.''

"How much did you talk about Helen?"

The excitement of remembering had caused David to pace back and forth in front of the wrought-iron table, but this question stopped him and he sat down again. It had brought something forward from the back of his mind: he and Frony had talked a lot about Helen while they were in Europe. Frony had asked him about her over and over again. She seemed to want to know every detail of their life together. How good she was in bed. What they talked about. How they had met. What they did on their first date. How long before they slept together. Everything, up until the time they separated. It occurred to David now that she could have been comparing their own beginning, their summer together, with his experience with Helen. Suddenly, and for the thousandth time, he remembered what Frony had said on the night of his fifteenth birthday, when they were at the river. *Remember me, David. Remember what we did. Nobody else can ever be first with you. Not for anything.*

He shook his head to clear the thought away and answered Glenn.

"We talked about her. Frony's like any other woman, Glenn. She wanted to know what her competition was like. Except there wasn't any competition; there never had been. I tried to tell her that." David didn't realize the significance of what he had said until he saw the knowing look on Glenn's face.

"So you told her, in effect, that you never loved Helen, or any other woman, because she had ruined you for anyone else," Glenn said with a little smirk of satisfaction, pleased that he had been right, that he had analyzed the situation accurately, and had made his point.

David sat silently, just looking at him. This had to be the most absurd conversation he had ever had, the most convoluted bunch of bullshit he had ever heard. Okay, Frony had gone off the deep end a year after D died. So what? A lot of women had mean bastards for husbands and lived with them anyway, for whatever reasons. A lot of them got a little goofy and had to take a rest cure of some kind, like Frony spending six months with the Walkers. Frony must have said some pretty weird things during those sessions with Madelyn. And she may have said that she had ruined him for other women. But that didn't make it true. Grace's image swept into David's mind. No, Frony hadn't ruined him for Grace. He forced his mind back to Glenn, and when he responded he was very calm compared to his former excitement.

"Glenn, do you have any idea how ridiculous this seems after all the time that has passed, almost five years, since Frony came to me in New York? And I've been in town, seeing Frony, for over a year. Is there any particular reason you've waited so long to tell me all this?"

"It's taken this long for me to realize you didn't know what happened to Frony. I didn't ever ask her if she had told you. I just assumed she had. And I've got a confession to make, David my friend." Glenn paused and smiled for the first time in an hour. "I can't understand it all, either. My love affairs have been pretty simple."

That David could believe. Glenn and Madelyn had adored each other since high school days. How simple it was when you never wanted someone you couldn't have. David smiled inwardly at the irony of Glenn's thinking things were complicated, when he didn't even know about David's affair with Grace.

"Do you have any particular reason for telling me now?" David persisted. Somewhere there was a motive—no, not motive, that was too negative, but a reason—for Glenn hitting him with all this. He suggested the only one he could think of, trying to sort out what Glenn was implying. "Do you think Frony is still so hung up on the past, on this ruination problem, that we won't ever be able to get together?"

Apparently that struck a nerve, because Glenn fidgeted, and David sensed something was coming that he didn't want to hear.

"Dave, I think she's setting you up all over again," Glenn blurted. Before David could react, he went on. "And I'm convinced she isn't even aware that she's doing it. On the surface she seems to be as rational as anyone I know. She works at the real estate office and keeps house and looks after Grace as best she can. All that seems completely normal, but Frony still has big trouble, emotional trouble she's tried to bury somewhere inside her head. She should have gone to a psychiatrist years ago." Glenn stood up and started to pace back and forth. "She still talks to Madelyn, and Madelyn tells me everything, of course. You wouldn't believe some of it. There was a long time—years—in Germany when Frony was completely celibate. D couldn't do anything and she just didn't have any sex. Maybe she was punishing herself, paying some kind of penance, I don't know. Can you imagine a woman like Frony without sex for all that time? It finally got to her and she got it on with quite a few of the guys in the American contingent in Berlin. One guy in particular. From what we could gather he was a huge bastard who was all cock and no brains—that's probably all she wanted—but it went on for a hell of a long time, up until, well, until D's death."

Glenn sat down abruptly and leaned toward David with his forearms resting on his knees. "I know you're not sleeping with Frony, Dave. I've acted like I thought you two were bedding down together because that's what I thought you wanted me to believe. According to what Frony tells Madelyn, and this part is pure theory from what we've been able to piece together, she's back into her celibacy role, with you now instead of D, because she's afraid she'll do the same thing to you again, promise you something she can't deliver, like she did when you were a fifteen-year-old kid. I know that doesn't make one goddamn bit of sense, but that's what I make out of it." Glenn looked down at his watch and was startled to see that it was twenty minutes to three. He slapped his knees and straightened in his chair. "I've got to go. Do you want to continue this after my class?"

David reached over and stopped him from standing up by pressing on his arm. "Just one more minute, Glenn. I've known there was something wrong with Frony, something keeping us from getting together. And—" David had to stop and swallow, his jealousy making it difficult to say the next part out loud—it was the first time he had mentioned this to anyone. "I also know she's seeing somebody else. Do you know anything about him?"

"I didn't know she was seeing anybody but you," Glenn said with genuine surprise. "Not since you came back. I know she went out with a few guys over the years, after she and Grace moved into her house. Nothing serious with any of them, as far as I knew."

"Did you ever see any of them?"

"Well, yes. Occasionally Madelyn and I would see her out someplace with someone we didn't know. We never met any of them, though. She never brought anybody around to pass inspection. I think they were just casual dates, Dave, just somebody to go out with. What makes you think she's seeing someone now, besides you?"

"I saw her down on Grove Street one night a few months ago. She was with a guy, a great big guy. I was just driving by and they were going into that seafood place in the middle of the block. I didn't get a really good look at him."

"Are you sure it was Frony? That's an unlikely place for her to be eating dinner."

"Yes, it was Frony. At first I didn't think they were together—they didn't seem to be talking to each other. But then he held her arm as they walked along the sidewalk."

"Any evidence that she's seen him since then?"

"No, just a gut feeling I have. There's something about the way Frony acts that even your ideas about her emotional problems don't explain. Maybe she's holding back with me because there's someone else."

Glenn stood up despite the pressure of David's hand, which was still on his arm.

"Look, I've got to go." He started walking toward the gap in the azalea bushes that served as both entrance and exit to the patio. "If you want to talk some more I'll see you at four o'clock."

"Is there anything you haven't told me?" David called after him.

He turned around and walked backward through the opening in the bushes. "Not that I can think of." He paused for a moment and then said, "Dave, if you want to know about Frony and this other guy, why don't you ask her?"

He disappeared behind the greenery. After a few moments David got up and walked out of the secluded little square and watched Glenn hurrying across the campus. That was a hell of a good question, he thought sourly. Why didn't he ask Frony? He suspected he knew the answer: because he didn't actually want to hear the truth; because he didn't want to be forced to make a decision, to have to *do* something; because it all had to do with his feeling for Frony and Grace and his own guilt. He didn't have the right to ask Frony the question. David walked home and lay down on the grass under the tulip tree in his backyard to try to sort out what Glenn had told him. The effort required a lot of remembering of how it had been with Frony—and Helen.

Chapter Six

Helen Connelly and David Fleming were married a year after she came to the newspaper in New York. She was a hustling young reporter who had a degree in journalism and a couple of years' experience on a midwestern daily. David was twenty-eight and she was twenty-five and she thought he knew everything there was to know about the newspaper business. At the time, he hadn't discovered that he really didn't like women who were viciously ambitious, who wisecracked about everything, and who managed to have a suntan even in the dead of winter. Every man in the city room thought he had pulled a great coup by marrying her. They considered her to be gorgeous, which David supposed she was, if you liked the type—honey-blond, long-legged, and thin as a rake, with breasts just big enough to fill up the palm of his hand. She was sharp enough, but her performance didn't live up to the bright patina of her appearance and personality. She wasn't very good at her job and she wasn't worth a damn in bed. From her David expected convulsive climaxes. Instead, he had to ask, "Did you come?"

Helen had read more about Darien, Connecticut, in novels than she had Scarsdale or Westchester, and, to her midwestern mind, that particular town represented the ultimate in New York suburban chic. So they moved from David's Manhattan apartment to Darien and she caught the seven-thirty with all the commuting men, wisecracking and showing her thighs all the way to Grand Central Station. She marched around the city on her brown athletic legs and in her sharply tailored career-girl suits with her flat little portfolio pressed under her arm. She had graduated to reporting general news—which she did rather poorly, because she had very little sense of discrimination when it came to the important facts of a story. However, she coaxed a bewildering amount of irrelevant information from scores of men by letting them look up her skirt while she asked her disorganized questions.

Weekend suburban life turned out to be pliable enough for Helen to mold into her concept of the American dream. She blazed around the countryside in an open sports car she had bought before she married and played tennis with a group of people David didn't know, and who had a lot more money than she and David had. The country club was out of their reach and she knew it, but she faulted him for not joining. She wanted to sit around the pool and display her lithe body as her hair bleached even blonder and her skin got even browner under the New England sun. Helen didn't really want to seduce anyone in the country club set—not to the point of actual bedding down—but she didn't know it. She was a teaser and she didn't know that either.

To Helen, David wasn't any great bargain, either, not anything like she had expected. She thought he was very dull, with none of the élan that a New York newspaperman should have had. He didn't belong in the social set she had managed to penetrate. He wanted more to his nonworking life than playing mixed doubles in the afternoon and eating charcoaled steaks in some young stockbroker's backyard at night. He didn't love the city, but after two summers in suburbia, he longed for it.

Just before Thanksgiving in the third year of his marriage, David took a two-room apartment on East Sixty-eighth Street, and Helen stayed in Darien. She also resigned from the paper and took a public relations job in a Wall Street brokerage firm. By the end of winter they had decided on a divorce settlement. She got almost everything—the equity in the house, the furniture, the car, the lawn mower, and half of his bank account. David ended up with about three thousand dollars, enough to finance the month-long European trip he figured he owed himself. The departure date was in late May, and three days before he was to leave Frony showed up at his apartment door. He just opened the door and there she was.

"Hello, David," she said, waiting for the recognition to come into his eyes. She was standing between two pieces of worn matched luggage, waiting for him to speak. There wasn't any hesitation on David's part, no stunned silence or stammering of her name. Frony had come back and the sixteen years evaporated as he stepped into the hall and took her face between his hands.

"Hello, Frony." David kissed her. When he stepped back to look at her again he was still holding her face in his hands. She was gloriously beautiful, more beautiful than he remembered. Her black hair accentuated the paleness of her flawless face and her wide gray eyes were so lovely, so strangely innocent, David couldn't stop staring into them. For the full minute they examined each other's face, he was aware of the soft rhythm of her breathing, the rising and falling of her breasts, the touch of her breath on his lips. Gently she took his hands from her face and held them. He wanted to kiss her again and to hold her against him. Before he could, she spoke.

"I called your office, David. They told me you're leaving for Europe Monday." They were still standing in the hallway, and she made no move to come into the apartment.

"Yes, I leave Monday night."

"Will you take me with you?" There was a note of urgency in her voice. The question was so startling that David didn't answer immediately. It didn't occur to him that he didn't have enough money for both of them. He just couldn't assimilate the meaning of the question. It was an enormous proposition. Frony and him together for a month in Europe. "I'll pay my own way," she said. "You don't have to worry about that."

David wondered what had brought Frony to New York, to his doorstep, but she didn't volunteer an explanation, and he didn't ask. He just accepted her as a precious gift.

The next thirty days were the most ecstatic of David's life. Two days in London—Buckingham Palace, Parliament, Piccadilly Circus, the Tower, the British Museum, and a half-dozen English pubs in two rambling days. Then south to Canterbury to see the place in the cathedral where Thomas à Becket had taken the knife. In the labyrinthine and catacomblike maze in the back of the altar he and Frony hid from each other in the darkness, like children.

They left the car in Folkstone and took the ferry across the English Channel to Calais. It was after dark when they boarded the Orient Express, and they were both still awake, lying in the dark on their second-class bunks and looking out the window, when the train stopped in Paris shortly after midnight. When they were far into the countryside east of Paris, David moved over to Frony's bunk and they made love on the Orient Express.

Thirteen hours from Calais they were in Visp, Switzerland, and two hours after that they were drinking wine in Zermatt, staring at the magnificence of the Matterhorn. For two days they tramped the hills at the base of the mountains, pausing often to look in wonder at the craggy granite peak. They sat on their balcony and drank wine, staring at it.

But two days were enough there, so they left, bound for France again, across the Alps to Chamonix, where they glimpsed Mont Blanc through the spring mist. From Chamonix they drove south—not through the wine country, because it was too early for the grapes—but to the east, through Albertville and Sisteron, the most direct route to Cannes.

At Cannes the women lay in the sun with only a patch at the crotch and two-ended spoons over their eyes. But no one on that Mediterranean beach could compare to Frony. Male heads turned to look at her, to admire her whiteness in the sea of tan. The other women were lovely, lithe, and beautiful, but David had brought the loveliest of all.

The dress Frony bought in Nice was white. It had no back and the neckline plunged almost to her waist. The knee-length skirt was a cloud of layered silk chiffon. And she bought white sandals with three-inch heels and delicate straps across the insteps. When she came out of the dressing room to model the dress and shoes for David, she twirled so that the skirt stood out and uncovered her stockingless legs to mid-thigh. She was glorious. What wonderful relics the dress and shoes would make of these golden days.

Frony, bare-legged and regal, floated through the great Monte Carlo casino in her chiffon dress and provocative sandals. Again men admired her and they made room for her at the tables. David watched her blow on other men's dice for luck, watched the excitement in her eyes reflect itself in her feet, which danced on the carpet by the crap tables. At the last possible moment they dashed down the broad casino steps and into a taxi to catch the train for Rome. Frony's chiffon skirt billowed as she collapsed into their second-class seat. The barefoot and breathless Cinderella had kept both of her slippers. They were clasped tightly in her hand.

Day after day they lingered in Rome, unable to get enough of it. The Forum, the Colosseum, the Vatican Museum, St. Peter's, the Church of the Maggiore, the Sistine Chapel (which saw them twice), the Spanish Steps, the Trevi Fountain, the excursion to Tivoli Gardens, the exhausting walks, the careening taxi rides, cappuccino in sidewalk cafés, their crummy hotel three blocks from the railroad station. They were captivated by it all. Frony and David would try to review what they had seen, helplessly groping for words expressive enough. When they failed they simply felt in their bones the things that couldn't be said.

They went south to Naples, Pompeii, and Sorrento, rushing through these to get to Capri and go through that tiny hole in the cliff that led to the most incredible of all caves, the Blue Grotto; again and again they bribed the boatman, stuffing lire into his outstretched and willing hand, to keep them longer on that small blue sea to shout their untuned songs against the echo-chamber walls, to keep them until all other boats were gone and they could swim naked in the transparent blue by the side of the boat.

In Florence, Frony bought Australian opals on the Ponte Vecchio and bargained in the open-air market for leather handbags she never actually bought. They stood in the Academy and stared at Michelangelo's huge-handed David, and had to catch their breath every time they turned a corner to another aspect of the Duomo's marble magnificence. But they were too ignorant for Florence. It had to be saved for another time. They had to move on.

They were standing in the Louvre, in front of *The Beautiful*

Gabrielle and the Maréchale de Balagny, the picture in which one naked sister is tweaking the breast of the other, when Frony asked him how good Helen was in bed. When he told her how unresponsive Helen had been, she seemed strangely pleased. "You had done it all with me, David," she said. "You remember what we did. We did everything." There was a strange release in her for having said it. Her eyes were softer after that and her hands more loving. She possessed him in a way that was different from the way it had been before, not more physical but more intimate. When they rode the métro she would sit with her hand on his thigh, and she would stop in the middle of the street and kiss him with lips softer, less demanding, than they had been before.

The night before they flew back to New York, Frony put on her white dress and they went to the extravagantly expensive Tour d'Argent for dinner, where for two hours she leaned over the table so that David and the attentive waiter could see the erect nipples on her breasts. In the taxi back to the hotel she pulled her skirt up around her waist and pressed David's hand between her legs. She hadn't worn any underwear at all. That night they didn't sleep. They finished all the wine left in their room and made love until they had to get up and pack to go to the airport. They slept across the Atlantic.

David didn't know until he picked up their luggage at Idlewild that Frony wasn't coming back to the apartment with him.

"I need to stop by the office a minute and let them know I'm back," he said when they were pulling out of the airport in a taxi. "You go on back to the apartment. The cabdriver will help you with the luggage."

He held out the apartment key, but she didn't take it.

"I have to leave, David."

"Leave? Why?" The idea shocked him. It had never occurred to him that she would leave. "Where are you going?"

"Washington. There are some things I have to do."

Some unfinished business about D, David supposed. Maybe something to do with his insurance. Or maybe she still lived there, had a house or apartment. He didn't really know where she lived. If he had asked her, she had never told him. There had been no talk in their month together of the past—except for her queries about Helen—or of the future. Some silent resistance in her had prevented questions. The present had been too precious to lose, so he hadn't asked. But things were different now; they were home, and the future was when she would come back to him.

She turned to look at him, took his hand, and pressed it to her face. "I won't be back, David. Not soon, anyway. I have to take care of Grace."

My God! Grace. He had completely forgotten about Grace. She would be fifteen or sixteen now. "Just stay tonight, Frony," he pleaded. "There are so many things we haven't talked about. Grace will be all right for one more day. Where is she? With friends?"

"Yes, she's with friends, but I have to get back. I don't want to talk anymore. Let's don't spoil things now, David. Now is the best time for me to leave." She removed his hand from her cheek, which had grown cool to his touch. She held his hand on the seat between them as they sat in silence on the way to her train at Grand Central Station.

After David put Frony's luggage in the rack over her seat in the chair car, he reversed the seat in front of hers and sat facing her. Their knees touched as he leaned forward to hold both her hands. "When will you come back, Frony?"

For a moment she looked out the window as if she hadn't heard him. David was about to repeat the question when she answered. "Not for a while. I told you I wouldn't be back for a while."

"Will you be in Washington? I can come down on the weekend, when you're settled."

"I'll only be there a few days, David."

"Well, how can I get in touch with you? Where can I write you? Or call? Do you have a number I can call?"

"No. Not right away." David waited for more, but she didn't speak. Her eyes fell from his face and she seemed to withdraw from him, to shrink back into her seat.

"Frony, why won't you tell me what you're going to do? I don't understand why you're doing this." He sat squeezing her cold hands on the train that was about to take her out of his life.

"It will take some time to work things out," she said. "When we get settled, I'll let you know. I'll write and let you know."

"Are you going to stay in Washington?"

"No, we can't—oh, David. The porter is closing the doors. You have to get off."

"Write as soon as you can." He leaned forward to kiss her, and she hardly parted her lips.

"Don't try to find me, David," she said as he stood up to leave. This sounded so ominous to David that he sat down again and wordlessly searched her face for the meaning of what she had said. He could tell she wished she hadn't said it, hadn't delayed his leaving. "I mean—well, I'll write. Wait until I write."

"I love you, Frony," David said, and as he got up to run down the aisle, he heard her say, "I know you do, David."

Reprise. "I know you do, David." She had said that before, lying in the sand by the river sixteen years ago. This was a repeat verse. Not, "I love you, David," but, "I know you do, David." She still hadn't said she loved him. Not then, not in Europe, not now, not ever. What had the last month meant? David went back to his apartment in an agony of doubt and confusion, and that night sleep didn't come easily. Images of Frony kept running through his mind. The woman David left on the train was not the same one with whom he'd drunk wine and made love the night before. He had left her in their small hotel room on Paris's left bank and said good-bye to a stranger on a train in Grand Central Station.

No word came from Frony, and so David's loneliness and melancholy drove him every night to the typewriter. If she had written, or called, he might never have written the book that allowed him to come back home. The book was autobiographical, about her and him and how they were when they were young, about losing her and finding her and losing her again, and the way he'd expected to see her standing at his apartment door every day for the next two years. He wrote of how he had searched for her everywhere except the place Frony came from, and how he'd seen her on street corners, on buses, in theaters. After four hundred pages of despair he found her again, expatriated in Europe where he had gone alone to retrace the steps and relive the passion. He found her in Florence, buying opals on the Ponte Vecchio. They bought a house in southern France, just north of Cannes, and lived happily ever after.

She didn't even read the book. She saw the movie.

That was when, three years after David put her on the train in Grand Central Station, she wrote to tell him where she was.

Chapter Seven

Lying under the tulip tree and thinking it through resulted in nothing more for David than the construction of a simple outline of Frony's psychological problems. He conceded that what Glenn had told him was undoubtedly true. Frony *had* slept around in Germany when she needed sex. She *had* come apart in the Walkers' living room after the trip to Europe. Maybe she *did* feel responsible for his divorce from Helen, and maybe she *was* expiating some imagined earlier sin by going back into the celibacy role where he was concerned. So Glenn had finally told him what he and Madelyn had come to believe about Frony's mental state, because they thought she was unwittingly setting him up for another fall. She had done it to him twice before, and she hadn't really known she was doing it then, either. One way or another Glenn and Madelyn had been witnesses; they had seen the hurt in him when he was fifteen, had read it in his book the second time.

Perhaps they were right. There was so little of what he thought there should be in his relationship with Frony, so little of what there had once been. Perhaps that was why he had come to need Grace so badly—to make up for what Frony withheld. But still he couldn't accept what Glenn was implying, that Frony's guilts had brought her to the edge of madness. Everybody had a guilt complex of one sort or another that had to be lived with. His own, about Grace, for instance. If it had been only a sexual thing with Grace, it wouldn't have bothered him so much; he had never worried much about the moralities of sex. But he was in love with Grace, and with Frony, and the dual nature of his love became an ethical problem that bothered him very much.

David sighed and sat up in the grass. He had lain in the same position for so long that his legs were stiff when he struggled to his feet and limped across the field toward the house. Something that he and Glenn hadn't talked about had begun to nag at him and he had some more questions.

Glenn had left the campus so David had to call him at home, which he didn't want to do. He could imagine Madelyn with her ear pressed to the receiver next to her husband's. David immediately disliked himself for having had such an ungenerous thought. There was no reason for him to resent Madelyn. She was just as much his friend as Glenn was. Had she pried into his affairs? Had she done any more than listen while Frony unloaded on her? He shook his head and dialed Glenn's home number, but when he answered, David couldn't help asking, "Are you alone?"

"Well, yes," Glenn said hesitantly. "Madelyn's in the kitchen."

"There's one thing that still bothers me, Glenn."

"Yes, what's that, Dave?"

"Why do we talk about D dying? I mean, why do we always say 'after D died'?"

"I don't quite follow. What do you mean?"

"It's well known he was a suicide, hanged himself in their basement in Berlin. The Hendersons told my folks and they wrote me about it. I never asked the details, didn't want to know. Was D a real mental case?"

The phone was silent. All David could hear was a deep sigh from Glenn and then the sound of his measured breathing. When he spoke again it was softly, as if he were cupping the mouthpiece of the telephone with his hand so that he couldn't be overheard.

"Dave, I believe anybody who kills himself is some sort of mental case. All we know is what we can put together from what Frony told us. D had a lot of problems, but he wasn't a raving maniac." Glenn paused briefly and then went on. "The bad part was afterward, but I guess there was no way for you to know. Frony wouldn't have told you."

He paused again, and the waiting was too much for David. Something pulsed through the wire connecting them that went into the nerves at the back of his neck. "Told me what, for Christ's sake?" he demanded.

"Frony found him when she came home after being with another man. She cut him down herself, so Grace wouldn't see."

God in heaven! D hanged himself and Frony found him after leaving another man's bed. Another guilt, David thought, to go along with what she thought she had done to me.

"Frony told Madelyn all this?" he asked, a tone of incredulity in his voice. It was hard to believe that Frony would confess to what she had done.

"Yes. It just came out with all the other stuff. There were times when she really didn't know what she was saying, Dave. It took us a while to figure it out, to piece it all together."

"My God! That has to be a huge part of this guilt complex you and Madelyn say Frony has. It's not just what she thinks she did to me—I know that's a good part of it—but the other part is what she thinks she did to D, what she drove him to. She's had six years of remorse to go along with the guilt."

David was thinking about Frony crawling out of the sack with some guy to go home and find D hanging by a sash cord, or whatever it was, and he was beginning to hurt over it, to feel her pain.

"Frony feels guilt about so damn many things, Dave, about you and everything that went wrong between her and D. She faults herself for things she must know in her own mind she couldn't have prevented. She probably couldn't have prevented his suicide by staying out of bed with *all* the guys she slept with in Germany. Everything she told us indicated D was already bent on self-destruction. She had a lot more than six years of living with these layers of guilt she's built up, but you're wrong about the remorse. She had no remorse about D. I'm convinced of it, and so is Madelyn. D's death was a release for her. She had no feeling left for him, not even pity. He'd destroyed anything that was left between them long before she ever got into another man's bed."

David couldn't argue the point. This dimension of Frony's

problem was too new for him, and Glenn had had a long time to think it through. While he was silent, considering it, a disturbing question came up in his mind.

"Was Grace around when Frony was making these confessions?" he asked. "How much does she know?"

"I don't think she really knows anything about it, Dave. When Frony started to come apart, Madelyn was able to get Grace off with a group of kids who spent two weeks at Claytor Lake. By the time she got back, Frony was over the worst part of it. I don't believe she even knows her father killed himself. Frony told her it was an accident, and that's the way the government people in Berlin handled it. Apparently they didn't want negative publicity about any of their people."

"It's hard to believe she doesn't know. The Hendersons knew and so did my folks; they told me about it."

"Maybe she really does. I'm not completely sure. I just don't think so. It's not something she'd talk about. Look, Dave, why don't—wait a minute. . . ." The phone had the peculiar nonsound of a hand pressed over the mouthpiece. David assumed Madelyn had come in and was talking to Glenn. After a minute or so he came back on the wire. "Sorry, Dave. Madelyn heard part of my end of this conversation. I told her about our talk this afternoon. Do you want to come over and talk with both of us about it? She knows more of the details than I do."

David thought the invitation over before he answered. Why not? Madelyn might be able to add some perspective to what Glenn had told him. He had no idea how he would even begin to talk with Frony about it. Madelyn could be a big help in that department, simply because she was a woman. "Okay, Glenn, but I've got to be back by seven. Frony's coming over for dinner tonight."

Nothing new came from the conversation with Glenn and Madelyn, but David was glad he took the time to review the details enough to get them straight in his head. Madelyn helped him with that. She sat on the sofa beside Glenn with her long legs crossed and her good-natured face smiling encouragement but turning serious at the right moments. Talking calmly, she offered what explanation she could to the questions that were still in his mind, especially the big one: How the hell could he get Frony to tell him about everything herself? Madelyn thought he could, but not all at once. He would have to lead her into it one step at a time, starting back at the beginning. Frony would have to admit she was in love with him when he was fifteen years old before she could tell him any of the rest of it.

What Madelyn suggested sounded reasonable. David could tell from the way she spoke, from looking into her intelligent face, that she had already given some thought to the way he should handle Frony. He felt much better when he left.

Frony always came to Parsons rather than have David come to her house. That really wasn't so strange, because she seemed to love the old place as much as he did. The first time he saw Frony after he moved into Parsons was through the screen door to the front porch, just as it had been the first time he saw Grace. She had come into his life again, unannounced, a repetition of her appearance at his apartment door in New York four years before. He kissed her and pressed her to him and cupped her breasts in his hands before they left the porch to come inside.

As he showed her through the house, he could tell how she felt about it. She examined everything as they made their way up to the widow's walk, where she surveyed the property in one slow circuit of the railed platform. For several minutes she stood looking south across the front lawn. "The river is over there," she said. It was a comment that required no response. She completed her thought. "You can't see it through the trees."

He was in Frony's house only once, a few days after she first came to Parsons, and he didn't give much thought to why he never went back. She hadn't invited him the one time he went there. He just showed up one afternoon because he wanted to see where she lived. The house wasn't small and it wasn't large; it was medium. Three bedrooms to go along with the living room, small separate dining room, kitchen, and two baths. There was a comfortable screened porch that overlooked the hedged-in back lawn. Frony didn't really show him the place. He made a quick tour while she was in the kitchen mixing drinks. After that she always came to Parsons. She would just say, "I'll be over about seven" (or eight or six thirty, whatever) when he called to make arrangements for them to see each other. She came to him; that was one of the few things that pleased him about their relationship.

But there were many things that didn't please him. Perhaps the most persistent single irritant was his inability to get Frony to talk about herself in any important way, especially about the past. They did talk about the trivialities of her work in the real estate office, but the job didn't interest her; she just recited what had happened that day or the day before, or some other day over the tiresome four years she had spent in the same tiresome job, and it bored them both. They talked about his work at the university and the progress on his book. Sometimes she talked about Grace (he came to feel intense guilt at these moments) and how she was doing in school. It was months before he realized that they never talked about anything that was really important to them. But in that time he had become restrained—Frony had that effect on him. He cursed himself for being so docile, for not forcing both of them back into their European mood. What the hell was he waiting for? No—not him. What was *she* waiting for? He felt like a fool, teased by a thirty-nine-year-old coquette who didn't remember that he had once been her lover.

David hadn't made any definite plans for the evening and he was determined not to go out. Not this night. This night would start the David Fleming therapy that would bring Frony back to what she had been on the Mediterranean beaches and on the streets of Rome and Paris. But first he would have to take her even farther back, to the summer when she had abandoned him. But carefully, with no resentment, to let her know they could talk about it, relive it without the agony it had cost both of them.

It was almost seven when he finished his shower, redressed in clean clothes, mixed a drink, and went out on the front porch to sit and wait for her. He was grateful she was late. It gave him a chance to practice his opening gambit, to work on the casualness of tone, but most of all to figure out exactly where he should start. He considered the most direct approaches first and mouthed them aloud as he sat rocking, sipping his Scotch, and smoking. The dread mounted that her car would appear in his driveway before he had decided.

"Do you remember," he would ask, "how we used to sit on the curb in front of Gil Thomas's house and tell ghost stories?"

No, that was too far back; he had been only nine or ten years old. Get right to it. That summer. Something about the movies. Something to do with their first intimacy.

"Do you remember the first movie we went to together? I mean, do you remember what was playing?"

He did. Vividly. But he remembered more vividly the shocking thrill of his palm against her thigh. He never remembered anything about the movie, other than the name, and he suspected she wouldn't, either. There was no subtlety in such a beginning. He would only be asking if she remembered the first time he'd had his hand inside her shorts.

"Remember the night when we were down on the beach by the river, and we thought there was someone in the woods watching us?"

Watching us what? Fuck. Absolutely not. He couldn't start that way. Anyhow, thinking about that night still made the hair stand up on the back of his neck.

He had to bring up the river—Frony and him and the river. But the best way was to work back gently. They would sit on the front porch after dinner and have brandy and coffee. Frony liked that, sitting in the dark, talking about the unimportant things they always talked about. Even when he could hardly make out her face, he could tell she was looking toward the river. She always did.

"You know, Frony," David would say, "when it gets quiet up here at night, you can hear the river. Listen." And she would hold her breath, listening for the river's sound. She would hear it, just as he did, although it might be just in her mind, as he sometimes thought it was in his. He would go on. "When it gets warmer, in midsummer, I'd like for us to go back to the river. I'd like to swim the way we used to when we were kids." He would have to amend that. He'd been the only kid; she'd been a woman. "When we spent our summer together," he might say. But that was the way he would start, with Frony and him and the river.

Frony was rarely late, so when she hadn't come by seven thirty, David began to feel a little resentful that she was unwittingly frustrating his plans. He got up, mixed another drink, and carried it with him as he walked down to the end of the driveway, hoping he could make her car appear on River Road if he looked for it hard enough. But he realized he wouldn't hear the phone if she called, so he walked back to the house and sat down on the porch again. By eight fifteen he had finished another Scotch. The liquor and his impatience were beginning to get to him. He called Frony at home and let the phone ring a dozen or more times before he hung up. Well, at least she's on her way, he thought. Twenty minutes more at most. David thought about making himself another drink, but he didn't. Instead he sat on the porch and lectured himself: Don't get loaded and louse up the first great David Fleming therapy session. He smoked and worked at being calm about Frony being over an hour and a half late.

The phone remained unanswered after another dozen rings when David called at nine. He drank his fourth Scotch at nine thirty, his fifth at ten, and at ten thirty he was drunk enough to say, "Fuck it," and go to bed with nothing in his stomach but Scotch whisky.

Frony and Grace were both in his dreams, sometimes singly and sometimes together, but this time it wasn't an inability to separate them in his nighttime hallucinations that was so frightening. It was something else, a startling difference of presence that kept Grace always in bold three-dimensional relief against the nightmare's background while Frony was indistinct, fading, and ephemeral, as she slipped in and out of the episodes his mind conjured. She faded from under him on the sand of the river beach to be replaced by Grace's younger body. But Frony was still there, standing like a white ghost against the dark outline of the woods, watching as they strained together, then vanishing into the deep umbra of moon-shade, absorbed by some rustling ominous shadow at the edge of the woods. She watched again from the side of the field as he and Grace made nighttime love under the tulip tree. And in back of her a lantern face hovered in the woods as she advanced to take

Grace's place. But when Grace was gone, so was her own wavering luminous body. There was only blackness and the face among the trees and the threatening shadows of the moonless night. Grace and Frony replaced each other on the widow's walk and on the streets of Paris and Rome. Grace's breasts rose proudly on the beach at Cannes while Frony looked down from the rail along the sidewalk. Frony leaped screaming from a wildly swinging runaway cable car on the Chamonix *téléférique* as he and Grace, who hadn't been there when she jumped, clung to each other in paralyzed horror. But they all survived to swim endlessly in the crystal waters of a Blue Grotto that had no entrance and no exit.

Chapter Eight

David awoke with a thundering headache and in a state of smothering depression. Segments of the dreams flickered oppressively through his mind as he lay in bed making a feeble attempt to analyze them. Was the transposition of Frony and Grace in the dreams only a reflection of his own inability to separate them in reality? Why was Grace's presence always so well defined, etched in such bold relief, while Frony's was receding, drifting out of focus into the vapor at the back of his mind? Were the dark and foreboding shadows, the threat of catastrophe that threaded the dreams, manifestations of his own feeling of guilt? Or were they adumbrations of things to come, prophecies of some danger that was an unalterable part of his destiny? David couldn't answer any of the questions he asked himself. Maybe he had been building up to those nightmares for a long time. Maybe he deserved them.

His stomach growled and he got up, put on a pair of undershorts, and padded barefoot down the stairs and into the kitchen. A glass of milk soothed his burning stomach somewhat as he scrambled eggs and fried bacon, but his hangover was still miserably with him after he had eaten and sat at the kitchen table drinking coffee and smoking one cigarette after another.

It was almost nine o'clock, and David toyed with the idea of calling and canceling the only class he had for the day, a graduate seminar that ran from ten until noon. There were only six students in the class, and they would all pass the course no matter what they did—or he did—this late in the semester. He would only control the level of argument as they critiqued each other's wild ideas about how far a newspaper's editorial page should go toward serving as the conscience of the community. God! The prospects of that two hours of bullshit made David's headache worse. The telephone beckoned to him from the wall in the alcove off the kitchen.

Canceling the class was easy. He called the secretary in the department head's office and asked her to put a note on the classroom door. No, he wasn't seriously ill, he told her, just a little under the weather. He'd be in Monday. Yes, he agreed (spinelessly, because he really didn't) the last week of classes could be the most important. If he got worse, he'd let her know so she could get someone to take his classes. But don't worry, he reassured her. He'd be there. As David hung up the phone he grimaced. Thirty years is too long to hold one job, Miss Pinella.

His headache was better immediately. He could add Friday to his weekend and sit for three days in front of the typewriter working around the hard spot that had stopped his book. He could also decide how indignant he was with Frony for standing him up, leaving him to get drunk by himself, forcing him to wait for another opportunity to start the treatment that would bring her back into his life where she belonged. When she called to explain, to apologize, how would he behave? Aggrieved? No, of course not. He'd always despised petulance. He wouldn't act indifferent, either. He was never urbane enough to carry it off, and she knew it. Jealousy would be the most accurate reaction, because the specter of Frony and the man he had seen her with kept coming into his mind. Frony and that big guy together, and David forgotten, rocking and waiting uselessly on his front porch. That was ridiculous! Frony hadn't forgotten. So how should he be? Inquisitive. That would be it. Inquisitive bordering on concerned: "I was really wondering what happened to you, Frony. I was getting a little worried." That's what he would say when she called.

For two days the phone didn't ring at all. David worked fitfully, in stretches that ranged from twenty minutes to three hours, and by

Saturday night he had produced five thousand words with only about a dozen holes that had to be filled in. The few times he left the house to work the kinks out of his legs in the backyard, he was still within earshot of the telephone's ring. Goddamn it! Why didn't she call? The things that Glenn had told him about Frony's mental state, things David, too, had come to accept, began to rattle around in his mind. The worry he had intended to mention almost casually when Frony called became real, a nagging intrusion that brought his writing to a near standstill. Only his obstinacy prevented him from picking up the phone and calling her.

Sunday afternoon David was writing, his conscious mind deeply involved in a characterization problem—while subconsciously he was still feeling lonely and neglected—when the phone on his desk rang, startling him.

It was Grace.

"David, I know you didn't want me to call or anything for a while," she began, paused briefly, as if expecting a rebuke, then pushed on, "but I just wanted to know if Mother is over there."

"Grace, I—"

"Oh, damn! I didn't want you to say my name. Is she right there? You can just say yes or no. If it's yes, I'll hang up." She waited two seconds. "Well, is it yes or no?"

"No."

"No what? She's not right there or not there at all?"

"She's not here at all, Grace. I wanted to—"

"Did she just leave? Were you together this weekend?"

"Grace! Will you slow down, goddamn it! I haven't seen Frony all weekend. As a matter of fact, I was supposed to see her Thursday night, but she didn't show. She stood me up."

There was silence at the other end of the line. Apparently Grace was thinking this over. "She didn't call?"

"No, I haven't heard from her since . . ." He didn't finish that. No sense going into it. "Well, I just haven't heard from her."

But she picked it up. "Since when, David? How long has it been since you heard from her?"

"Early in the week. I don't remember exactly."

"The day I was there? The day I came over after classes?"

"That was Wednesday, Grace. It was earlier—Tuesday, I think."

"That's been five days, David. You haven't heard from her in five days?"

David detected alarm in her voice and realized she wasn't just checking on him, unable to leave Frony and him alone. "What's the matter, Grace? You sound worried."

"I called Mother Thursday night and she wasn't home. I assumed she was with you. I mean, I didn't know anywhere else she might be, so I thought it was likely she was with you."

"Did you try calling her at work Friday?"

"No. I wasn't worried Friday." She really did sound worried, more than when she had started talking.

"Why are you worried now? Hasn't Frony ever gone away on a weekend since you moved into the dormitory?" He was being cynical, thinking about four years of weekends when Frony might have gone off with someone besides him.

"Well, yes. Winter before last she went on a ski weekend in New England. But she told me about it beforehand. She would have told me, David, and she would have told you. Anyhow, she didn't show up Thursday night. She wouldn't just stand you up. You know she's not like that."

David was still back at the ski weekend, wondering whom Frony had gone with. He didn't even know she skied. It took a little time for him to work through his jealousy. Of course, Grace was right—Frony wasn't like that. Even considering all the problems he'd recently discovered she had, she wouldn't just go off without telling Grace, or him. She would at least have shown him the courtesy of calling and lying about why she couldn't come over. He hated himself briefly for that thought. Jesus! He *was* indignant about being stood up.

"David?" Grace was impatient with his silence.

"You're right, she's not like that," he finally agreed. "Grace, do you want to come over here?"

"No, I want to go home. Will you take me, David? I'm afraid. . . . I don't want to go by myself." She wasn't just worried anymore; she was frightened. David caught her urgency.

"Do you have a key to the house?"

"Yes."

"Can you be out in front of the dorm in ten minutes?"

"Yes. I'll be waiting for you."

Grace sat rigidly beside him during the twenty-minute drive. Neither spoke, not even when she climbed into the car, until they were well away from the campus. David said only, "Let's don't speculate, Grace. There's probably a simple explanation for—well, for why we haven't heard from Frony." After he said it, he wished he hadn't, but he was compelled to say something. It sounded incomplete, and he regretted his own admonition not to speculate because it seemed a natural thing to do, until he realized that he couldn't think of a single plausible reason for five days of silence from Frony. Grace didn't respond; she just sat twisting her white-knuckled hands together in her lap until he stopped the car in front of Frony's house. They both saw at once that Frony's car was in the garage.

They searched every room, every closet, every square foot of the basement and yard. They looked under the beds and in the bushes. They found no mutilated corpse, which was what David knew Grace had expected, and there was no evidence of struggle, no bloodstains on the carpet, no ransom note. The last thing searched was the car. But Frony wasn't in it, not in the front or back seat, suicidally dead of carbon monoxide poisoning, nor was she stuffed in the trunk, dead of some brutal physical attack. Frony was just gone.

Grace was close to hysteria. She stood trembling in the driveway, staring into the empty trunk of the car. David put his arm around her waist for support as he led her into the living room and forced her to sit on the couch. He found a bottle of brandy in a kitchen cupboard and poured a half inch into two water glasses. Standing in front of her, he put one of the glasses to Grace's lips.

"No, wait!" she objected.

"Just sip it." He pulled the glass away when she grabbed his hand and filled her mouth with the burning liquor. The brandy from the glass sloshed down the front of her dress and spurted from her mouth as she choked on what she was trying to swallow. "For

Christ's sake, Grace! Take it easy." A brandy stain spread on the right leg of David's trousers. Tears coursed down Grace's cheeks and he felt like a bastard for being so abrupt with her. He sat down and put his arms around her, but she stiffened and pulled away.

"I'm all right now, David. Just give me a minute." She took the glass from his hand and sipped until it was empty. When she spoke again, her voice was solemn and steady. The hysteria was gone. "I want you to call the police."

The same thought was in his mind, but it seemed such a drastic thing to do that he wanted to postpone it. He had never called the police for anything. Besides, he hadn't rationalized enough; he hadn't had time to think it through. Did he really think something sinister had happened to Frony? The grisly thoughts that had entered his mind while they were searching the house seemed exaggerated, now that he was sitting on the sofa in this immaculately clean living room with the afternoon sun streaming in through the windows. He just wasn't ready to call the police.

"Not just yet, Grace. Let's try to figure a few things out first. Have you called the Walkers?"

"No, I didn't have any reason to," she said a little defensively. "I thought Mother was with you all weekend. Remember?" Her voice had a sharp edge to it.

"Okay. Don't get upset with me. I just wanted to make sure. I'll call them now." He got up and crossed the room to a small writing desk that held the telephone. Halfway through dialing he stopped and asked Grace, "Do you remember how many pieces of luggage Frony has?"

"I'm not sure. I think so."

"There was some luggage in that big closet in the back bedroom. How about seeing if there is anything missing while I call the Walkers?" She nodded, and he finished dialing.

Glenn answered the phone, and David was casual as he asked if he or Madelyn had heard from Frony over the weekend. David didn't want to get Madelyn into the act—she'd been dramatic enough lately over his painful love affair. Glenn spoke briefly with Madelyn and then volunteered that they hadn't heard from Frony in over a week. David was grateful that he didn't have to explain any further than saying that he had called her a couple of times without getting an answer. Grace came back into the living room as he hung up. Her face had brightened and she seemed immeasurably relieved by what she had found.

"Her small case is missing," she announced almost joyfully. "I'm sure of it. She bought herself matched luggage for Christmas two years ago. Blue. I've looked in all the closets and the storage room. The other pieces are in the bedroom closet and the old luggage is in the storage room. She took the small case."

She took the small case! What volumes that simple declaration spoke to David. Frony had been gone for four days, maybe five, and she had left without telling her daughter or her erstwhile lover. She had left them to worry, to come to the edge of panic, while she went off (David had no doubt) with some other guy, probably that son of a bitch he had seen her with on Grove Street.

Grace plopped down on the sofa with her arms flung out to either side, palms up, her legs straight and spread in front of her. Her skirt was halfway up her bare thighs. It was a slouch of emotional exhaustion. Her head rested on the back cushion as she looked at the ceiling. She sighed deeply.

"I wonder why Mother did that," she said, and then expanded on the rhetorical question. "Why would she go off without telling me"—she took her eyes from the ceiling and looked at David, then finished—"or you?"

It was his turn to sigh, which he did as he sat down in the straight chair in front of the writing desk. The thoughts running through his mind were so complex, he knew it would take a while to sort them out. He was convinced that Grace hadn't detected any mental abnormality in her mother, probably because the symptoms were too old and too subtle, and because Grace had relatively little contact with Frony these days. She was physically removed, living in a campus community where she thrived on her newfound independence. David knew that Grace loved her mother, but he also knew she was sawing away at the emotional umbilical that had to be severed before she and Frony could be liberated from each other, could begin their lives apart after so many years of dependency. So maybe he could convince Grace that Frony had simply reached the point where she didn't have to explain her comings and goings—to either of them. He could have tried if his jealousy hadn't been bothering him so much.

"I don't know. Maybe she just had an opportunity to get away for a few days and took it." It sounded lame and David knew it.

"You don't really believe that, do you?"

"No, I don't."

"What do you really think, David?"

He couldn't say it directly. He would have to skirt around the edges and come up to it indirectly.

"Grace, do you know anybody else—any other man—besides me that Frony goes out with?"

Grace's head abruptly came off the back cushion of the sofa, and surprise registered on her face.

"What makes you think she's going out with somebody else?" she asked, and when David didn't answer immediately she went on. "As far as I know she hasn't been out with anybody but you since you came back. Has she said something about another man?"

"No, she hasn't, but I saw her with a guy down on Grove Street a couple of months ago." David repeated essentially what he had told Glenn about seeing Frony go into the restaurant with a big man.

"You mean that seafood restaurant down on Grove—the Sea Room?"

"Yes, that's the one."

"That's a pretty crummy place. Have you ever taken her there?"

"No. I'm not big on the kind of seafood you get around here."

"She's not, either. Especially the greasy stuff you get in the Sea Room. Fried stuff. It's been frozen so long it takes a week to thaw out. That place is strictly el cheapo, and it's in a shitty part of town, too. Why would a guy take somebody like Mother to a dump like that?"

Why, indeed? David thought. Frony had too much class for the Sea Room.

The conversation wasn't going anywhere, but it had, at least, brought Grace back from the brink of hysteria. In the ten minutes they had been talking, the sun had dropped behind the trees across the street, and the room had taken on a more comfortable twilight tone. David went into the kitchen and made drinks with Frony's liquor. When he came back he sat on the sofa beside Grace, and they both lit cigarettes. After Grace had taken a couple of drags and sipped on her drink, she asked a question.

"Did you ask me about Mother seeing someone else because you think she's gone off with some guy?"

"The thought crossed my mind."

"The same guy you saw her with, maybe?"

"Christ, Grace! I don't know. Maybe so. Her car's still here. She had to go with somebody." There was an edge of irritation in his voice and Grace turned to look at him.

"I think I've struck a nerve, David. I know you don't like it, but *I* think the idea of my mother sleeping with some guy besides you is great. Now maybe we—"

"Goddamn it, Grace!" David exploded. "You're the only Bennett I've slept with in the last five years, and I'm up to my ass with everybody thinking Frony and I are always in bed together."

Grace just sat and stared at him with the smoke from her cigarette curling up into her astonished face.

"You mean to tell me—"

"Yes, I mean to tell you."

"Oh, David, not since you were together in Europe?"

"No."

"Oh, God! Am I relieved," Grace said, and the relief was apparent; it flooded her face. She clapped her hands together like a child. "I didn't want to compete with her in your bed, not with all those memories on her side. That's what they are, David, memories. I said it was just the two of us now, you and me. Will that be enough for you?"

David hadn't been looking at her, but now he turned to look into her excited eyes.

"I don't know, Grace. Let's not press it for a while. I think we're going to have plenty of time to work on it."

She leaned over to bury her face in the hollow of his shoulder.

Presently her arms slid around his neck and she raised her open mouth and kissed him.

"Will you take me to Parsons?" She pulled back to look soberly at him, and when he hesitated, she urged, "I don't want to stay in the dorm tonight. Please, David. We don't have to—you know—do anything."

For the first time all afternoon David smiled. She had him and she knew it. The solemn look faded from her face and she returned his smile. A barrier between them had been breached with the relief they both felt that Frony was not murdered, that she had just gone off with someone—inadvertently stepping aside to let them get on with their lives. He knew that in Grace's mind, her mother's inconstancy toward him made him fair game. Despite her knowledge that he had suffered an unwanted celibacy (where Frony was concerned) for five years, she welcomed the discovery that there was no actual carnal competition between herself and her mother. Strangely, David found he welcomed his own discovery of it. The itching patina of guilt that had varnished his feelings over the last months now slipped away, and with it went most of the jealousy he felt about Frony and whatever new bedpartner she might have selected. How could he be cuckolded by a woman who wouldn't allow him in her bed? What euphemism did he use to describe, to Frony and himself, her image fucking in the form of her daughter? Suddenly David realized that he really didn't care, because he couldn't tolerate being that much of a fool or that much of a bastard. His love for Grace had to be real. He was basking in the radiance of her smile.

Chapter Nine

Grace sat close to David during the ride back to Parsons. At her suggestion, they detoured down Grove Street past the Sea Room. The restaurant was closed on Sunday, as were all the others in this part of town, and it was impossible to see into the murky interior past the large unlit neon sign that hung in the narrow plate-glass window. Paint-peeling doors bracketed the entrance, apparently leading to staircases sandwiched between the storefronts—staircases that led to second-floor apartments.

"What a dive!" Grace turned up her nose as if she could smell the place. "I don't believe Mother would even go in a place like that."

"Well, she did. I can't imagine why, either."

"Maybe the guy wanted to buy it, you know, through the real estate office."

"Frony doesn't sell real estate, Grace. She just answers the phone and types letters."

Grace was silent for several blocks, until David turned south, off Grove, and headed toward River Road. Then she asked a question he had expected her to ask earlier. "Do you think Mother went out with that man more than that one time?"

The question had run through his mind a hundred times since he had seen them together. What did he really think? He didn't know, but his instinct told him she must be seeing someone else. "I don't know, Grace, not for sure. I just think she was going out with someone. He's the only one I ever saw."

David regretted having taken the detour down Grove Street. The glow he felt sitting on the sofa in Frony's living room was beginning to fade, and he didn't want to lose it. Grace sensed his reluctance to pursue the subject of Frony's other man friend, whoever he might be. She pressed against his side and ran her hand to the top of his thigh, where she squeezed gently. "What are you going to feed me?" she asked as they turned onto College Road. Her voice was clear of the afternoon's anxieties.

They ate the steaks David had intended to cook with Frony Thursday night, and then they made love on a blanket in the middle of the field. Before they went inside David asked Grace to lie still and he stood up to look down at her. Her body was chalk-white in the moonlight, a beautiful reclining Diana with a cloud of black hair. Frony was nowhere in his mind; there was only the love he felt for her reincarnation, supine at his feet. As they walked back to the house, Grace paused to look toward the woods. Remembering, David looked himself. There was no pale lantern face among the trees.

The thought of the nine o'clock class David would face in the morning returned him to the reality of his unfinished lecture notes. It would take twenty minutes to put them together, so Grace followed him into the study to sit and wait for him to finish. She went to the couch in front of the fireplace and sat with her back against the armrest and her legs stretched out across the cushions. One bare arm rested along the couch's back, and she smiled at David as he stood at his desk and thought of what a magnificent adornment she made for this bare room. She was still naked, and so was he, except for his shorts.

When he looked down, the surprise of finding the note on his desk registered immediately on David's face, and as his eyes ran over the first several lines, that surprise turned into shock. The change of expression was so sudden and complete that Grace detected it at once.

"What is it, David?" she asked.

But he couldn't answer. He couldn't even deflect his eyes from the terrible piece of paper that had been so carefully placed in the center of his desk. He could only sink into his chair, pick up the note with trembling fingers, and reread it:

Dear David:

I'm sorry to have taken Margaret out of turn. I really had planned for her to be next to last, right before you. However, none of the chronology is right except for William, who was, of course, first. Not everyone fits the pattern; there were too many of you. Glenn should have been before Dwight, but for reasons you could probably understand, I was especially eager for Dwight. He was the worst of all.

Although the war cheated me out of Howard, it was so long ago I've stopped thinking about it. But none of you who are left will cheat me, David. I have a message for you all. Read these lines to them, David. Read them to Glenn and Madelyn and Gilbert and Dick.

Like one who, on a lonely road,
   Doth walk in fear and dread,
And having once turned round, walks on,
   And turns no more his head;
Because he knows a frightful fiend
   Doth close behind him tread.

I am that fiend, and you all will walk in fear and dread until I come for you. But take comfort in one thing, David. You will be the last.

Grace had come to stand behind him, and as she leaned forward to read the note, her breast pressed against his shoulder. He felt the shudder of terror go through her, heard the moan of despair and horror rush from her mouth.

"Oh, my God! Margaret! That's Mother!" Her voice was rising. "He's taken her. Who wrote this? Who took her? What does that mean, David, he's taken her out of turn?"

She was shouting in his ear, the hysteria of earlier in the afternoon returning.

David stood up and held her quaking body tightly against his own. The shock of what he had read was so profound that he couldn't think through it. He couldn't tie one terrible sentence to the next. All he could do was try to calm Grace.

"I don't know what it means, Grace. No, wait—" She was pushing at his chest, trying to free herself. He jerked her back against him and held her until she stopped struggling. "Goddamn it, be still and listen to me! Your coming apart won't do either one of us any good. Do you understand me?" The harshness in his voice was an instinctive act of bravado, a mechanism to protect while he struggled with his own fear. So he held her in this strained, unloving embrace until the riot of apprehension in his own mind could subside enough to let him act. When she had become almost limp in his arms, he pushed her away from him and looked into her face until she nodded that she understood. "Now, go in the living room and get your clothes," he instructed. "Get mine, too, and bring them in here." She hesitated. "Don't be afraid. Whoever was here is gone." He didn't know that—for certain. His confident tone was part of the bravado. But he sensed that whoever wrote the note was not ready for a direct confrontation—the timing wasn't right.

David walked with her to the door of the study, then returned to his desk, picked up the telephone, and dialed Glenn's number. While the phone rang he looked at his watch—it was just after eleven. Madelyn answered.

"Have you and Glenn gone to bed?" David asked, not even identifying himself.

"David? No, we were just about to, though. Do you want to talk to Glenn?"

"Yes, please." He tried to keep the alarm out of his voice, but Madelyn must have sensed it. He could detect a note of urgency when she called Glenn to the phone.

"What's up, Dave?" he asked so pleasantly that he immediately made David feel better.

"I'm going to ask you to do something that will sound strange, Glenn, but please do it without asking me a lot of questions. I want you and Madelyn to come over here—over to Parsons—right now. I'll explain when you get here. Will you come?"

"Of course, we'll come." He didn't hesitate at all. "It will take about fifteen minutes. Anything else? Should I bring anything? I mean, do you need anything?"

"Do you have a gun?"

Here there was a small pause before Glenn answered. "Well, yes. You mean a pistol?"

"Yes. Bring your pistol."

"One question, Dave. Will Madelyn be in danger?"

"No. Not now."

"We're on our way."

Grace had returned to the study and dressed while David talked on the phone. She stood watching him as he pulled on his slacks and shirt and stepped into his loafers. The simple act of dressing seemed to have calmed her, but now she needed something else to do.

"Go make us a pot of coffee, Grace," David instructed, "and bring a bottle of brandy in from the bar, with some glasses." She didn't move, so he went over and put his arms around her. "We're going to do what we can, honey. You heard me talking to Glenn. They'll be here in ten minutes. Now, go and do what I asked you to do."

"Why don't you call the police?"

"I will. I promise I will. But I want to talk to Glenn first." That seemed to satisfy her, and she turned and walked out of the room.

The note was unsigned, of course, and as David read it over and over again, he noticed that it was not written in script. It had been carefully hand-printed in strong vertical letters on plain white bond paper. Although the note's language seemed stilted, there was a strange literacy about it. And the poem—whoever wrote the note hadn't authored that—David had read it before, years ago. Glenn would know, he thought, English literature was his métier. But there was no question about the intent of the grisly letter—to have them all, David and his childhood friends, live in fear, dread the darkness of every night until he killed them, one by one. But who was this brute who knew them all? Glenn and Madelyn and Gilbert and Dick, he had written. Someone from . . . The doorbell rang. David's preoccupation had been such that he hadn't heard the Walkers drive in or walk onto the porch.

Glenn and Madelyn looked at him soberly through the screen door and followed him down the hallway without a word after he beckoned them to come inside. Glenn carried the pistol awkwardly, self-consciously, with his hand wrapped around the cylinder.

There was more sitting room in the parlor, but David preferred the study because no one could see inside. He couldn't avoid a creepy feeling that they were being watched, regardless of what he had told Grace. The Walkers sat on the couch and he pulled a chair and the coffee table from across the hall. They looked surprised when he rolled the swivel chair from behind his desk as an indication that a fourth person would join them. The surprise faded from their faces as Grace came in with brandy and glasses on a tray. They seemed to accept her presence without question. Glenn stood up; he was still holding the pistol.

"Hello, Grace," he said—the first words spoken since they had come in. "Here, let me help you with that." He dropped the pistol on the couch and took the tray, holding it for an indecisive moment before placing it on the coffee table.

"Hello, Glenn, Madelyn." She had come to call them by their Christian names during the six-month period of Frony's collapse. "The coffee's ready, David. Should I bring it in?"

"Yes, bring the coffeepot. We'll plug it in here to keep it warm." After she returned to the kitchen, he spoke to the Walkers. "Let's wait until Grace gets back. This will take some time, and you might as well have some coffee. You won't be going to sleep for a while."

"That sounds pretty ominous, Dave," Glenn said and picked his pistol up from the sofa where he had dropped it. The action was a reflex and he seemed a little embarrassed by it. "Is there any immediate threat that Madelyn and I should know about?" He couldn't resist looking over his shoulder into the semidarkness at the other end of the poorly lighted study.

"No. I don't think so. I'll explain everything, but it will take a little time."

"David, can't you—" Madelyn began, but Glenn interrupted.

"Let's just wait, honey. Dave wants Grace here when he starts." He sat down beside her on the sofa and patted her hand affectionately. An almost imperceptible shudder of nervousness and fear ran through her. David sat wondering how he could go through this without scaring the hell out of her.

The coffee was poured, and he had to begin.

"You remember I was supposed to see Frony Thursday night, after I left your place. She was coming here. Well, she never showed up."

David told them in complete detail what had happened from the time he sat waiting for Frony on Parsons's front porch until he and Grace had finished searching for her. "We finally discovered that one small piece of her luggage was missing. We were damned relieved—assumed she had just gone off with someone without telling anybody."

"That's why you called this afternoon to ask about Frony?" Glenn asked.

"Yes, I called you from her place."

"You didn't mention that you hadn't seen her Thursday night."

"I didn't see any point in mentioning it. You said you hadn't heard from her in a week."

"Well, if you haven't heard from her since—"

David interrupted Madelyn because he could tell she wasn't quite following.

"None of us had heard from her in five days, not since Tuesday night when I talked to her on the phone. But after we discovered one of her bags missing, we really stopped worrying. I mean we . . ." How could he keep from getting lost in one digression after another? He was't doing a very good job of telling the story, and he could sense Grace's impatience. "Look, let's just say we thought Frony had been thoughtless enough to go off on a long weekend without telling anybody."

"You *thought*. Don't you think so now?" Glenn asked. He was alert to something that was yet to come, something that would justify the pistol.

"No, but let me finish. Grace and I came back here to eat dinner. Then we . . . went out into the field for a while." He caught a knowing look in Madelyn's eyes as he got up and walked over to pick up the note from the desk. He had the feeling that she knew about him and Grace, and if Madelyn knew, so did Glenn. Well, what the hell! We're all grown folks! David exclaimed to himself. But he couldn't help flushing slightly as he handed the note to Glenn. "I found this on my desk when we came back inside."

Glenn and Madelyn leaned close, their two blond heads almost together, as they both began to read. A muscle in Glenn's jaw jutted under his pale skin as his eyes worked down the page, and Madelyn's fingers, resting on Glenn's forearm, dug into his flesh. She pressed closer to his side and leaned forward to bring her nearsighted eyes closer to the paper. Her chest rose and fell sharply as her breathing quickened. After several minutes she raised her wide eyes and turned to look at Glenn. His face was grim, but otherwise expressionless, when he, too, looked up from the brutal, threatening page. Madelyn was the first to speak.

"My God in heaven, David!" she exclaimed. Disbelief was in her voice. "Is this real? This must be some cruel joke. Who would—"

"I don't think it's a joke, Madelyn," Glenn said evenly. He had been studying David's face, and he could see the trouble in it. "You've had a little time to think about this, Dave. Do you have any idea who it is?"

Before David answered, he pulled his chair next to Grace's and took her hand between his. He could tell she was about to crumble. Her eyes were darting from one to the other of them, looking for help.

"It has to be someone who knows all of us, knew us years ago, when we were kids playing together. I haven't seen the others— Gilbert, Dick, Howard—D, for that matter . . ." Grace's hand jerked out of David's as a nervous spasm went through her, and she began to tremble again. He put his arm around her shoulder as Madelyn jumped up to try to calm her. "Pour some of that brandy, Glenn," she instructed. Grace twisted her head when David put the glass to her lips.

"I don't want the goddamned brandy," she screamed. Her eyes were blazing. "You're sitting here going over all this shit while

Mother's . . . while she's . . . Why the hell don't you call the police?'' She began to sob convulsively. With Glenn's help David got her to the couch and forced her to lie down. She curled on her side with her hands over her face. Tears streamed between her fingers as Madelyn knelt beside her, cooing and comforting her as she would a child.

Glenn pulled at David's arm and tilted his head toward the other end of the room. The two men walked into the shadowy end of the study.

"Why *don't* we call the police, Dave? I mean, why don't we call Gil Thomas?''

It took a few seconds for David to connect what he was saying. "My God! I completely forgot about Gil being on the police force. What fucking irony! Him being one of us, one of the threatened. He's a detective, isn't he?''

"He's head of the homicide unit.''

Homicide. There it was, the true meaning of the grotesque note, the complete threat defined in one word. To David "homicide'' had never sounded like a euphemism for *murder.*

Chapter Ten

Gilbert Thomas didn't look anything at all like David's memory of him. He was no longer the fat kid they had called "Brother" when he lived down the block on Seneca Street. David had pictured a plump, small-town cop with a sweaty face and a baggy uniform. What came through the front door was a crisp-looking plainclothes (light-gray Palm Beach suit) detective, about five ten, a hundred and seventy-five compact pounds with a sharp-featured, intelligent face and thinning brown hair.

"Hello, David," Gil said and clasped David's hand briefly, then Glenn's. "Glenn, Madelyn," he acknowledged. Then he looked past them at Grace, standing a few paces to the rear. An expression of puzzled semi-recognition came to his face.

"Gil, this is Grace Bennett, Frony and D's daughter," Glenn said as they all shifted aside to let Grace greet the policeman she had begged them to produce.

"Hello, Grace," he said gently, and David could tell by his eyes that he was thinking back twenty years, remembering the long-legged, black-haired Frony. Poor bastard, he was probably in love with her, too. "I'm Gilbert Thomas, an old friend of your parents'. You're over at the college now, aren't you?"

As Grace mutely nodded, still too unstrung to speak, Gil seemed to transfer enough of his calmness to her that she managed a faint smile. For several seconds they looked unblinkingly at each other. The effect on Grace was amazing. The mixture of dread and fear and anxiety drained from her face. It was more than calmness he was transferring; it was his strength, although he didn't touch her, not even to shake her hand. David observed the effect and realized Gil represented something to Grace that none of the rest of them did. He was authority, competence, the solution to their problem—he was the doctor of law and order, brought in to save their lives. So to reassure her, all he had to do was stand before her and show that there was no fear in his eyes.

"Okay, Glenn," he said as he turned back to the two men, "let's get on with it. Where do I sit down while somebody tells me why you got me out of bed after midnight."

David led the way into the study, where Gil immediately selected the more comfortable of the two chairs, and Glenn, Madelyn, and Grace sat on the sofa. They all looked at David, who had been trying to make up his mind where to start. After pondering the decision for another moment, he began with the search of Frony's house, trying to tell it exactly as he had told the Walkers, and he ended by handing the note to Gil. David must have read it ten times since he'd found it, and his lips almost moved to recite its contents as Gil read. Minutes went by, and as the others sat silently and watched the detective studying the single sheet of note paper, they began to shift and fidget in their seats, impatient for him to do something, to say something. He hadn't spoken a word since David had begun his horror story.

"Who the hell is William?" he asked finally as he looked up from the note, first at David, then at Glenn and Madelyn.

"We don't know," David answered for all of them. "We've been over and over every sentence, every phrase, in that goddamned thing. None of it makes sense. The only thread is the eight of us lived in the same neighborhood when we were kids. But there was no William, no kid we called Bill. Notice how formal that letter is. He calls Frony 'Margaret' and D 'Dwight.' "

"Okay, let's don't get into any more of that sort of thing now," Gil said rather sharply. "Our immediate problem is finding Frony. I suppose all of you have had your hands all over this piece of paper." He looked at each of them in turn and watched their faces burn as they realized they had probably ruined any chances of his picking up fingerprints from the letter.

"No, I can't, but you're assuming that whatever we did, whatever colossal sin we committed, had to be back then, when we were kids. Why couldn't it have been later?"

"That's not reasonable, Dave. We all split up and went our separate ways. I'll bet there's hardly anyone we all know in common that we met after D and Frony got married and left town."

There really wasn't anybody else. All the grown-ups and other kids they had known had been benign people, phantoms that floated in and out of their lives almost unnoticed, peripheral and unimportant to their group.

"Okay, Glenn. You've made that point," David conceded. "What else?"

"Who is the only person you and I—all of us—have ever known that was as big as the man you said you saw with Frony?" Glenn didn't expect an answer, because he was going to answer this himself. "Son had to be six and a half feet tall, maybe more. He must have weighed two hundred and fifty pounds when we knew him, and he was only about twenty years old."

"You're leaving out one very important factor, my detective friend," David challenged. "If the conclusion we reached last night that my Grove Street man and Frony's Berlin man are one and the same, then that puts our miraculously recovered half-wit in Frony's Berlin bed six years ago. Do you want to give me a couple of reasons why that doesn't wash?" David waited just long enough for Glenn to start to respond before he held up his hand to stop him. "Allow me, if you please." He got up and paced to the other end of the study and back. "Number one, what you're saying implies that Son has been out of Whitfield for over six years. Number two, you're saying that he was mentally capable of getting past the government people and becoming part of a military or diplomatic contingent in Germany. Number three, you're saying that he was Frony's bed partner over a long period of time—if that were true, how could she not know it was old Simple Son who was slipping it to her?" He stopped pacing and sat on the corner of the desk facing the bookcases where Glenn leaned against the shelves in arm-folded patience.

"Am I correct in assuming you ain't buying that part of my theory?" Glenn asked in mock seriousness.

"You are one hundred percent correct. I ain't buying."

"All right, let's leave that alone for a while." Now Glenn began to pace, and he asked his next question from the far end of the study. "Who was the only other person besides the ones in that murder note who got the shit scared out of him sitting on the curb and listening to those ghost stories? Here, let me read you something from your own book." Glenn had returned to the desk and was running his finger down a page in the book. "*In our childish cruelty we would make every situation more horrible and whisper an embroidery of dreadful detail into Simon's recoiling ear.*" He looked up from the book and asked, "Who had more reason to hate all of us for what we did to him when we were kids? We didn't know what we were doing, but don't you remember how we tormented the poor bastard? Think about it, Dave. You remember how we scared each other. Can you imagine how terrifying it must have been for Simple Son?"

David did think about it—the row of them huddled together on the curb, goose bumps on their bare legs, shivering in the warm air of the southern night, each in turn with his lips close to Son's ear, slipping poison into that puny brain. They were guilty of being children, and that was all. Everyone knew that children were cruel. But that was too poor a defense to mention to Glenn.

"If anybody has thought about it, I have, Glenn. Or did you miss the theme of 'Ghost Stories'?" David was back in his desk chair and he tapped the open book with his finger.

"No. I didn't miss the theme. I was just emphasizing a point—the last one I want to make. Son had the motive—revenge. Son was the *only* other person who was always around when the rest of us were together. Son is the *only* one we all know who fits the physical description of the Berlin man and the Grove Street man. We said last night it was possible these two were the same person, right?" Glenn spread his hands on the desk and leaned toward David on stiff arms. Their faces weren't more than a foot apart and David could feel Glenn's breath when he spoke. "Simple Son is out there somewhere, and he intends to kill us all."

There was no doubting Glenn's conviction that he had made his case. The points he'd made were difficult to refute. Everything he'd postulated would have made absolute sense, if it hadn't been for one thing—Son was an imbecile. How could that shambling, mind-crippled hulk of a man-boy they had known twenty-five years ago be anything but what he was then?

David couldn't stand the pressure of Glenn's staring down into his incredulous face, waiting for his arguments, waiting to be told where he was wrong. With some effort David broke Glenn's lock on his eyes and got up to pace behind the desk.

"Glenn, whoever wrote that note was literate—not sane, but literate. Son wasn't insane. He wasn't someone who had once been normal and then gone off his rocker. Those people can be nuts at one minute and lucid as hell—literate—the next. Son's bread just wasn't baked. Never had been. People like Son stay that way. I know everything else you say makes sense. Everything seems to fit perfectly, down to the motive for someone wanting to kill the eight of us. But you're asking me to believe—have you ever heard of anyone as feebleminded as Son getting to the point where he could—well, it just doesn't happen."

"How do you know it doesn't happen?" Glenn wasn't yielding.

"Okay, let's just say I never heard of it happening. I asked you before. Have you?"

"No, I haven't, but that doesn't mean it can't happen." Glenn finally backed down a little to admit, "We're laymen where that sort of thing is concerned, Dave. We just don't *know*, either of us, whether it could happen or not. If it's impossible that Son recovered, then my theory is shot. Look, we both know how we can find out."

"You mean call Whitfield and see if Son is still there." The thought had occurred to David even as he was formulating his arguments against Glenn's theory.

"Yes."

"Let's do it, then." David got up, and when Glenn started to follow him into the hall, he said, "Stay here. I'll get the phone from the living room and plug it in over there." He pointed to a receptacle in the wall behind the desk.

David returned with the phone, called the operator for the Whitfield number, and had just sat down with his finger poised to dial when the realization came to him that he couldn't ask for information about someone named Simple Son Hammond.

"Do you remember Son's real first name?" he asked Glenn.

Glenn stared at him blankly and without answering got up and walked into the kitchen to ask Madelyn.

"Madelyn says it's Ralph," he reported when he came back.

"She must have thought that was a peculiar question to ask her."

"She did."

For fifteen minutes they alternated trying to persuade the people on the other end of the line to tell them how they could find out about a patient at Whitfield. The people were all uniformly adamant in declining to give them any information whatsoever over the telephone. David slammed the phone into its cradle in frustration when he got his final negative response.

"Goddamn it! We'll have to go up there."

"Yes, I guess we will," Glenn agreed, "and we should go as soon as we can."

"Maybe Gil should go with us."

Glenn didn't look forward to a repeat performance in trying to convince Gil of his Son Hammond theory, but he nodded and said, "Okay, we'll wait awhile. But if we don't hear from him by noon, I want to go anyway."

At eleven thirty a sergeant from the homicide division called to say that Captain Thomas would be in touch with them later in the afternoon. No, he wasn't available in any way at this time, the sergeant insisted, but he would be with them later in the afternoon, definitely.

Just after twelve thirty David and Glenn pulled out of the driveway in Glenn's car and took the shortcut along College Road to the highway. Whitfield was just over a hundred miles almost due north, and they expected to get there before three o'clock.

Madelyn and Grace had shown a definite lack of enthusiasm for being left alone, and the two plainclothes policemen Gil had stationed in front and back of the house didn't think Captain

Thomas would like David and Glenn running around loose without someone to keep an eye on them. They told the women they would be back about seven or eight o'clock and they told the policemen they would be back in about thirty minutes, maybe a little longer. These negotiations had taken about an hour.

It was a relief for both of them, especially David, to get outside, away from the house. Except for the trip with Grace to search Frony's house the day before, he had been cooped up inside for over three days. For the first ten miles after they got to the highway, David just looked out the window at the countryside. Everything was late-spring green. He hadn't really remembered how lovely these rolling hills could be at this time of year.

Glenn drove with a certain grim determination, remaining silent; that suited David just fine. A lot of stuff was running around in his head, and he had some thinking to do. For the next twenty miles he pieced thought fragments together. Then he opened the copy of *Frankenstein* he had brought along and began to go over some parts he had marked to reread the night before. There were connections between Mary Shelley's horror story and the real-life horror they were experiencing; he was convinced of it—if only he could order the thoughts that slipped so elusively past each other, almost but not quite connecting, inside his head. Very suddenly two details fell into place, came together, and lay comfortably side by side in the front of his mind. David sat up straight from the relaxed slouch he had assumed.

"You said last night you'd read *Frankenstein*, Glenn. How long has it been since you read it?" The question was a prologue to what he really wanted to talk about.

Glenn thought for a minute, then replied. "I was in high school, so it was over twenty years ago. I want to read it again when we get back tonight."

"Do you remember who the monster's first victim was?"

"No." Glenn detected the excitement in David's voice and turned his head to give him a quick glance.

"It was Victor Frankenstein's little brother."

Glenn ran this fact through his mind, but the significance of it escaped him. He waited briefly to see if David would elaborate, and when he didn't, it became obvious that he was waiting for Glenn's reaction.

"Now that you remind me, I do remember it. But I'm not getting any farther than that. Obviously, there's something else you have in mind."

"Do you remember what the little brother's name was?"

"No, I don't."

"It was *William*."

This time Glenn's head snapped around so violently that his hands jerked on the wheel and the car swerved dangerously before he could straighten it out.

"Christ!" David exclaimed. "Take it easy!"

Glenn looked intently at the road, but his mind wasn't on his driving. He was busy making the same mental connections David had already made.

"Holy Jesus!" he swore just above a whisper. "The William in the note and the one in *Frankenstein* and the Billy in your story are all the same. At least, they are the same in the mind of the person who wrote the note."

"I think that's it. Now if we've made that connection correctly, what does that suggest about my relationship with the crazy bastard that wrote the note?"

Glenn drove in silence for a mile, trying to work out an answer to David's question. He finally confessed that he couldn't. "I don't know, Dave. I need more to work with."

"Okay, try this. Why was the note sent to me and not to one of the others of you?" David paused to let Glenn absorb the question before he continued. "Why did the note say I would be the last to die? Remember, in the book, Victor Frankenstein was the last to die."

"You mean that for some weird reason he's identified you with his—the monster's—creator, Victor Frankenstein?"

"Yes, and that's why I think he—"

"Wait a minute, Dave. I want to go back to another point. Why did you invent a little brother for that story? It was inconsistent with the rest of it. You mentioned him and killed him off immediately, so why put him in there in the first place?"

"It was a shitty story, Glenn." David was a little piqued at the criticism. "One of the first ones I wrote. I don't even remember why I put him in. Maybe a symbol of something I had lost in my youth. Anyway, that's not important now. Let's suppose you're right; I'm the parallel to Victor Frankenstein. I started to say a minute ago that I thought that's why he plans to save me until last."

"I didn't remember that the monster killed Frankenstein."

"He didn't. Not directly. But Frankenstein died from chasing the monster all over the Arctic ice cap. It was the monster's final revenge for being created such a repulsive brute."

"I guess I keep thinking of the nothing-like-the-book movie version," Glenn confessed. "You don't look anything like Basil Rathbone."

David returned Glenn's quick smile, grateful that they both still had a sense of humor.

"Now, get ready for this," David warned. "I don't want you to wreck the car. You remember the line in the note that said '*Glenn should have been before Dwight*'?" The question was rhetorical, more of a statement that would be expanded. "That would have made you the second victim instead of D, and that would have made our theory consistent with the book, because the monster's second victim was Henry Clerval, Frankenstein's best friend."

Glenn thought for a minute, then nodded. "That's why I was supposed to be after William instead of D. I'm your best friend, so I'm Clerval's counterpart." He mused for thirty seconds before he went on. "You didn't actually have a brother named William or Billy. Do you really think he killed someone else—some kid—anyway?"

"I've been thinking about that. If he did, it had to be over six years ago, before D. Remember, the note said *of course, William was first*. Then again it could just be something in his head, an aberration. You know, Glenn, this guy might have known of some kid who died before D did, someone he named 'William' to suit his own purposes. We don't even know what level of rationality we're dealing with. But maybe Gil could check on it—you know, see if there's anything about a kid being killed, even strangled, about that time."

"What time? It could have happened a long time before he killed D, and it could have been anywhere, not necessarily around here."

"Yeah, I suppose so."

"Why did you say 'strangled'?" Glenn asked.

"That's the only way Frankenstein's monster killed his victims," David answered, turning to a page in the book where he had underlined part of a sentence. "Frankenstein's little brother was strangled. His father found him and says, *'The print of the murderer's finger was on his neck.'* Clerval was throttled to death and so was Frankenstein's new bride, Elizabeth. I don't think any of us has to worry about being shot or stabbed to death."

They were both silent for a few miles. David assumed Glenn was taking the same small solace in this limitation on the prospective modes of their execution.

When Glenn spoke, he made a grim observation. "Son strangled his mother."

Chapter Twelve

Dr. Lawrence Betchel greeted David and Glenn with the antiseptic cordiality peculiar to doctors and ushered them into his office. He was a rather ordinary-looking man of middle height with thinning brown hair and pale blue eyes. David guessed his age at about fifty. He seemed slightly nervous.

"I understand you have come to see one of our patients—an old friend from some years back," Dr. Betchel said pleasantly enough after his two visitors had taken chairs in front of his enormous highly polished desk.

"Yes, we have, Doctor," Glenn confirmed and was uncertain how to continue. "Actually, it has been about twenty-five years since we've seen him."

Glenn immediately regretted having admitted they had neglected their "old friend" for all those years. David regretted it, too, when he saw the doctor's eyebrows lift in surprise.

"Twenty-five years! What makes you think he's still—I mean, he may not still—" Dr. Betchel was having a difficult time getting out what he wanted to say. "Why, you must have been just kids the last time you saw him." He was passing judgment, and they knew it. All three of them were uncomfortable.

"Well, yes. We were," Glenn conceded. "But it's important that we see him now, Dr. Betchel. We'd like to see Ralph Hammond."

The effect of this request on Dr. Betchel was startling. He dropped the thin gold pencil he had been slipping back and forth between his fingers and leaned forward to look through his narrowed pale eyes at David. Glenn had made the request, but the doctor ignored him.

"Mr. Fleming, are you researching a new book?" he asked with none of the cordiality of moments before.

The question was so unexpected that David didn't immediately understand what he meant.

"You mean now?" David asked.

"Yes."

"Why, no. Of course not." The response carried sufficient indignation to be convincing. Dr. Betchel relaxed enough for David to go on a small offensive. "That was a peculiar question to ask, Doctor. We just want to see a boyhood friend that I admit we have neglected for a very long time. What would Ralph Hammond have to do with my researching a new book?"

Now it was Betchel who hesitated before he answered. He had retrieved his pencil and resumed his nervous fingering of it, watching it slip through his fingers instead of looking at either of the two men across his desk.

"Did you always call him Ralph? I mean, when you were kids." The question was so crude that David was disappointed in the good doctor for making the test so easy.

"Doctor," he said as evenly as he could manage, "I didn't even know his first name was Ralph until today. We always called him Son when we were kids. He lived right across the street from me. I've known him all my life."

Dr. Betchel's face brightened instantly, and he got up and came around to lean casually against the front of his desk.

"I'm sorry I questioned your motives, Mr. Fleming—and Dr. Walker. We have to be very careful here. For some reason a mental hospital holds a strange fascination for the general public. The press—reporters or writers of any kind—make me very nervous." He smiled his apologies at David. "I was skeptical because I thought you would have known about Son Hammond—he was before my time, but they called him Son here, too. He hasn't been here for years."

David could feel Glenn's knowing eyes on the side of his face and resented the satisfaction he took for being right. David also resented the excitement in Glenn's voice when he asked, "How many years, Dr. Betchel?"

"He was discharged in 1941," the doctor said without hesitation.

They were both so shocked they couldn't speak. 1941! For God's sake! That was over twenty years ago, and the doctor knew the exact year, without thinking, even though Son had been there before his time. David had to ask him about that.

"Why would you remember Son's release date so precisely, Dr. Betchel? You weren't even here then. There must have been thousands of patients. Why would—"

Glenn cut him off with a question he considered more direct. "How could you discharge him after just a few years? Son was an imbecile and a murderer! He killed his own mother. He would always have to be institutionalized. Did you send him somewhere else?"

Instead of answering, Dr. Betchel leaned forward and pushed a button on the sleek intercom on his desk.

"Yes?" a hollow-sounding female voice responded.

"Hold my calls for a while, Marie. I'll let you know."

"Yes, Doctor."

Betchel went to a file cabinet, took out a fat folder, and reclaimed his seat behind the desk. Before he opened the file, he looked at his watch, which prompted Glenn and David to glance quickly at theirs. It was just after four o'clock.

"Gentlemen, I'm going to review Son Hammond's history at this institution for you. It was a remarkable case. Of course, I won't disclose the confidential aspects, but a lot of information is available because the case was the subject of several papers in medical and psychiatric journals. It was a landmark case in some respects—altered certain neurological procedures to the point where—" Dr. Betchel realized that he was becoming discursive, so he began again. "Look, there is no way for me to tell you about this without using certain medical and psychiatric terms you probably won't completely understand. In some ways they're not important, so don't worry about them. Just try to get the gist of what I'm saying. I'll give it to you in narrative form"—he waited for David to smile his appreciation, one storyteller to another, before he went on—"and I'll appreciate it if you hold any questions you might have until I've gone through it. I have to leave in about thirty minutes, and we may be a little pressed for time."

The two of them nodded that they understood and waited for him to continue.

"I'm sure you are familiar with the circumstances that brought Son here in early September of 1936. Yes. Well, we won't dwell on that. There was some apprehension at first about homicidal tendencies because of what he had done, of course, but in larger measure, it appears from the records, because of his physical size. He is described as being six feet seven and one half inches tall and weighing two hundred and forty-six pounds when he was admitted.

"At this hospital the intake physician—the doctor who oversees admissions—is a neurologist. In 1936 that position was held by Dr. Hugh Cornell, who had been on staff about four years. He was very thorough in all his post-admission examinations and did a complete neurological workup on Son before he sent him off for psychological testing. During his examination of Son he had noticed some imbalance of the eye muscles, specifically that Son seemed to have some trouble looking upward. He also noticed that the pupils of Son's eyes were somewhat small. Dr. Cornell gave considerable thought to this and noted in his records that this was unusual in someone who appeared to be just a nonspecific mental retardate—in other words, just feebleminded.

"Cornell decided to bring Son back for another look, but not before he retrieved Son's medical records from downstate and made three or four full skull X rays and some—I hate to say it—rather primitive EEG's. In those days they had only a few channels, four or five. Well, anyway, the X rays really didn't show anything, but the EEG's showed a curious slowing of the frontal areas. That is, the signals from the wires hooked up to the forehead regions never seemed to have as much speed consistently, or the frequency wasn't as high consistently, as for other areas of the brain.

"The slowing phenomenon was fully substantiated when Cornell ran EEG's on his own equipment, and he decided to run another series of X rays. One of the X rays showed a very faint indication of calcified flecks in the area of the pituitary gland—just over it, in an area of the brain called the sella.

"The medical terms will get pretty thick as I try to explain what this means, so just hang on and follow the best you can.

"Anyway, this discovery led Cornell to wonder whether this was a potentially correctable problem with Son. He suspected a craniopharyngioma. This is a congenital abnormality, a very slow growth of extra tissue in the area of the pituitary gland. It is, in effect, a tumor. Such tissue formations put pressure on the third ventrical of the brain and could alter some of the eye movements. Of considerably more interest to Cornell, however, was the effect such a growth could have on Son's behavior patterns. If it were a tumor of any size, it could prevent the fluid from draining effectively from the lateral ventricles, which in turn would compress the upper lobes of the brain. Cornell speculated that this could account for Son's learning disabilities. That is, he would look for all the world like someone simply retarded from birth—poor memory function, little or no language function, trouble with controlling impulses—with little negative effect on motor skills.

"In any event, Cornell had built himself a pretty exciting medical theory. He trotted his X rays over to the general hospital section and talked to a couple of neurosurgeons on the staff about a neurosurgical workup that would include arteriograms and pneumoencephalograms. They do that by taking—well—pictures when air is bubbled up from the spine into the head. Well, the surgeons weren't too enthusiastic—thought the procedure could be too risky, especially in a long-term problem like Son. Actually, Cornell's X rays weren't too convincing. The surgeons suggested to him that the calcium flecks weren't in the brain at all, but in the outer table of the skull.

"Cornell was a very persistent man, however. He kept working on his theory and read up on it the best he could—there wasn't a hell of a lot in the literature on the subject back then. It took him about a month to remember a procedure—completely experimental at the time—that might solve his problem. A friend of his from medical school days had come up with the idea of using a moving X-ray tube that could send a beam in a single plane through various parts of the body, including the brain. The image obtained could be reconstructed on a crude analog computer. This was really the beginning of computer-assisted tomography—very important in today's diagnostic techniques.

"Well, anyway, they got their pictures—Cornell had to take Son all the way to the West Coast—which showed that the lateral ventricles were dilated. That could mean—uh, well—let's say it supported the tumor theory. The tumor could be blocking the flow of spinal fluid—the cerebrospinal fluid the brain makes to bathe itself. If the fluid isn't absorbed at the proper rate, the lateral ventricles dilate and the upper lobes of the brain can be compressed. The uppermost part of the brain stem—the diencephalon region—is responsible for certain motor controls, eye movement, for instance. It also controls mood and other nonmotor functions.

"Now Cornell had the evidence he needed to convince the surgeons. They decided they would take a frontal bone flap out, lift up the frontal lobe of the brain, and, very simply, look in to see what they could find. When they did, they saw it sitting there—the tumor—easy to circle and ligate. They pulled it out, en bloc, and found a relatively uncalcified long-standing craniopharyngioma, just as Cornell had predicted. You can imagine how excited he was.

"Son had a small complication that scared the hell out of Cornell. He showed a left-side weakness after the operation—a slight paralysis on the left side. They had gone in on the right side—the nondominant hemisphere—and operated from that side. Physical therapy didn't help much, so, after eighteen days, they went back in and drained some collected subdural fluid. After that the change was truly astonishing. Son was making verbalizations that to their knowledge he'd never made before. They pulled out all the stops—speech therapy, tutoring. Son learned to read and write in six months. Keep in mind that no part of Son's brain was ever really damaged. When all the tissue was allowed to renew normal metabolic function, he was just filling in gaps. His mind was like a giant computer which had short circuits in certain areas. His brain was like a sponge, soaking up knowledge, filling in pieces, making connections.

"Son was at high school level four years after the operation— passed high school equivalency and was certified just before we released him. He wasn't brilliant, wouldn't have been even if he'd never had the tumor—but he was of above average intelligence. According to Cornell, he pretty much educated himself. About all he did was listen to the radio and read—hundreds and hundreds of books in the nearly five years he was here. Cornell made some notes about the types of books he read—almost exclusively fiction but some pretty heavy stuff. Seems he had an unusual reading proclivity—books on the supernatural, necromancy, that sort of thing. It worried Cornell for a while, until he realized it was a natural regression—going back for something Son figured he'd missed when he was younger. But still, paranoia in a man that big could be—"

"Dr. Betchel," David interrupted, "I'm sorry, but I'd like to get a little detail about the books that worried Dr. Cornell. Are they listed by title in the records?"

"No, not specifically by title," Dr. Betchel said after referring to one of the papers in the manila folder. "The observation about reading preferences was just a footnote in Cornell's paper."

"Is there anything else in the paper about—" How in the hell could David ask him the obvious question without getting so involved that he would have to go into all of it? Maybe if he let the doctor think it was curiosity he had piqued himself. "Well, I've always been interested in that sort of stuff myself—considered writing a novel along those lines. . . ." God, that sounded weak. "Anyway, you mentioned Dr. Cornell's being worried about paranoia in Son. Do you think he could have identified with any of the characters in the books he read?" David didn't want to get any more specific.

"Mr. Fleming," Betchel said with a chuckle, "you told me you weren't researching a new book." At least he misunderstood David's motives the way David wanted him to.

"Oh, no. Of course not." David returned the chuckle. "But we're both interested in Son and what happened to him. Everything you've told us, the way Son was cured, is next to incredible. An absolutely astounding medical—psychiatric—achievement."

"Ninety-nine percent medical," Dr. Betchel said modestly. He looked at his watch and sat forward in his chair, prepared to terminate the interview. "I'm sorry, but I have only a few more minutes."

"Just a few questions, Doctor," David said quickly. "Was there any evidence of serious paranoia in Son?"

"No. Not serious. Cornell noticed that he would become quite bellicose when he was taunted by anyone, especially the younger patients—the children. He was especially sensitive about his size and the somewhat ugly scar the operation had left on his right forehead. There was no reported physical violence. He was quite docile even when his coordination improved and he became more physically active. You have to realize, Mr. Fleming, that all of us are paranoid to a certain extent. We imagine small persecutions that don't really exist. True paranoids—as opposed to paranoid schizophrenics—can be very strong and decisive, very cunning. They can also be very charming. Adolf Hitler was a true paranoid." Betchel was expatiating even with the shortness of time. He had gotten more into his field and seemed eager to compete in some small way with the strictly medical people who had performed Son's miracle. He realized he was drifting into a lecture he didn't have time for, so he came back to the subject. "But Son got over his regressions for the most part—"

"Regressions?" Glenn spoke for the first time since Dr. Betchel had begun his recital. "What kind of regressions, Dr. Betchel?"

It was evident from the doctor's small show of annoyance that he wished he hadn't said anything about regressions. "Oh, just occasional states of depression. Most patients who are institutionalized for long periods have them. In a way, they're considered normal."

"Is that when Son's behavior would have these overtones of paranoia?" Glenn persisted.

"More the other way around. The paranoia would become evident and then—look, this is a very complex mechanism—"

"I know, Dr. Betchel," Glenn said and stood up. "You've been very patient with us. Do you have any idea why such a remarkable case—and one that was medically well-publicized—never made the local papers? I've lived here all my life, and I've never heard about this before."

"Publicity in scientific journals rarely leads to news stories elsewhere. We at the hospital certainly wouldn't announce something like this to the mass media. Some people would understand no more than that a murderer has been released into their midst." Dr. Betchel's face had taken on the same disdainful expression it had held when he'd earlier mentioned newspaper reporters.

"Yes, that makes sense. Thank you very much, Doctor," Glenn said. "I don't suppose you'd have any idea what happened to Son after he was discharged?"

"No. If Dr. Cornell were still alive, he probably could give you those details." Dr. Betchel stood up and walked around his desk to where they were standing.

"Dr. Cornell is dead?" The question showed David's obvious disappointment. "I had hoped—uh—how long ago did he die?"

"Ten or twelve years ago. I don't remember exactly. Tragic thing, too. He was on a weekend trip downstate to see the old plantations. Freak accident. He fell into one of those huge dry well things they have in back of some of those old plantation houses. Thing must have been thirty or forty feet deep. Broke his neck. I think they closed them all up after a little boy died the same way a year or so later."

Glenn's reaction was exactly the same as David's. They couldn't talk, but stared incredulously at the doctor, then turned to look at each other. There was no clairvoyance in either of them, no divination. They didn't need those gifts to figure it out. If it hadn't been for the boy *a year or so later*, it would have just been an unfortunate accident. Dr. Cornell could have been clumsy. But not the two of them; it had to be more than a coincidence.

The doctor wrung their hands and walked them to the door.

"Hate to rush you off," he was saying, "but I've told you about all I know. Probably more than you wanted to know. Sorry for the medical jargon. The rest is just more of the same that doesn't mean much to a layman. Good luck on locating Son. I'd kind of like to know what's become of him myself."

David regained his ability to talk just before the doctor closed the door. "Oh, Dr. Betchel, do you remember when in 1941 Son was discharged?"

"Yes, it was in May."

"Thank you, Doctor. We appreciate the time and the information you've given us."

Holy jumping mother of God! David's mind reeled at the thought of it. May of 1941! So Son could have been in the woods by the river that summer, watching Frony and me fuck in the sand. He could have been in Frony's bed in Berlin and with her on Grove Street. His lantern face could have shone in the woods at the edge of the field. It really could have been Son—yes, it had to be him. There was no one else. He had been watching them all for over twenty years.

Chapter Thirteen

Neither Glenn nor David spoke until they were well out of town. Glenn drove in deliberate silence, his face starkly serious as he stared at the highway, arranging his thoughts. The lush countryside David had admired earlier slipped unnoticed past the windows. His mind was entirely occupied with about a half-dozen connecting but strangely disjointed facts. They had a doctor who didn't know what he was talking about, because Son wasn't a mild paranoid. He was a raving lunatic. They had a doctor who had cured Son of imbecility and got a trip down a dry well as a reward. They had a kid who had got the same trip, and he guessed it was with the same help from their old friend, Simple Son. They had two women they weren't doing a very good job of protecting, plus the one woman he had loved all his life and whom he felt certain he would never see again. They had two amateur detectives who had better get their asses back home and tell the professional everything they had found out.

"We'll be home before dark," Glenn said, as if he'd read David's mind.

But David's thoughts had shifted back to Cornell and the boy. Had he jumped to a ridiculous conclusion when he assumed that Son waited all that time to kill the doctor who had been his benefactor and then waited another year for the boy, who was undoubtedly innocent of any crime against him? If it was ridiculous, why had Glenn instantly, simultaneously, jumped to the same conclusion? Several miles of concrete ran under the car before he spoke to Glenn about it.

"Do you think there's a chance we're wrong about Son killing Cornell and the boy?"

"I've been wondering if there's a chance we were *right*. I know we thought exactly the same thing back there in Betchel's office, but maybe we're—" Glen thought for a minute while he drove. "Well, maybe we're so keyed up on trying to prove our theory that we're getting ahead of ourselves. Those two deaths *could* have been coincidental accidents."

David mulled that over for a while.

"Do you really think they were?" he asked after he had watched another mile of Virginia countryside slide past his window.

"No." Glenn turned to give him a sober shake of his head.

"Okay. Let's just assume we're right. Why do you suppose Son killed Cornell? I'm supposed to be Victor Frankenstein."

"If you'll remember, you made that deduction yourself, about your being Son's creator," Glenn reminded him. "Of course, Cornell was the logical one. He literally invented the Son that's out prowling around now. I've got a very good idea why he's transferred to you, but I'd like to hear what you think."

"I think he screwed up when he killed Cornell, whose neck I'll bet was broken from strangulation before he hit the bottom of that well. I've got two theories on that. If he had his Frankenstein plan before he killed Cornell, he probably sat around mentally kicking himself until he kicked Cornell completely out of his memory. He didn't want to admit to himself that he'd killed the guy first who was supposed to be last. I'm inclined to think that he didn't formulate his plan until after he'd killed him. He would want to start fresh, and he'd need a new Frankenstein. I got elected because there weren't any other real candidates. He probably doesn't even remember the surgeon who actually opened up his head and took out the tumor. Anyway, he decided to start over again and restricted himself to the people who had tormented him when he was so helpless. Obviously he must have read my 'Ghost Stories,' so he wanted to start with my fictitious and innocent little brother. My God, I wonder if he went after a kid to kill or if one just happened along at a bad time. In either case, he must have put Cornell out of his mind. He doesn't count in the plan.''

"I agree with the second theory, that he probably didn't come up with his Frankenstein plan until after he'd killed Cornell. Maybe killing him made Son think of it. That leaves the question of *why* he killed him.''

"Okay, I asked the question in the first place, but I've got a good idea on that one. Want to tell me what you think?''

"All right, but I'll be putting some of it together as I go along, so bear with me.'' Glenn waited for David to nod before he went on. "Betchel said Cornell was killed about twelve years ago. That would put Son in his middle thirties.''

"Hold on,'' David interrupted. "Let me get this time thing straight. That would be in the early fifties, after all of us had pretty much gone our separate ways.''

"That's right. You were in New York and D and Frony were already in Europe. Dick McKenna may have still been in town—I can't remember—but Howard was dead. The only ones who never really left were Madelyn and me, and Gil, of course.''

"I didn't mean to slow you down. Go on.''

"Okay, where was I? Oh, yes. The way it figures, Son had been out of Whitfield nine or ten years when Cornell died. I'm betting he was a miserable son-of-a-bitch. He considered himself huge and ugly. After years of struggling to find a place in life, he wasn't really accepted. Women were afraid of him. Besides that, he knew he wasn't mentally normal—he was intelligent enough to know that much—but he didn't really know what was wrong with him. The depressions became more frequent. He couldn't remember what it was like to lead his imbecile life, but he began to long for it. In his mind it was simple and untroubled—he had expunged his mother's murder from his memory—compared to the torment he unwittingly manufactured for himself after he had been *cured*. Somebody had played a cruel trick on him, made him imperfect, almost but not quite like anybody else. Who was responsible?'' Glenn stopped his recitation and waited for David to answer.

"Cornell?''

"Who else? So he decided to kill him, to make Cornell pay for what he'd done."

"Jesus!" David exclaimed. "That's so close to what I worked out, I can't really add anything to it. I just wonder where in the hell Son *was* all those years. He apparently didn't come home. If he had, you would have seen or heard about him at one time or another."

"There really wasn't any reason for him to come back home. His father sold the house and left town shortly after Son was sent to Whitfield."

"Yes. I remember when he left. He never even came over to say good-bye to my folks."

They stopped talking about it because there wasn't much else to say. The monotony of the road ahead and the humming of the tires caused David to drowse into head-bobbing semiconsciousness. Pictures of Frony flashed in slow sequence onto his closed eyelids. He saw her bare-legged and radiant, in white sandals and white chiffon, standing at the Monte Carlo gambling tables . . . beautifully bare-breasted, lying on the beach at Cannes . . . tall and elegant, striding down a street in Rome . . . naked and urgent, thrusting her hips toward him on the sand by the river . . . crumpled and broken, dying at the bottom of a huge dry well. . . .

David's terrified eyes snapped open just as Glenn was turning onto College Road. They were less than a mile from home and, David realized with a flood of relief, less than a mile from Grace. And for the first time he accepted the reality that no matter what happened, Frony was lost to him. She had been taken out of his life by a justice of the peace long ago and by her own inability to handle being in love with a fifteen-year-old kid. He had lost her twenty years ago and Grace knew it better than he did. She had said it out in the field less than a week ago. *"I just want to be sure you're not in love with something you've created out of twenty years of memories,"* she had said, *"something that doesn't really exist after all this time."* Reality was less than a mile away. The woman he loved was safe at Parsons, waiting for him.

* * *

Gil Thomas was sitting on the front porch, slowly rocking back and forth in one of David's old wicker rocking chairs.

"I can tell by your faces that you have something you can't wait to report," Gil said so mildly that he almost disguised his irritation with them. "You can tell us all about it while you eat. Madelyn says you probably haven't eaten anything since breakfast." He got up and walked past them through the front door. When they got to the kitchen he was setting up a tape recorder on the kitchen table.

As Madelyn and Grace filled their two plates from the food warming on the stove, David drew Gil into the hallway and asked in an undertone, "Is there any news about Frony?" Glenn came up to join them in time to hear the question.

"No, nothing"—he paused—"yet." The pause was ominous instead of encouraging.

David honored Glenn's proprietorship of the theory by interrupting only rarely as he told the story. Madelyn interrupted more, especially at the beginning, to protest her inability to believe what she was hearing about Simple Son.

"Son Hammond!" she exclaimed at one point, shaking her head in rejection. "My God, Glenn! You can't be serious."

"Let's wait till he's finished, Madelyn," Gil said with enough quiet admonition in his voice to silence her. "I don't want a lot of extraneous stuff on this tape. Go on, Glenn."

Grace hadn't said a word since the two men had returned. Now she sat beside David with her hand on his forearm and watched Glenn with wide gray eyes. At certain times something he said caused her strong fingers to dig into David's arm in momentary muscular spasms.

Gil just listened until Glenn finished and David said he had nothing to add. He snapped off the tape recorder and leaned back in his chair. The others waited for thirty seconds while he ruminated.

"That's the goddamnedest story I've ever heard," he finally said.

"Well, what do you think, Gil?" David asked. "Are Glenn and I nuts?"

"I don't know. I've got to have a little time to digest what you've told me."

"Is there any particular part of this that bothers you?" Glenn asked.

"The whole goddamn thing bothers me, Glenn. You and David make a good case for your theory—and that's all it is right now—but it's preposterous to believe the Son we knew could be capable of—"

"But he's *not* the Son we knew, Gil," Glenn argued. "He's—"

"I know. He's not an imbecile anymore. The doctors transformed him into a killer who still holds a murderous grudge against a bunch of kids for scaring his ass off with ghost stories." David started to protest, but Gil went on. "I know I'm being unfair to the doctors. That was an overreaction. My big problem is that I really can't say you're wrong. If you're right, a lot of things start to come together. We've got a motive and a suspect who fits the physical description of the Berlin and Grove Street men. Right now Son is our only candidate. I'm just having a little trouble swallowing the whole story. I'll have to send a man out to ask the doctor a few more questions."

"What do you think about Cornell and the kid being killed in the well?" David asked. "I'm beginning to have second thoughts about that myself. Maybe it was just coincidence."

"It probably was, but I think there may be something on that in our records."

"Records? What records?"

"The general records in our central file. If my memory serves me, we looked into a couple of accidental-death cases that happened a lot like the way you say Cornell and the little boy died—falls into some kind of well. I wasn't involved in checking out either of the cases, but I'm sure somebody in the department made out reports on them."

"Do you remember where these accidents happened, Gil?" Glenn asked.

"I think it was Huntington—yes, I'm sure it was. You know, the old run-down place on the river about fives miles east of town. It's one of the few plantation houses from the Revolutionary period that hasn't been restored. I always wondered why the Historical Society ignored that place."

"You mean Cornell and the little boy were killed at Huntington?" Madelyn asked in disbelief.

"I didn't say that, Madelyn," Gil corrected quickly. "I just remember that a couple of people were killed from falls into a hole of some sort out in back of the main house. Who they were remains to be determined. Look, there's nothing more we can do on this tonight. I'm going back downtown to get these tapes transcribed." He paused to look at Glenn and David with stern policeman's eyes. "I'll appreciate it if you two don't take any more excursions without letting me know. If I'm not around when you call, ask for Jack Evans, Lieutenant Evans. He knows what's going on and he can either help you directly or get in touch with me."

"Gil, how long do you want Madelyn and me—and Grace—to stay here?" Glenn asked as Gil made a move toward the door.

"A while longer," he answered noncommittally. "We'll talk about it tomorrow."

The afternoon had been long and boring for Madelyn and Grace. They were restless for some kind of physical activity, but had nothing to do other than walk around the house and grounds. Whenever they were outside, their movements were closely monitored by the wary eyes of the two policemen Gil Thomas had left to watch over them. So they spent most of the afternoon in rocking chairs on the front porch making cautious conversation, each carefully avoiding any serious penetration into the things that really occupied their thoughts. During the course of the afternoon Madelyn made a few pungent observations about their two "heroes" going off and leaving them to shift for themselves.

So when the detective's parting comment presented them with the prospect of being virtual hostages for an indefinite time, Madelyn resolved to break the somber mood that had gripped them. At her insistence they played cards on the living-room floor until one by one they all became too tired to concentrate on the game. Finally, Madelyn pulled Glenn to his feet, said good night, and led him upstairs.

"I'd better go upstairs, too, David," Grace said. He faced her and put his hands gently on her shoulders. He leaned forward to kiss her, but she pulled away. "No, David, I just don't feel like—I can't—"

"No, no. I understand how you feel. We can wait for—until everything is cleared up." David didn't want her to leave, not just yet.

She had started to get up but now settled back onto the floor.

"David, Madelyn has known about us for a long time." She said it as if she were suddenly compelled to confess. The surprise on David's face caused her to hurry on. "I told her about it right after the first time. And she told Glenn, if you're wondering."

His face burned with the embarrassment of their knowing. No wonder they had reacted so mildly to his confession the night before. They had known all along. His reluctant admission that he had taken Grace into his bed must have amused them. They had nodded, had given small benevolent smiles to the citified seducer playing the fool. But that was the strange part, the smack of approval in the way they reacted. It suddenly occurred to David that his two old friends were pleased Grace was his lover. She was Frony's replacement, the daughter who could love him replacing the mother who couldn't.

"What did Madelyn say when you told her?"

"She was happy, David. That's what was so strange. She hugged me and then sat me down on the sofa in her living room and asked me all about it." Grace's eyes were wide with the dismay she remembered feeling at the time. "Oh, she didn't ask about—all the intimate details. She wanted to know how it started, how long we had been seeing each other, how I really felt about you, how you—"

"What did you tell her—about how you felt about me?"

Grace hesitated, then said solemnly, "I told her I was in love with you, David."

That's what David thought she had said. He just wanted to hear it.

"Did she ask how I felt about you?"

"Yes, she asked me."

"What did you say?"

Grace looked away from David's face briefly, then turned back to hold his eyes with hers. "I told her you weren't in love with me yet—but that you would be." She looked away again. "What should I tell her if she asks me now, David?"

"Tell her you were right," he said, and before she could react he asked another question. "Was Madelyn glad or sorry to learn that you were in love with me, Grace?"

"Oh, she was pleased. She said it was the best thing that could happen to you." Grace leaned forward, animation dancing in her face. "She said I'd be good for you."

"Did she say how?"

"We talked about you and Mother, David!" She sighed deeply after she'd said it. Her eyes, which usually looked at him so steadily when she spoke, were again cast aside. Before she went on, she turned her head to look gravely into his face. "Madelyn didn't—doesn't—think you and Mother are going to make it. She doesn't think you and Mother could ever—" She stopped so abruptly that David looked around to see if someone had come into the room. A shiver of apprehension ran down his spine. They were still alone. He took both her hands and squeezed them.

"What's the matter, Grace?"

"I'm feeling so goddamned guilty, David. Do you realize this is the first time today we've said anything about Mother? Nobody's said anything about her and the awful thing that's happened. I know I said I believed she was dead, but I don't really believe it. That's why I can't mourn." Her eyes implored him for an assurance he couldn't give.

"We've avoided talking about Frony because we don't know anything, Grace, not because we haven't thought about her. I don't want to build you up to expect too much, but you're right; it's too early to mourn."

"What do you honestly think, David? About Mother, I mean. Do you think she's dead, that he's already killed her?"

David knew he would have to answer carefully, so he took a little time. "There's no rational way I can justify it, but I think she's still alive. It's a gut reaction that I can't explain, just something I feel."

Grace's face brightened at the small encouragement.

"That's the way I feel, and that's what it is—a feeling, just some intuitive sense, that she's still alive."

"Don't let your instincts take you too far, Grace. You can build your expectations too high."

"You're wondering what I will do if we're wrong about Mother, aren't you?"

"I just want you to be able to handle whatever comes." He avoided answering her question directly. "When I told you not to expect too much, that's what I really meant, being able to handle it even if Frony—even if we don't find her in time."

Grace mentally adjusted to what he had said, then leaned forward until their faces were only inches apart. "If you're around, I can handle it," she declared with such resolution that David was convinced she really could.

"I'll be around," he assured her and took her face in his hands and kissed her. "I'll always be around."

There it was, the commitment he hadn't been able to make—not because he didn't really know he was in love with Grace, but because of his own emotional indecision. He knew it now, had accepted it in the car that afternoon when he was coming back to her.

"Always, David?" she asked.

"Grace, do you remember the other night, out in the field, when you said, 'I just believe that it's you and me now'?"

"Yes, I remember."

"You were right; I just didn't know it at the time. It *is* just you and me. I realize now that I've spent over twenty years of my life wanting something I couldn't have, not ever. Madelyn was right, Frony and I weren't going to make it. I know now it was over when she decided she couldn't wait for a fifteen-year-old boy to grow up. And Madelyn was right about something else. You're the best thing that could have happened to me. And we're going to make it. After all this is over, we're going to make it."

Tears glistened in Grace's eyes as she sat unmoving, leaning on her rigid arms, until a light shudder ran through her. The rhythm of her breathing changed, quickened. In one fluid motion she stood, slipping out of her clothes, leaving them in a bundle on the floor in back of her. Her eyes never left his face. David stood up and peeled off his clothes as she stood in front of him, gloriously naked, her breasts moving in the new quick cadence of her heated, open-mouthed panting. When she stepped forward, he kneeled and wrapped his arms around her hips. His face pressed into her belly, and he felt the soft beginning of pubic hair against his lips. The rhythm now was in her groin, and as the motion started, she clasped her hands behind his head and pulled him into her.

She moved forward, pushing against him, forcing him back until he released her and rolled onto the floor. She followed him down, kneeling over him.

"David! Oh, Christ! David!" She pressed herself hard into his face, a signal to stop, to let her recover. She raised herself to slide down him until she could reach his mouth with hers. They mingled their juices as they kissed, their mouths wide to accept the probing tongues. Then she turned so that he could move over her.

Now. Do it now, David! Another instruction from over twenty years ago. *Go slow, David.* But he couldn't. She was too insistent, too close. So was he.

Grace lay with her head on his shoulder and her arm across his chest. They hadn't spoken. The spell, the afterglow, was still strong in them as they waited for their pulses to become regular again. She shifted her head, and he felt her lips move against his throat.

"I love you, David."

I love you, Frony.

I know you do, David.

"Say that again, Grace."

"I love you." She propped up on her elbow and rested her head in her hand, watching him smile. After a while she asked, "Are you going to say it?"

"What?" he teased.

She bent down and bit his lower lip. "Do you love me?"

"Desperately."

"Then, say it."

He reached up and cradled her face in his hands. "I love you, my darling heart." His smile was gone, and his voice almost broke when he continued, because he wanted her to believe him. "I'll never let you go."

Her tears fell on his cheeks.

She loves me! David exulted. God, how different this is!

Grace climbed the stairs with her clothes in her hands. David stood at the base of the stairs admiring the way she moved. When he snapped off the light, moonlight flooded through the windows into the darkened living room. Jesus! he thought. We fucked with the shades up. Well, the watchful detectives no doubt had a set of erections to keep them company. As he followed Grace up the stairs, he wondered if anyone else had looked, with leering maniac eyes, through those windows.

Just as David was drifting into sleep Grace's mouth moved close to his ear. "Why did Mother do what she did with a man like that Son Hammond?"

His stupor kept him from comprehending. "What? I don't understand what you mean."

"In Berlin, before Daddy died. Remember what you said, what Madelyn and Glenn told you about Mother sleeping around. If that man she was with so much was really Son Hammond—and if, like Glenn said, he's the one who killed Daddy—how could Mother do that?"

David didn't know. Maybe she was sick, confused. That's what he told Grace and urged her to go to sleep, to forget for a while. What *about* Son, if that was him back in Berlin? Had she known who he was? Did she actually know that the man she was fucking was old Simple Son, the shambling imbecile from Seneca Street? Maybe she did, maybe she was Son's first woman, as she had been David's, and maybe she knew it, and there was some weird connection in her mind. David wondered if Son would tell him before he strangled him and threw him down the well.

Chapter Fourteen

Gil came straight back into the kitchen, where they were sitting around the table with lighted cigarettes having an after-breakfast cup of coffee. He was carrying a medium-sized brown paper bag, and they could tell by the look on his face that he had something to tell them.

"Bring the coffeepot into the study, will you, Madelyn?" He turned to leave the kitchen, saying over his shoulder, "And bring an extra cup for me."

He led them down the hall and took his place behind David's desk. The rest of them sat down and looked at the brown paper bag in the center of the desk while he stirred a spoonful of sugar into his coffee. When he finally spoke, the paper bag still lay ignored where he had placed it.

"I've got a few things to report," he began, leaning slightly forward to speak directly to Grace. "A little something on your mother, Grace, and I'll hurry up and get to it. But I want to let you know what I've learned about Dick McKenna. The answer is, not much. About two years ago his mother died and left him a small inheritance, just over twenty thousand dollars. He claimed it and took off for parts unknown. His aunt, the sister Mrs. McKenna was living with, hasn't heard from him. She thinks he went to the West Coast, but she's not sure. We'll eventually find him, but it will take some time. We will have to assume he's out of harm's way, at least for the time being, if he's that far away.

"Now." Gil paused as he pulled the paper bag toward him and

began to open it. "I want you to come look at this, but please don't handle it. I have to send it to the lab." He held the corners of the bag and dumped the contents onto the center of the desk. It appeared to be a pale peach-colored woman's jacket. With deft fingers lightly touching the material, he arranged it so that they could examine it. David recognized it instantly as the jacket to a light summer suit of Frony's. She had worn it to Parsons several times.

"That's Mother's!" Grace cried out in surprise. Then her voice changed, filled with apprehension. "Where did you find that? Have you found her? Is she—"

"No, no, Grace. Nothing like that," Gil cut her off. "Just wait a minute and I'll explain." He looked at the rest of them. "Anybody else recognize it?"

"Yes. It's Frony's," David confirmed. "I've seen her wearing it a number of times."

"Madelyn?" Gil asked.

"Yes. It's part of a summer suit. I remember when she bought it." She bent over to look at the label. "There. The Angela Shop. And it's one of a kind; that's all they sell, so you won't see yourself coming and going—"

"Where did you find it, Mr. Thomas?" Grace interrupted impatiently.

"We found it last night in one of those small apartments over the Sea Room Restaurant." He waited for this to sink in. The others looked at him blankly. "That's where David saw Frony and the man—"

"Wait!" Glenn interrupted. "Do you agree with David and me that the man was Son?"

"I'm not sure yet." The detective didn't elaborate. "I was going to say that this man—whether it was Son or not—had been living in an apartment over the Sea Room, up to sometime last week."

Something clicked in David's mind. Now he understood. They—Frony and the man he believed was Son—weren't going into the Sea Room at all. When they had disappeared from view he had thought they were going in the restaurant door, but it must have been the other door, the one opening onto the stairs that led to the crummy apartments with dirty windows and torn blinds. His stomach turned when he thought of Frony wallowing up there with a huge homicidal maniac. What squalor! It was worse than eating in the Sea Room.

"That means Mother was there, doesn't it, Mr. Thomas?" Grace was saying. "I mean, that's where he took her, isn't it? I think she had that suit at home up until last week."

"Can you be sure of that, Grace?" Gil asked. "It's important."

"Well—yes. I don't have enough room for all my stuff in the dorm, so I leave some of it at home. We keep a lot of our clothes in the same closet. We're exactly the same size, and sometimes we wear each other's things. I'm sure I saw that suit in the closet when I went home to get some of my summer things to take to the dorm. That was about two weeks ago."

Gil thought for a moment. "That's close enough," he said, and then answered Grace's earlier question. "Yes. I'm sure that's where he took her."

"You said this guy—Son as far as I'm concerned—had been living there up to sometime last week, Gil." Glenn reminded him. "That means, of course, that he's not still there. How do you know when he left?"

"I don't really know. I'm just speculating. Let's say Frony went with him willingly. We don't really know what their relationship was. But after a couple of days she must have got the message—he didn't plan to let her go back home. She was *taken out of turn,* as the note says—in effect, kidnapped. For some reason I don't think he would have stayed there for more than a day or so after he took Frony. I wouldn't if I had just kidnapped someone." Gil thought for a moment, then went on. "The place is Spartan as hell, but it has the appearance of being kept fairly straight. Now there's a collection of dust on everything, a certain mustiness that goes along with not being lived in for a while."

"How did you find out he was living there?" Glenn asked.

"One of my men got onto it. I asked him to go down to the Sea Room and ask around about a big man and maybe an attractive woman who came in there occasionally to eat. Nobody could tell him anything until last night when the late shift came on. The cashier said he'd never been in to eat that she remembered, but she'd seen him walk past the place a few times. It was her idea that he might live in one of the apartments on the second floor. We checked out four occupied apartments, but we had to find the landlord to let us in when we discovered that two were apparently empty. We found the jacket in the second one about eleven o'clock last night."

"Was there anything else besides the jacket?" Madelyn asked.

"Not a thing," Gil said meaningfully. "The place was clean as a whistle, except for the dust."

He was waiting for them, expecting them to deduce something from what he had said. But they missed it, couldn't make the connection. He hadn't given them enough to go on. So he gave them more.

"The jacket wasn't hidden in any way," he offered, "not under the bed or in the back of a bureau drawer."

"Where was it, then?" Madelyn asked.

"It was on a hanger in the middle of the closet."

David got it first. "And he left it there on purpose, for you to find?"

"Yes. I think that is very possible, David," Gil confirmed. "I think he may have wanted us to find it."

"Do you realize how absurd that is?" Glenn asked. "I know Son is some kind of psychopath, but why would he deliberately give out such a clue? It gives you a starting point. Does he want to get caught?"

"What do you think about that, David?" Gil had his own opinion; he just wanted to see if David would confirm it.

"I think you're testing my deductive powers, Lieutenant Thomas," David responded with mock formality, "or maybe you want a sample of Fleming fiction. Okay, I'll give it to you the way I see it, the way I would write it." He waited until Gil Thomas nodded for him to go on. "I don't think Son wants to get caught, but that's not the point. He doesn't believe he *can* get caught."

"Why do you say that, Dave?" Glenn asked. "Surely he knows that Gil—the police department—is involved now. He's not just up against a bunch of terrified amateurs."

"It makes my fiction more consistent if he does know; that's part of his role playing. He's playing the part of Frankenstein's monster, isn't he?"

"Well, yes, what we've figured out so far points to that," Glenn agreed, "but why would he make it easy for Gil to come after him?"

"If you'll remember, Glenn, Frankenstein's monster was bigger and stronger than mortal man. He was even on a par intellectually, the way Mary Shelley depicts him. He was an ugly beast, but he was also superhuman. So in this role Son's not in the least afraid of us. And he does know Gil is a policeman. He wants him to keep coming on. He wants us all to keep coming on until he can— well—I think he's getting impatient. He's waited too long already."

"There might not be as much invention in what David proposes as you might think, Glenn," Gil said after taking a few moments to absorb what he had heard. "This man—okay, Son if you insist—seems to be playing a deadly serious game with us while he's playing out a part he's cobbled together from bits and pieces of Frankenstein." The detective stood up behind the desk and began carefully folding Frony's jacket. "I stayed up half the night reading that damned book after I left here last night."

"Mr. Thomas, I'd like to go see the apartment," Grace announced when it became apparent that Gil was preparing to leave. She and Madelyn had gotten lost in the theorizing, and they were getting restless. Madelyn's crossed leg had begun to bounce.

"We'll all go," Madelyn decided for the rest of them. She rose from the sofa before Gil could object.

The prospect of visiting the apartment appealed to David. He would like to have a look at it himself. "Yes," he supported. "I think we should all go." He started to suggest that they might find something the police had overlooked but thought better of it when he saw the sour look on Gil's face. The detective wasn't thrilled with the prospect of leading the whole troop into the Grove Street apartment.

"Well, now, I'm not sure that's such a good idea," he protested. "My men haven't—"

"Why not?" Madelyn snapped. "We're not going to screw up any of your clues. You said the place was bare as a bone. Anyway, we need to get out of this house for a while."

"Okay. Okay." Gil held his hands up placatingly to Madelyn. "We'll all go in my car if you promise not to fool with the siren and the police radio."

Madelyn returned his smile and led the way out to the police car.

It was easy for David to see how he had made the mistake of thinking Frony and Son had gone into the restaurant. The door leading to the apartment was only five or six feet from the restaurant door and was recessed only slightly from the outside façade of the building. The stairs were so narrow that while he and the others were climbing them, David wondered how anybody could ever get any furniture, a refrigerator for instance, up and down them. The upstairs hallway, lighted by a single small-wattage bulb, wasn't much wider than the stairwell. The two couples shuffled along behind Gil until he stopped to unlock one of the doors.

The room they entered at almost dead center was L-shaped and served as sitting room and kitchen. The fabric on the butt-sprung sofa and matching chair was long since threadbare and the coffee table in front of the sofa and the drum table to the right of the chair were missing thin strips of veneer. What kitchen equipment there was—an ancient refrigerator, a small range, and a sink—lined the back of the L to the left. A chrome-and-plastic dinette set filled the rest of the space. Nowhere on any surface in this room was there decoration of any sort, nor were there any windows.

The single window in the bedroom looked out on the alley that ran in back of the building. Son had apparently supplied his own bed—a box spring and mattress on a steel frame—because it was oversize in length. The bathroom door was directly opposite the foot of the bed and next to that was a doorless closet. The closet opening was covered with a piece of printed cloth.

Gil had been overkind when he described the apartment as Spartan. It was crummy, and a faint odor of fried fish seeped through the floorboards from the restaurant kitchen below.

During the five minutes they had moved as a group from one section to another of the small apartment, nobody had thought of anything to say. After they had gone in single file to examine the bathroom, their silent inspection brought them all to stand staring down at the neatly made bed. The same vivid picture formed in all their minds. This was the only place for them to sleep and Frony had been here for some time, perhaps several days. Had she been a willing captive? David wondered. He shook the vision out of his head.

"I don't believe any of this," Grace said in bewilderment. She looked from one to the other of them. "What can a shitty place like this have to do with any of us? How could that fucking bastard bring my mother up here?" Her voice was raw with anger. They all felt it, an anger that went along with the absurd circumstances that could bring the five of them here to stare down at this strange bed, as if they were looking into an open crypt. What, indeed, did this run-down apartment in a run-down part of town have to do with any of them? What an obscene son-of-a-bitch Son Hammond was! David felt his threat more strongly than he ever had before.

Grace turned and jerked aside the cloth covering the closet opening. A half-dozen wire coat hangers were bunched together in the middle of the clothes bar.

"This is where you found it?" More of a declaration than a question. Grace knew what they all thought, that it hadn't merely been found, discovered; that it had been left there as an encouraging clue, something to keep them coming on.

"Yes," Gil answered and added, because the simple one word didn't seem enough, "right in the middle."

All of them, even Gil, craned to look into the empty closet.

"Let's get the hell out of here," Madelyn murmured. She led the way out of the bedroom and out of the apartment. None of them paused to take a last look around.

The only words spoken on the trip back to Parsons were those Gil undertoned into the mouthpiece of his police radio. Clipped police language, to let them know where he was. The rest of them slumped into their own depressed silences, regretting that they couldn't keep the pictures of Son's sleazy apartment from flashing across the screens of their minds. Grace's drawn face told David she wished she hadn't gone.

"I'll come in for a minute," Gil said after the car had stopped in the driveway and his passengers had emerged, stiff legged, from their cramped seats. "Here. Let's sit here," he said as they approached the house. "I think we all need some air." He sat on the edge of the porch and they settled, two on either side, on lower steps. "I looked into the two deaths down at Huntington. There wasn't much in the files, but there was enough."

"Meaning?" David asked when the detective paused.

"Meaning—I came closer to accepting your and Glenn's theory about Son when I learned Cornell went down that well in the summer of 1950. It was closed out as accidental death. So was the kid's death in the spring of 1952."

Glenn asked the question first. "What was the kid's name?"

"William Marshall," Gil answered without any attempt to dramatize. "Billy Ma shall."

"Well, at least that i ts the theory, if we discount Cornell as a mistake in Son's timing," Glenn said grimly. "Son said William was first, the way it was in the book. Victor Frankenstein's little brother."

"My little brother," David corrected. "That boy's name was what really convinced you Glenn and I might be right, wasn't it, Gil?"

"Yes, it was," the detective admitted. "But we really have no way of knowing whether he went out and hunted for a kid named William, or whether he killed the first kid who came along, and the name just happened to fit. Another thing—you and Glenn made so much of the fact that the deaths should be by strangulation to be consistent, that I had my doubts. There was nothing in the medical report about suffocation. That's generally the cause of death from strangulation. Both victims did have broken necks, but the assumption was that their necks were broken from the fall. No autopsy was performed in either case. The cause of death was too apparent to raise any question with the coroner."

"Well, we may be nit-picking about Son strangling all his victims," David pointed out, "just because that's the way it was in the book. But he probably is strong enough to break a grown man's neck with his hands. What do you think, Gil?"

"It's been done," he agreed.

"Who was the Marshall boy?" Grace asked. "Was he someone any of us would know? I mean, did he live anywhere around here?"

Grace voiced a question that had bothered David ever since Dr. Betchel told him and Glenn about the second death in the Huntington well. What was the connection? Why would Son pick out some kid at random, an innocent, to start his pattern of revenge? Part of the answer was taking shape in his head when Gil answered her.

"I don't think any of us would have any reason to know him. The Marshall family farms the land on the other side of the road from Huntington. Some notes in the report on the case indicate that he was just a farm kid who sometimes went over to the Huntington grounds to play. He'd been there many times by himself."

"I don't believe there had to be any connection between us and the boy," David volunteered. "Remember, my little brother, Billy, in the story, was fictional. There wasn't a candidate to fit the role in Son's scheme of revenge, so he had to find one. The Marshall boy was just unfortunate enough to be around when Son slipped into his own role of Frankenstein's monster. I'll bet there was something about that boy that reminded Son of me when I was a kid, something that would allow him to believe he was my little brother."

"He did have auburn hair," Gil confirmed, "according to the records."

They all sat silently for a full minute, thinking their separate thoughts, waiting for someone else to speak. It was obvious to the others that Gil had something else to say, or he would have left to get on with his police business.

"I think it will be better for you and Madelyn to go back home." He was speaking to Glenn. "Grace will be better off there, of course. This place is too big for my man to watch, and I have to take one of them off each shift for a while. One will be enough at your place." He turned to David. "What about you? Will you go stay at the Walkers' for a while?"

David shook his head. "No, Gil. I'm going to stay at Parsons."

Grace was shocked. "You're not going to stay here by yourself, David!" She didn't wait for him to answer before she turned to the detective. "Can't you leave someone here with David, Mr. Thomas?"

"No. I just don't have—"

"I'll be all right here," David insisted. "Anyway, I'm supposed to be last on Son's list." He smiled to break the tension, but Grace didn't think it was funny. She glared at him.

"I'd feel much better if you would leave here. How about moving into a hotel in town for a few days?" Gil tried again, although it was apparent to him that David wouldn't leave Parsons voluntarily. The resignation was reflected in his voice when he said, "Okay, David. Just try to stay put. You'll make our job a lot easier if you don't go anywhere."

The detective lightly slapped his knees and stood up. The others stood and followed him across the lawn to his car. He beckoned and one of his men started toward them from across the front lawn.

"Wade Felder—the tall one—will stay and follow you back to your house this afternoon." He was talking to Glenn. "A new man, Jim Bascomb, will relieve him around seven this evening. Why don't you get ready to leave here about the middle of the afternoon, three or four o'clock? When you get back home, stay together and stay inside as much as you can, especially after dark. I know this is a pain in the ass, but it can't be helped." He turned to David. "I don't know what to advise you, except to be careful. I want you to call Glenn before you go to bed, just to report in." He hesitated and smiled. "Don't say anything you don't want me to hear—both your phones are tapped."

The shorter of the two men from Gil's protection unit circled the car and got into the front passenger seat when Gil opened the door and got in himself. As he backed out of the driveway, he waved and said, "I'll be in touch."

It was almost five o'clock when they left, all three in the front seat of Glenn's car because the back seat was loaded with the stuff one of Gil's men had retrieved from Grace's dormitory room. Felder's unmarked car, a light-green Plymouth sedan, stayed fifty yards behind Glenn's as David watched them out of sight down River Road.

Chapter Fifteen

By six o'clock David had discovered that he didn't like living alone anymore. Two days of having three other people in the house with him had taken all the charm from the solitary life he had led since his split with Helen. Now the study seemed twice as gloomy as it had before. The pile of manuscript pages for his new book intimidated him from where they lay on the desk. He looked sourly at them for a few minutes, his eyes refusing to read the top page, and then put them in the desk drawer. There was a feel about having other people in the house with him that was gone. Some light vacuum had come into the place. It hulked emptily around him with no sound at all, no echo of another voice or the sound of a foot on any floor.

He was lonely.

He needed something to do with himself.

He needed a drink.

He needed to get the hell outside while there was still some daylight.

The front porch was better. A cigarette and glass of Scotch kept him company as he rocked away another half hour. But he couldn't sit and rock any longer than that. With a second drink he circled the house several times and walked to the back of the field to peer down over the escarpment to the narrow rocky creek below. What a fall that would be! He shrank back from the edge and looked over his shoulder. Nerves. He laughed self-consciously at his sudden fear of being sent headlong over the cliff. Be careful, Gil had said.

Don't get drunk and fall out of your own backyard, he told himself.

He needed something to do until the sun went down and he was forced back inside. He couldn't work on the book now. But something else . . . an idea came to him. Ah, yes, a journal! Write it all down; everything from the beginning, but make it current. He would start with Grace's phone call on Sunday when she was worried about Frony, and then go back when retrospection was required.

There was more than an hour of good sunlight left, so David set up a lawn chair and a snack table for his drink in the field by the tulip tree. He used a clipboard in his lap and wrote in pencil. He could transcribe it on the typewriter later. Before it got too dark to see what he was writing, he filled eight pages of lined tablet paper. He was just getting into the interview he and Glenn had with Dr. Betchel at Whitfield, and it was a good place to stop. It was too complex to write down as quickly as the other events he had already recorded. He would have to give more thought to this part before he went on.

His Scotch had sat neglected and was warm and watery from the melted ice, so he emptied the glass as he walked back to the house. He'd have one more before he went inside to work on the journal in the study. The field was dim with twilight when he came back fifteen minutes later with a new drink and a thick sandwich. He couldn't think those medical thoughts on an empty stomach.

But he really didn't think medical thoughts. One thing that stuck in his mind was Dr. Betchel's revelation that Son had left the hospital in 1941—in May. It had to have been Son in the woods by the river. He would have to include that in the journal, even though it was speculation, his own conviction. His thoughts brought him to look into the woods to the west of the field. They were dark now, and he strained to see the lantern face that had been there a week ago. The dark fringe was unbroken, with no movement among the trees, nothing to betray the presence of a giant madman who would throttle him last of all.

He shook his head and looked up into the sky, which was only slightly brightened by the waning moon. It was time to go in, too dark to be comfortable. He had left no lights burning in the house, and it looked ghostly against the southern sky. There was a thrill of danger in being left alone to face the dark menace of that cavernous old house. A shudder of fear ran down David's spine.

What was that?

There, on the widow's walk.

Again. There it was again. A white fluttering—on the widow's walk.

Some ghost in his mind. No. It was still now. A form standing at the rail, watching him. Moving back, fading. Gone. Had he seen an arm lifted to beckon him?

The light lawn chair crashed behind David as he bolted forward, almost falling as he ran across the grass, slippery with early evening dew. He took the back porch steps in one leap and violently opened the back screen door, which slammed against the wall and rattled closed behind him. He bounded up two flights of stairs, to the second and third floors, three steps at a time, and jerked open the door to the last flight—to the widow's walk. With hesitation, a slight faltering in his pace, he climbed up this last stairway. Apprehension thudded in his chest; the fear of what he might discover filled his straining eyes as they came even with the platform of the widow's walk. Rail posts obscured his view. Taking the last few steps in one lunge, he stood spread-legged and gasping on the widow's walk floor, searching wildly for the flutter of white.

Nothing! Only an empty thirty-foot square, slightly luminescent in pale moonlight.

He circled it twice, stopping at each side and corner to search the grounds below. Nothing moved. There was no rustling in the shrubbery, no change of shadow. Everything was still.

Using the back staircase, he searched the house room by room—the maid's quarters on the third floor, the six bedrooms on the second, the big main rooms on the first, the small cellar under the kitchen floor—every corner and every closet, leaving lights on in each room as he abandoned it for another. He stopped and listened attentively, breathlessly, as he searched. There was no other sound but his own coursing blood. The silence rang in his ears. He was alone.

The house was a blaze of light as David walked the grounds in ever-widening circles, braving even the outer fringe of woods on the dark west side. His fear was gone as he righted the lawn chair and sat down to smoke a mangled cigarette from the crushed pack in his shirt pocket. The widow's walk was bright from the backlighting of a three-hundred-watt floodlight at the front of the house. An empty, harmless, geometric square of railings and posts.

No beckoning ghosts. No mind-made apparitions.

Perspiration cooled on his skin and he shivered in the night air. But he smoked another cigarette, doubting what he was so positive he had seen, wondering how he could have conjured such a vision in his thirty-six-year-old mind. Why not? He had done it when he was ten. The cigarette burned his fingers and he flung it on the ground as he got up to go inside.

He wouldn't tell Glenn when he called. Maybe he would mention it tomorrow; he'd have to think about that. What he needed was a shower and maybe another Scotch to put him to sleep. He'd get back to the journal, too. All that should be enough of an opiate to send him off to dreamland.

David didn't work on the journal. He just sat slumped in the lounge chair and tried to think about it through the haze of alcohol and fluttering white ghosts, sipping his way to ten thirty and the phone call to tell Glenn he was going to bed. He was too drunk to worry about being murdered in his sleep.

His hangover was colossal, worse than the one Friday morning after Frony hadn't shown up. God, that was less than a week ago! David got up, walked to the bathroom, swallowed three aspirin, and returned to bed with a cold washcloth pressed against his forehead. For thirty minutes he lay hating himself, wondering if he was becoming an alcoholic. He had consumed more booze in the last week than in any similar period in his life. There was some comfort in the thought that there hadn't ever been a similar week in his life. As he lay suffering, he resolved to solve his future problems without any alcoholic assistance.

The headache eased, and David got up and took a shower, a long one with the water as cold as he could stand it. When he walked into the kitchen, it was after ten. He had slept for over ten hours. The phone rang just as he was plugging in the coffeepot.

"Why didn't you talk to me last night?" Grace asked without any prologue. Not "Good morning, my sweet lover."

It didn't exactly register.

"What?"

"You don't sound so good. How do you feel?"

"Shitty."

"Good. It serves you right. An old fart like you shouldn't drink by yourself. That's one of the first—"

"Don't lecture me, Grace. I don't feel up to it."

"Sorry. I was hoping you'd say you got drunk because you couldn't bear the thought of being there without having me on your living room floor."

"Don't say 'fuck,' Grace. The phone's tapped."

Now she giggled outright. "Are you listening, Mr. Thomas?"

"Don't be impudent. You're not even twenty-one yet. Go ask Madelyn if I can come over for lunch."

"Of course you can. I was going to ask you. That's one reason I called."

"What other reason?"

"To find out whether you'd been strangled in your bed, you bastard."

She hung up. David realized he had said "don't" to her three times in less than two minutes. No wonder she called me a bastard, he reflected. He was grateful for the tone of good humor when she'd said it.

David spent the rest of the morning typing up his journal and making notes on what he remembered of the interview with Dr. Betchel. He had nothing but coffee in his stomach, and he looked forward to lunch as he drove to the Walkers' shortly before noon.

After lunch the two men went into the Walkers' small study. Glenn liked the idea of the journal and wanted to read the part

David had completed. He made a few annotations in the margins of the typescript, and the two of them later argued quietly until they agreed on several points Glenn had questioned. Together they worked on the interview with Dr. Betchel, going over and over each part until they were satisfied nothing of real significance had been omitted. By five o'clock they were both tired of it. David collected the papers scattered on the desk and closed them in a manila folder. Glenn went into the kitchen and mixed them drinks.

"You plan to start on another headache?" he asked as he handed David his. No remonstrance was intended; he chuckled as he said it.

"Twice a week is all I can stand. Anyway, I made a resolution about that just this morning." David smiled and lifted his glass in salute. "Cheers."

"What are the women doing?"

"They're back in the bedroom." Glenn took a long swig from his drink, then said, "Grace is going through some pretty wild emotional swings, Dave. You know how hard she's trying to handle what's happened to Frony, but it's always on her mind. She tries to put on a good face around you—I heard that bright conversation she had with you on the phone this morning—but it doesn't last. The depression hits her and she caves in until Madelyn can get her out of it."

David *did* know how hard Grace was trying. He could understand that this period was bitterly difficult for her—probably impossible without the support Madelyn was giving her. Thank God for Madelyn! And for Glenn—David wasn't sure how grown up he would act without the support of his old friend.

"Glenn, I think you know—or suspect—how I feel about Grace." He felt a little self-conscious about what he was going to say and dropped his eyes from Glenn's face. "She is the love of my life, and I've been such a fool that I've only just discovered it. I know what she's going through, and it bothers the hell out of me that I can't be more help getting her over the rough spots. I hope Madelyn knows how grateful I am for what she's doing."

"She knows, Dave," Glenn said quietly, then slapped his thighs and stood up. "Well, that's enough of that serious talk."

"Maybe I should say good-bye to the ladies," David said, looking toward the study doorway.

"You're leaving?" Glenn asked when David drained his glass and stood up. "I thought you'd stay and have dinner with us."

"Now that I'm not being guarded every minute, there are a few things I want to do." One thing anyway, David said to himself. The urge to drive down to Huntington had come over him while he and Glenn were working on the Cornell death section of the interview with Dr. Betchel. He had decided not to mention it to Glenn because he probably would want to go, and then they would have to contend with Madelyn and Grace. And Gil's man, Wade Felder, would be on the radio as soon as he found out they had sneaked off. David didn't want any more of Gilbert Thomas's disapproval. "Besides," he added, "I have a lot of food at home to eat up." That was true. Gil had somehow arranged for enough supplies to last the four of them a week or more. "I'll bring some of it over here tomorrow. Maybe Madelyn will invite me to stay for dinner."

"Consider yourself invited. Lunch, too, if you like," Madelyn said as she and Grace walked into the living room where the two men stood.

Grace protested loudly when she realized David was leaving. She stood in the doorway with her hands on her hips, and David could feel the daggers she was looking into his back as he walked to his car.

Traffic thinned as David passed the tract-house subdivisions that had been built along River Road east of town. As the countryside became rural, the tenseness went out of his shoulders and he relaxed against the back cushion of the car seat. God, how he hated to drive in traffic! It made him too nervous to think about anything but saving his skin. Now it occurred to him that he hadn't really thought about last night's ghostly episode since his headache mercifully evaporated shortly before noon. And he hadn't told Glenn about it. Why not? he wondered. But what the hell had he really seen—what was there to tell him? That he'd seen a ghost on the widow's walk? Glenn would think he was going soft in the head. Maybe he *was* getting a little silly, silly enough to imagine things. Maybe he'd try it out on Glenn tomorrow, just to get his reaction, maybe not. It didn't seem as real in broad daylight. Real or not, he wanted to be back in the field that night by nine o'clock, just in case.

The land to the east side of town rolled more gently than that to the west, but the rises formed crests along the river from which perpendicular bluffs of some thirty to forty feet fell to the river's edge. Huntington sat atop one of these broad crests a half mile south of River Road with its back side to the river. The grounds in front of the house had never been farmed and the trees that had grown up on what was once a vast expanse of greensward obscured all but portions of the roof.

David turned onto the rutted gravel road that led to the crumbling remains of a tall stone gateway at the center of the property. The opening was closed with an aluminum gate, chained and padlocked to an iron loop protruding from one of the stone pillars. On either side barbed-wire fencing stretched to the ends of the property line and turned to mark its boundaries to the east and west. He was about to get back into the car when he noticed that an end of chain hung, unattached, behind a horizontal bar in the gate. Looking more closely, he discovered another chain end tucked between two loops which were wound around the edge of the gate. The gate was not really locked; it was tied shut. David unwound the loops and the gate swung open with a gentle push. He got back into his car and drove through, then closed the gate, securing it with one loop of the light chain, and drove carefully toward the huge house in the distance.

Ahead the drive rose with the slope of the hill for several hundred yards, then veered off to the right to lead to the outbuildings west of the house. This course had undoubtedly been changed over the years from the broad drive that David imagined had led directly to the house's front entrance. However, there was no evidence of the earlier road at the turning point as he drove past.

The front of the house became fully visible when the tree line ended fifty yards from the front portico. Stopping the car, David got out to have his first good look at Huntington. The size of the house amazed him. Constructed of rust-colored brick and perhaps one hundred and fifty feet across its front façade, it consisted of a two-storied square central building, two flanking wings, also two-storied and almost as large, and two connecting corridors. Stone steps led to the front portico of the central building, and four large columns, paintless and gray from weathering, supported a second-floor porch surrounded by a dilapidated balustrade. The double-doored entryway was topped by a fanlight and bracketed by two more columns at the outer edges of the portico.

David's interest in the house was secondary to his interest in the outbuilding that held the murderous dry well. He returned to the car and drove up to the largest of three outbuildings at the right of the house. It was also of brick and approximately thirty by forty feet. There was no door or window on the front side, so he circled it and discovered a door covered by a sheet of corrugated steel roofing on the side facing the house. The metal sheet was attached to the doorframe by rusting nails, and he easily pried it away with the tire iron he retrieved from the car.

As he loosened the nails, his ears picked up a peculiar echo from the immense hollowness in the earth. He could feel the presence of the pit before he ventured inside. A rush of coolness, and an odor, dank and rotting, washed over him and stung his nostrils as he took one halting step into the gloom. For some time he stood adjusting his eyes to the darkness. In the faint light from the open doorway the rim of the well gradually came into view, two short steps from where he stood. Carefully he slid his feet across the brick floor until he came to the edge, shivering involuntarily, teetering with vertigo as he peered into the pool of blackness that yawned at his feet. Then he shrank back. Careful, you fool!

As slowly as he had approached it, David backed away from the well. He returned to the car and retrieved the five-cell flashlight he had wedged under the front seat. The strong beam of light dug into the blackness to reveal the well's damp floor forty feet below, then slid up the far wall some twenty feet away. No parapet wall protected the cylindrical well, which was constructed of brick, with random patches of concrete. Clusters of green mold spotted the damp walls and floor. Directly opposite each other at the bottom of the well were two arched openings, doorways, that appeared from his oblique viewpoint to be about four feet wide and seven feet high. Brick paving extended through these openings as far as David's light would reach. These doorways puzzled him. Where could they lead? Were they entries to passageways to the other buildings, or perhaps to subterranean crypts? An impulse to descend into the well sent him in search of some knotted rope or ladder that he thought must certainly be hanging from a peg in this or the other outbuildings. But the large room at the end of the building was virtually empty, as were the other buildings. He came back to circle the well twice, cautious on the slippery floor, probing every surface with his light, until he finally just stood staring at the circle of light on the well's floor. Images of Cornell's and Billy Marshall's crumpled bodies alternated in the yellow spot.

Outside, the shadows had become long in the late-afternoon sun. It was almost seven o'clock. The day's gloaming was close and David still wanted to explore the house. He entered through a window on the left of the back portico, which was identical to the one at the front of the house. The window had been forced before, and the upper portion of the latch dangled from a single screw. David was in a large back foyer which led to the center hall of the house through double French doors. The center hall was enormous. Tiled in Italian marble, it extended between paneled walls past double-door entries to the morning room and drawing room on the left and the library and dining room on the right. All these rooms were paneled in mahogany, except the morning room, which showed traces of the gilt and pastels that had lightened it in years past. High-manteled fireplaces on each room's interior wall looked out on complete emptiness. About midway in the hall a stairway of carved mahogany rose to a window-lighted landing, then turned and wound to the rooms above. The corridor to the east wing, entered from the dining room, led to the kitchen complex and second-floor servants' quarters, and the corridor to the west connected the main house with guest quarters, a sitting room, and two large bedrooms.

Returning to the center section of the house, David climbed the stairs to the bedrooms on the second floor, all empty except for one. In this one was an overlong bed identical to the bed in the Grove Street apartment, two worn upholstered chairs, two small tables that held kerosene lamps, and a battered chest of drawers.

Just inside the doorway David gawked at what he had found. Another lair for Simple Son. Suddenly it made so much sense for Son to have come here to Huntington that David wondered why Gil hadn't thought of it and sent someone out to investigate.

And there was no mistaking it. On the dressing-room floor was a blue overnight case, and in the closet hung Frony's clothes, clothes familiar to David. Other clothes, a big man's clothes, hung beside Frony's.

The discovery was stunning, oppressive; he couldn't stay in the room. Downstairs, he wandered from room to room, trying to sort out in his mind what he had found. This was truly Son's lair. He had probably been here for years, using this run-down plantation house as his base of evil. And what about Frony? Had she come here as an unwilling captive, kidnapped? But did kidnap victims pack little blue suitcases? Had she come willingly? Had she been here before? How often had Son brought Frony to that riverward bedroom where the glass door opened to the porch over the back portico? How often had she stood on that porch in the dark, listening, as she did on the Parsons widow's walk, to the river's sound? No. She couldn't hear the river from Parsons, only glimpse its gleam through the trees.

David sat on the deep window seat in the study, engrossed in the thought, absently playing the flashlight beam across the paneling by the fireplace. At first he didn't see it, or it didn't register through the clutter of thoughts that so absorbed him. The spot of light had flicked over it a dozen times before the irregularity, the dark vertical seam, caught his eye, and he got up to examine it. The discontinuity in the wall, a six-foot-high three-quarter-inch protrusion, was the edge of a door that was not quite closed. He pulled at it with his fingertips and it swung slowly, reluctantly, open, groaning on its hinges, and it sounded like the opening of every secret door in every haunted house his mind had ever invented. I have discovered a secret passageway! David silently exclaimed. To what? The only thing he could think of was the well. What if he had discovered the passageway to the well!

The descending corridor with its twenty stone steps was narrow, less than three feet wide; but several paces from the bottom of the steps it turned obliquely to the left and widened to perhaps five feet. The arched brick ceiling was a foot over David's head, and he could walk comfortably on the declining brick floor. He had judged the center of the well to be fifty yards from the back of the house, and now he counted fifty-six paces before he came to the tunnel's end. To his surprise he entered a small room that was square, except for the far wall, which was formed by the convex arc of the well. The arched opening he had observed from above was directly in front of him and he walked through the anteroom onto the well's floor. Thudding echoes of his footfalls came from the circular wall as his soles slapped the moist bricks. Turning in the center of this giant cavern, he followed his flashlight's spot in several circuits of the dripping walls. He snapped off the light and stood in stifling darkness. Only a faint glimmer came from the open door of the wall's covering building. The panic of disorientation came over him—he felt small, helpless, vulnerable, at the bottom of this pit. The voluntary blindness was unbearable. He shuddered and snapped on the light.

An identical square room was on the well's other side, the river side, and a passageway led from its far wall. For a hundred feet—until David came to a heavy door, standing halfway open—the floor seemed perfectly level. Just on the other side the floor sloped downward more steeply than the passageway from the house. The footing became difficult and he held the light's beam on the floor directly ahead, sliding his feet carefully along the slippery, uneven bricks. The bobbing circle of light picked up an edge of water, and, startled, he swung the beam upward. The tunnel's sides formed long wedges that ended when the ceiling dived below the water's surface. For a time David stood listening to the water's gentle lap against the sides of the passageway, trying to understand why the southern opening could be below the river's surface. Why was there a passage to the river at all? Or to the house? What were the little rooms for on the sides of the well? Or the well itself—what purpose had it served?

David couldn't imagine.

And he didn't care. He would research it later. Now he was too anxious to get out into the open air. His retreat was made in as much haste as he could manage. Within five minutes he was standing on the back portico, breathing deeply, looking at his watch. It was seven thirty. He had been inside the house and down inside the earth less than three quarters of an hour. It had seemed much longer.

The landfall toward the river in back of the house was very gradual. Calculating the course of the southern passageway, David noticed it ran under a family burial plot. As he passed through, he examined the half-dozen grave markers that still stood. The most recent death recorded was 1832. One flat stone, the size of the grave, was on the edge of a small wash, the stone itself probably causing the erosion from water running toward the river. It was elaborately but indecipherably inscribed. David knelt and rubbed away enough dirt and moss to make out the first name, *Rosamonde*. Standing on the stone, he thought of Henry the Second's Rosamonde, who had so irritated his queen eight hundred years before. That was the most pleasant thought he'd had all day, and he smiled at its inanity before he jumped to the ground several feet below.

No evidence of the river's opening to the passageway could be seen from the top of the bluff. David didn't know what he had expected, but he was disappointed. Surely there had been an indicator of some kind in years past. Perhaps the river's level had been lower two hundred years ago and the opening was exposed. Even in his geological ignorance he couldn't accept that. Even he knew that over time rivers cut their channels deeper and gradually lowered their levels. He would research that later, too.

The sun had reached the top of the trees on the river's south bank. There was barely an hour of daylight left, and David wanted to get back to Parsons. Gil would want to know what he had found in Huntington's back bedroom, and he wanted to be in the field when darkness came. He hurried back toward the car. Just as he was quickening his steps even more, gaining momentum to jump the two-foot rise to the flat gravestone, he noticed a patch of blue cloth protruding from the crumbling earth under the stone's lip. This dirt was freshly turned, and digging at it with frantic fingers, he uncovered the arm within the blue sleeve, and later, with the help of a broken spade from one of the outbuildings, he uncovered the bloated, strangulated face. David screamed when the recognition flooded into him. The hot rush of vomit burned in his throat as he turned away from the corpse of Dick McKenna.

Chapter Sixteen

Gil Thomas wasn't at home and he wasn't at police headquarters. "The message is urgent, damn it, urgent," David told the policeman on the phone. "Yes. Get his ass on the radio, and have him call me. No. Have him come to Parsons. He'll know. Just tell him to come to Parsons." It's dark now, you dumb bastard, and I have to get out in the field. David didn't say that last part, just thought it.

There wasn't time to call Glenn, to explain. It would take too long, and it was already night. He would call Glenn later.

He left the house completely dark and sat in the lawn chair looking at the widow's walk. This was the way Son wanted it; not him there on the top of the house, waiting. He knew David would be there, playing the game his way, looking for his sign, his apparition to appear as it had last night. So David sat and smoked in the wan moonlight, knowing he couldn't stop what was going to happen.

After one cigarette and half of another he saw the vague thing on the widow's walk become more distinct through the rising cigarette smoke—just a grayness against the night sky at first, and then the white form, moving, halting, moving again until it came to the railing and was still. And as he moved toward the house—not running this time, because he felt no sense of urgency, no need to run—it remained for a while and then receded, delaying the moment of discovery until he could cross the field and climb the three flights of stairs.

She was still standing at the railing, still looking into the field, her face obliquely seen, almost obscured by the cloud of black hair. How magnificent she was! How straight she stood, her face in lovely profile, her breasts slowly rising and falling with the rhythm of her breathing. And, yes. Yes. The white chiffon dress. White sandals on stockingless legs outlined underneath the diaphanous cloth. Even with the moon at her back the dress seemed luminous from the thirty feet that separated them. She turned toward him and for long seconds they stood motionless, not speaking or gesturing, just looking at each other across thirty feet of space and a lifetime of joyous and painful memories.

"Hello, David."

He moved to stand beside her at the railing, and as she looked up to him the moonlight brightened her beautiful face and her gray eyes glistened. Was there the glint of lunacy in those eyes? Had she slipped over the edge into the madness that had threatened her for so long?

"Why did you run away last night, Frony?" he asked softly.

"Because it wasn't time. He said it wasn't time."

"Son said that—said it wasn't time?"

"Yes. But not Son—Ralph. He's Ralph now."

"Is it time now? Is tonight the time?"

"I think so, David. He will tell you."

"Is he here?" David turned to look toward the stairs. They were still alone.

"Yes, he's here." There was a finality in what she said, a strange satisfaction in her voice, as though something long awaited was about to happen.

David wanted one question answered before Son appeared. "Why did you leave me, Frony?" He was thinking of the two other times, long ago, when she had left him—not the last time, the night he had waited for her at Parsons.

"I had to, David. He said I had to; he needed me."

"I needed you, Frony." Then he had, when he couldn't love anyone else.

"Maybe those other times, David"— she seemed to understand—"when I had to leave. But not anymore. Now you have Grace."

He was shocked. Guilt flooded into him. She knew about Grace and him. Had he done this to her, pushed her over the brink by making love to her daughter where Son could see? Of course he would have told her. David could see again the lantern of his face in the woods, watching.

"Frony, I didn't mean—"

"Don't you see? You've been waiting all these years for Grace. You thought it had to be me, because of what we did, but it was Grace you've been waiting for. I know that now. I'm glad you found each other. Now I don't have to worry about it anymore." She paused, and her vacant eyes looked past him toward the river. "David, do you remember a long time ago, when we used to go to the river? Now you can start over—you and Grace—like it was then."

Words he couldn't say scalded his throat. Did he remember how it was then? Not a day had passed that he didn't remember. No darkness had ever blotted out her face, no sleep had been merciful enough to deliver him from the dreams. Now she had come back to set him free. It was all right now. Grace was her gift to make up for all the agony. She *was* mad! But how generous she was in her madness.

"I came to tell you good-bye, David."

God, how he wanted to save her! How could he deliver her from the beast . . . save her for Grace? His old passion for her was gone, lost in their past struggles, buried in their long absences from each other, but the love was still there, in the memories that would always be part of his life.

David reached for her face and cupped it in his hands. For a moment he stood staring into her dim gray eyes. Just one more question to be answered, before Son came, so he could finally know the truth.

"Have you ever loved me, Frony?" He searched her face and detected no understanding in her eyes.

"Of course she loves you, David. That's why I took her from you." The baritone was deep, rumbling across the widow's walk.

The shock of it caused David to step back from Frony, almost stumbling, as he whirled to face him.

Son stood at the top of the stairs, outlined against the darker southern sky, clearly visible as he faced the moon. David had forgotten his enormity. His arms, as big at the biceps as a woman's thighs, hung from his short-sleeved shirt. But his bigness was all in proportion. He tapered from incredibly broad shoulders to a trim waist. The fabric of his trousers was tight against his well-muscled legs. The features of his face were regular, yet there was a terrible ugliness about him, a contortion of malevolence about his mouth, a peculiar lack of symmetry to his upper skull. The right side of his forehead bulged grotesquely from hairline to eyebrow.

"Let her say it, Son."

"No. It's too late for her to say it now."

"Why did you have her meet me up here alone?" Temper was rising in David, anger taking the place of the fear he knew he should be feeling. "So you could hide and listen to us, watch us like you've done before?"

Son didn't seem irritated by the insinuation in David's voice. "I wanted her to tell you good-bye so you'd remember seeing her one last time. I wanted you to remember it all, David, in the time you have left." There was no mistaking the menace of his words. "I wanted her here when I told you what you want to know." He paused and raised his arm. "Come over here, Margaret." David touched her arm and started to follow her as she moved away. "No, David. You stay there." Son stepped toward him and he stopped. "Sit down. There, on the floor. I have to answer all your questions tonight. This will be the only chance for you to know."

Frony's dress made a swirling circle on the floor as she sat down with her legs under her. Son waited until David had sunk to the floor before taking his place beside Frony. As David sat peering at them across the widow's walk, he thought how unreal this situation was—less real than any fiction he had ever invented. How could he be sitting on this platform at the top of his house, waiting in the darkness for a giant he had known years ago to tell why he was going to murder him, watching while Frony—who should have been sitting on his side—slowly caressed the maniac's thigh with her hand? David's skin crawled with the revulsion he felt at seeing them together. Was she so far from sane that she didn't know Son was going to kill her? He sat helplessly, despising them both, until he mastered his anger.

"Tell me why, Son. Why are you doing this?"

"Ralph, David. I am Ralph now. Son was before, the imbecile you tormented."

David wanted to defend himself, all of them, against Son's charge, but it would be futile. Son wouldn't understand—wouldn't want to understand—anything other than what he already believed. The venom of rage and frustration was in David's voice. "Who is this Ralph, this killer you've become?" he demanded. "Tell me why you're better than what you were. I want to hear it all—before you murder me."

"No, David. It's not your turn, not yet. I told you—in the letter—that you would be the last. But, yes, I'll start at the beginning, before you killed my mother."

Before you killed my mother!

My God! My God! How had we missed it? He blamed us for that! Matricide was too awful to blame on himself, so he blamed us for it. We were responsible. He was just the instrument. That was our guilt—his mother dead in her ghostly white nightgown— not from his strangling fingers, but from our whispering, tormenting voices. His revenge was not only for what we did to him but for what we caused him to do to the only person he ever really loved, the only person who could love him.

"Son—Ralph. You know we didn't—"

"Yes, all of you. Dwight, Margaret, Glenn, back under the streetlight in front of Gilbert's house."

"We were just a bunch of kids, Ralph," David protested. "We didn't have anything to do with . . ." But he couldn't go on. Because in their childish cruelty, they *had* done it on purpose. They *had* poked and jibed and whispered into his terrified and feeble mind. David could hear the whimpering beginning of Son's anguished wail.

"I remember," Son began. "Even before the operation." He lifted his hand to touch the bulging right side of his forehead, the ridge of ill-fitting bone. "I remember the rest of it—when you described Frankenstein's monster. You looked at me and I saw your face. You said, *'Big as old Son, strong like him, and he couldn't talk, only grunt and growl, like old Son.'* You and your stories made me into a monster, David. Then you held my hand and delivered me home to claim my first victim. I can still see her lifeless eyes staring up at me from the floor. She haunts me." He looked past David, lost in his remembering. Frony's hand was still on his thigh, and she stared past David, too, as if she could see the dead face of Son's mother with the marks of his fingers still on her throat.

"You were there, David. I remember seeing you in the doorway, before your father knocked me unconscious. And you were watching when they took me away. It was over a year before I remembered—no, longer than that. Two years. After I had begun to read. Then I remembered all of you and what you did to me."

"But surely you remembered we were just kids." David tried again to justify what they had done. He was pleading for his life, and for Frony, for all who were left. The jarring reality of Dick McKenna's grossly bloated face came to mind. Where was Gil? He would have to keep Son talking until Gil got his message. "You must have remembered other things about us, Ralph. Not just those nights but the other games we played. We were innocent. We didn't hate you—we just didn't understand that you—"

"That I was an imbecile, Simple Son the imbecile." Son leaned toward him as he spat out the words, glowering rage twisting his face. "You wrote about me that way in your book. And you killed me in the end, killed me with your words. But I am resurrected now!" Son shouted his pronouncement across the space between them, but as suddenly as it had come, the passion drained away and he relaxed against the stair post. "No, you didn't understand. You don't understand now. Do you know what happened to me at Whitfield?" He waited for David to nod before rushing on. "Did they tell you they made a whole and rational man out of a drooling half-wit? I was almost deceived myself. The doctor wrote his papers and put me on display, gave me tutors and books, and pronounced me *normal*. But he hadn't taught me how to forget, only to remember. He hadn't taken my mother's swollen face or your tormenting voices out of my dreams. And he hadn't protected me from the fear in a child's eyes or the loathing on a woman's face that the mere sight of me evoked. I despised him for this, and I came back to twist his neck and throw him into the pit."

Son broke off his narrative and leaned slightly toward David. A low chuckle rumbled in his throat. "You knew about Cornell, didn't you? Well, David, he wasn't the only one I despised. When I saw him lying at the bottom of the well, I could still see your jeering face, even after all those years. I was still your dumb brute, your monster. You had invented me before you were ten years old."

Raving! Son is raving was all that came into David's mind. There was no continuity, no consistency in what he accused them of doing to him.

David couldn't think of any way to stop him, to control the jeering, convoluted account of the crimes Son was convinced they had all committed against him.

"My father never came to see me when I was in Whitfield." Son was calm again. His narrative had started at a new place, almost as if the violent accusations of moments before were forgotten. His tone now was almost reminiscent, regretful. "I knew when I got out that he would be gone. I didn't even go to the house. I took a bus from Whitfield and I didn't get off until it was on the river side of town. I didn't want anybody to see me. I went to the river and found that little boat—you remember the boat, David. I crossed the river and went into the woods."

"And you stayed there, didn't you, Son?" David had to interrupt. The rustling in the woods came back to him too vividly. "You lived in the woods and came to watch us, Frony and me."

"Yes, I lived there in a shack. You were too afraid of the woods to come in and find it. And I watched you every time you swam. I saw Margaret naked the first time you did. I saw you in the sand together. . . ."

"You saw us fuck," David said brutally. He resented Son's elegance, his lack of vulgarity. "Did you jack off while you watched, Son?"

The huge, ugly face clouded with anger, and Frony, who had sat passively beside him, turned and put a lightly restraining hand on his chest. It calmed him.

"Don't call me Son, David," he warned. The other aspect of David's derision he seemed to ignore. "She was the first woman I ever saw that way. I learned at the same time you did about what a man and woman do together. That's when I decided that Margaret would be my woman. And I wasn't going to let you keep me from having her. *'Shall each man find a wife for his bosom, and each beast have his mate, and I be alone? Are you to be happy, while I grovel in the intensity of my wretchedness?'* " Son's voice rang with emotion. It was several moments before David realized he ·was quoting from Mary Shelley. He must have learned long passages from the book. But how he had distorted them to suit himself!

David realized what lengths Son must have gone to, in order to claim Frony for his own. Had he been cunning enough to seduce her when she was an emotional cripple in Germany and then deliberately drive her mad? Had he murdered D and told her about it to drive her over the brink with guilt? Had he destroyed her so David could never have her?

David had to know. He calmed himself before he spoke.

"Ralph, tell me how you came to be in Germany. Tell me how you found Margaret after all those years."

"I never lost her, David. I was more constant than you. Wherever she was, I was there, invisible to her. The invisible giant—can you believe that, David?—the nimble and furtive giant, not the shambling, obvious fool. I was with her in Norfolk and Washington, and when the foreign service sent Margaret and Dwight to Germany, I went, too. That's when Margaret saw me, knew that I was there. But she didn't know who I had been. I was Ralph, not Son. You see, David, I was in the foreign service, too, and I was with them almost every day, watching and waiting. I was Dwight's driver for four years."

Christ Almighty! Listen to the triumph in his voice. Four years of plotting to kill D. How many years did he fuck poor deranged

Frony before he whispered it into D's ear, just as he crushed his throat?

"Did D—Dwight—know who you were?"

Son smiled. "Not until the end. He had to know then. He had to know why he was going to die. He was the first; just as you will be the last."

"But he wasn't the first, Ralph." David wasn't thinking of Son's mother, or Cornell.

"Oh, yes, that's true. Little Billy. You found out about him. I was afraid you wouldn't." Son seemed pleased that he knew about this most senseless of all the murders.

"He wasn't my brother, Ralph. I never had a brother."

Son waved the comment aside impatiently. "Don't be a fool, David. You can't deceive me. I knew about him because of your story—the one you wrote about me. You said he had died, but I didn't believe it. You said I had died, too."

In that instant the terrible revelation came to David that he was responsible for the death of Billy Marshall. He had supplied the list of all Son's victims.

"Billy was innocent, Ralph."

"Of course he was innocent," Son almost shouted in agreement. He leaned forward again, forcing his voice across to David. "Just as Justine was innocent, and Clerval, and Elizabeth."

What does he mean? David repeated the names again and again in his brain. All of them were innocent. My God! All of Mary Shelley's characters were in Son's mind. Justine, the innocent governess, who was hanged for the murder she didn't commit; Clerval, Frankenstein's friend, murdered even though he didn't know the monster existed; Elizabeth, his bride, killed on her wedding night. All were innocent. But Son was mad; David knew he couldn't argue for the innocence of those who were left.

"Why must you go on with your destruction, Ralph? I know about Dick. I found his grave. Cornell, Billy, Dwight. You have destroyed as many as the monster. And now you have your mate. You have taken Margaret as your woman, taken her from me, your Frankenstein. Wasn't that his ultimate crime, depriving his creation of a mate? Why do you need more revenge?"

Rage distorted Son's face. He came to his knees and leaned forward on his huge arms.

"*You can blast my other passions; but revenge remains— revenge, henceforth dearer than light or food! I may die; but first you, my tyrant and tormentor, shall curse the sun that gazes on your misery. Beware; for I am fearless, and therefore powerful. I will watch with the wiliness of a snake, that I may sting with its venom. Man, you shall repent of the injuries you inflict.'*"

David sat in open-mouthed disbelief as Son again quoted the monster's words, denounced him with the intensity of that fictional assassin. Then Son came across the widow's walk with an incredible quickness. David had only begun to rise when Son's massive hand found his throat. As the single arm pulled him to his feet, David's hands instinctively went to Son's wrist. It was like a bar of steel.

"You ask me about revenge?" he hissed in David's face. "I have no woman; she is your woman. I never took her from you. I couldn't. She has always belonged to you. That's the last thing I wanted to tell you, to show you. It's time now for you to know."

He reached up with his other hand and snapped a handcuff to David's right wrist. His grip on David's throat relaxed as he spun him around and pulled his arms together behind his back. Son snapped the other side of the handcuffs to David's left wrist. The choking hand had brought David to the edge of unconsciousness, and Son pushed him down the three flights of stairs and into the back field before his brain cleared enough to wonder about the handcuffs. It seemed ridiculous that Son could have them. He must have read David's mind.

"Gilbert won't be coming here tonight, David," he said as he shoved his prisoner ahead of him. "Don't hope for him to save you. You have no savior. I am invincible."

Had Son been there, David wondered, somewhere in the house, listening when he called the police station and left the urgent message? Where could he hide that I wouldn't feel his monstrous presence? David asked himself.

The significance of what Son had said was slow to penetrate the fog in David's brain. When it did—with a shocking, terrifying jolt—David stopped and turned to face him. Frony was beside him as he stood looking into David's face, anticipating a question, smiling, waiting for him to ask it.

"Are these Gil's handcuffs?" Fear now numbed David to all but the realization that Son was indeed invincible.

"He gave them up reluctantly. There was some valor in him, David."

"You killed him?" He couldn't believe it. When had there been time? It was only yesterday that Gil had advised David to be careful.

"I'm surprised you didn't know," Son said, still smiling. His face was hideous. "You said you found Richard's grave. There was a newer one, closer to the river."

All David could do was stare at him until the smile faded from Son's face and he motioned abruptly with his hand to continue into the field. Just before they got to the tulip tree David felt the cold weight of a light chain slip over his head and around his throat. Startled, he lunged forward and the chain tightened. Spears of pain shot through every nerve. It was a choke chain. Son had David on a leash, like a dog.

"Careful, David. It's not your time," he warned and relaxed the tension on the leather thong he held in his hand. As he wrapped the leash around the tree trunk and tied it, he said, "I selected this place because of your fondness for it. Now *you* can watch, but not from the woods—here, close—where you can see the ecstasy on Margaret's face."

Son moved outside the moonshade of the tulip tree, and as he began to unbutton his shirt, Frony lifted the dress and pulled it over her head. There was nothing under it. She stood completely naked in her white sandals until Son finished undressing, then she kicked them from her feet. Son guided her as they came closer to David, standing side by side. They were both magnificent—Frony as perfect as she had been over twenty years ago, and Son the bigger-than-life replica of a Herculean statue, except for the giant cock that hung between his legs. In the long moment they stood before David, he examined their faces. Reflected moonlight showed the gleam of lunacy in their eyes.

A slight movement of Son's hand on Frony's side directed her. She sank to the ground and lay on her back looking up at him. She lifted her knees and spread her legs. She held her breasts in her hands. David strained to see, choking himself as he leaned forward. Son moved toward her until he stood between her legs. He began to kneel, but she stopped him.

"No, not yet, David. I want you to look at me." She widened herself with her hands.

Not yet, David!

She wasn't here at all. She was back on the sand at the edge of the river, making a fifteen-year-old virgin boy wait too long. Her madness had taken her back that far.

Not yet, David. The shock of hearing it again caused him to lurch against the chain. He closed his eyes in pain, and when he opened them, Son had turned to show him the hatred on his face. You see how it is, his eyes said to David. She is your woman—has always been. It is always with you—on the beach by the river.

Son grew enormously erect as he watched her begin to squirm on the ground. The great bar of his sex stood straight out from his groin, and she stared at it with fascinated eyes. The heat was in her, and she began the motion, thrusting her hips upward, wanting him. She held out her arms.

"Now, do it now, David."

She gasped when he entered her. So did David. When Son's motion quickened, she admonished him, "Go slow, David."

David shuddered at the grotesqueness of what was happening, but he could not look away. They were sideways to him, and he could see Son's great shaft pumping into her. Son held himself up on stiff arms; huge knots of muscle ridged his shoulders. Frony's head rolled from side to side, and she picked up the pace, lifting her hips from the ground, bucking into him. She circled his neck with her arms to give herself purchase.

"Now, David. Harder."

The frenzy of orgasm was in them both. He slammed into her as she wrapped her legs around his and lifted herself from the ground, going with him as he withdrew, afraid he would come out of her before her time. The low moan started deep in Son's chest and it was answered by Frony's rhythmic "Ah, ah, ah. Yes. Oh, yes." The shudder of climax went through them both and the motion slowed. Son's arms trembled. Two strokes, three. He went down on his elbows, covering her, flattening her breasts.

Tears burned in David's eyes when Son rolled off her and he could see her shining body in the moonlight. She turned toward Son and put her hand on his flat belly.

Jesus Christ!

Her hand was on the belly of the surrogate lover, of the insane killer. And David, lashed to a tree in his own backyard, wept the bitter tears of frustration and helplessness.

Son's malign eyes held him as he untied the leash. David could see the pulse of rage that beat in that deformed temple. How he despises me! David thought. How I despise him!

Son's hand was tight on the collar as he pushed David ahead of him toward the rim of the cliff. Frony, still naked like Son, walked beside David and, for the last several paces, took his hand in hers. When they could walk no farther, they stood on the edge of the gorge. Frony turned and pressed against David, her arms circling his waist, her breasts against his chest. He leaned back to look into her face. The death wish was in her eyes.

The noose tightened and Son spun David toward him at the brink of the precipice. Frony's arms fell from around David and she stood smiling, mindless, looking at him and Son.

"You have deprived me of her, David," he hissed in his prisoner's face. "Now you can be deprived of the thing you always possessed." He shoved and David sprawled on the ground.

Horrified, helpless, David watched as Son swept Frony up into his monster arms and, turning toward him, grinning hideously, hesitating an awful moment, flung her into the dark chasm.

As David lunged toward him he heard her voice. What was it she called up out of the darkness? Had she called his name before she crashed onto the rocks below? Was that what he heard as he rammed his head into Son's side, before Son's arm circled his throat and the blind fury was choked out of him?

But Son had said it wasn't his time. So the great thigh-arm relaxed, briefly, long enough for Son to see in David's eyes that he understood when the monster said, *"I shall be with you on your wedding night."*

Chapter Seventeen

Glenn's voice was calling from a great distance, but David could feel his warm breath right there on his face.

"Dave! Can you hear me, Dave?"

Not so faint now, the voice came closer to where he was. Glenn's hands on his and Glenn's face swimming through the fog of this terrible dream with Frony's arms flung out and her back arched as she fell.

"Christ! I thought you were dead." Enormous relief was in Glenn's voice. He was leaning over his friend, peering anxiously into the white face, when David forced open his eyes.

And with the sight of Glenn's face came the flood of reality, pushing aside the amorphous figures that had haunted the two hours of unconsciousness.

Gil is dead! And Frony! He threw Frony over the cliff! But he couldn't speak. No words could be forced from his swollen throat.

He could see Glenn clearly now, kneeling beside him, his arm around his shoulders, his own mouth working to help form the words.

"He killed her, Glenn," David croaked through the pain in his throat.

Glenn didn't understand.

"What? Easy now, Dave. Take it easy. Wait till I get you inside, then you can tell me what happened."

Glenn's arm under his shoulders helped him to sit up. David's hand went to the welt on his throat. The chain was gone, and the leash, and, of course, the handcuffs.

But David couldn't wait. There wasn't time. He shook his head impatiently.

"Frony," he said as deliberately as he could and pointed to the edge of the cliff.

"Down there, Dave? Frony's down there?"

He nodded, two sharp dips of his head, and came up on his knees. Glenn understood enough to walk beside him as he crawled on all fours to the edge, not ten feet away, and to stand beside him peering into the blackness below.

"We can't see, Dave. We'll have to go down there."

After the first halting steps David could walk alone. He swept Frony's dress and sandals from the damp grass as they crossed the field. Glenn started to speak but didn't, deciding to wait until David was ready to tell him what had happened. The trembling weakness left David's legs and he took the back-porch steps two at a time. Inside, he turned into the kitchen and took a jar of honey from the shelf. He spooned a gob into his mouth and put another spoonful in a glass with warm water from the tap. The effect of the honey on his throat was immediate. By the time he came back downstairs with his gun, he could talk without much pain.

"We'll take your car," he said over his shoulder as he led the way down the hall toward the front door. He carried the glass of honey-and-water mixture in one hand and the pistol in the other. "Did you bring your gun?"

"Yes, it's in the car," Glenn answered.

"What about a flashlight?"

"Yes."

"Start the car; I'll get mine."

Glenn's pistol was on the seat of the car when David got in, and he sat on the barrel. He pulled it from under him and felt the heft of it compared to his thirty-two.

"My God! What caliber is this?"

"Forty-four." Glenn started to say something else but David interrupted.

"Why did you come to Parsons, Glenn?"

"Because you didn't call. You were supposed to call by ten thirty, eleven at the latest. Remember? It's after midnight now. I tried calling Gil to see if he'd heard from you, but he wasn't there." Glenn hesitated a moment, then asked, "Are you going to tell me what happened?"

They were turning into College Road and were less than a minute away from where they would have to stop to search for Frony.

"I'll tell you everything after we find Frony, Glenn. Son was here—you've probably figured that out—and he had Frony with him. He damn near killed me, and he made me—that son-of-a-bitch—he made me watch while he fucked her. He chained me to the damn tree and made me watch." David could feel his throat tightening and he sipped several times from the glass of honey water. "He didn't even put his clothes back on—that fucking bastard—and he made me watch when he threw her over the cliff."

"You picked up her dress. So when we find her, she'll be—"

"Naked. Yes, he threw her over the cliff naked." For some reason David added, "She didn't even scream."

Glenn pulled off the road just before they got to the narrow two-lane bridge that crossed the creek. When David came around to the driver's side of the car, Glenn caught his arm to stop him.

"You know she couldn't have survived the fall, Dave. It's almost two hundred feet."

David looked up at the sheer wall of the escarpment. "Yes. I know, I just want to find her before anyone else does."

"We can't move her before the police . . . maybe we should have tried to call Gil again."

"Gil is . . ." No. David didn't have time to tell him now. "I wish I had brought a blanket," he said as he started down the incline. "We don't have anything to cover her up with."

But they didn't need it, because they didn't find Frony.

A half-dozen times David stopped to calculate where she would have fallen, shining the powerful beam of his flashlight up to the fringe of trees at the top of the cliff. *That's where Son stood—right there exactly—or maybe two more trees to the right, or left.* They searched in places where they knew she couldn't be. The shallow creek, only a few feet wide, couldn't hide her body. And there were no blood-soaked rocks, no dark stains on the pebbly beach by the creek.

The two searchers stood together; their flashlights, dangling from their hands, made restless pools of light on the sand.

"Son came and got her," David said. "He's taken her to Huntington."

"Huntington?"

God Almighty! David exclaimed to himself. He doesn't know about any of it, and there isn't time to go through it all.

"Glenn, I have to go to Huntington. If you want to go with me, I can tell you on the way about everything that's happened."

"Son's at Huntington?"

"Yes."

Glenn hesitated for a moment before he said, "Maybe we should call Gil and let him know we're going. He'll want to—"

"Gil is dead, Glenn."

The flashlight in Glenn's hand jerked upward to shine in David's face. It was involuntary, and he saw the conviction in David's eyes. Glenn accepted Frony's death, because he was used to the idea; they had talked about it for days. But Gil! How could Gil be dead? He was too strong. He was a professional, for God's sake!

"Son killed him? When?"

"I don't know. Today. Sometime today."

"He told you that? Son? Son said he killed him?"

"Yes. I know Gil's dead, Glenn. We'll find him buried by the river at Huntington."

Gil was dead! Glenn had to believe it, because David said he *knew* it, without doubt. And he *knew* where he was buried—by the river at Huntington. And Frony! Thrown into the void to lie crushed and naked at the foot of the cliff until Son had retrieved her to perform whatever maniacal rite he enacted with his victims. Two more empty spots in the row of those who had sat shivering on the curb in front of Gilbert's house. Except that there were *three* empty spots. David hadn't told him about Dick McKenna.

"David, why don't we call the police, call the man Gil told us to call—Jack Evans—and have them go with us?"

"Because Son won't be there if the police come. We'd just be postponing what we have to do. He didn't kill Gil because he was a policeman; he killed him because he was one of our group." David turned to leave, angling his flashlight beam back toward the road. "Look, I have to go. I have to finish it tonight. He knows I'll be coming, and he'll be waiting for me. I think it might be better for you to stay with Madelyn and Grace."

A long, steady look convinced Glenn that David was speaking rationally, and that he spoke the truth. "I'm going with you." Glenn started walking rapidly back to the car. "Come on, I want to stop by your house and call Madelyn."

Glenn drove without the deliberation David had noticed at other times they had been in a car together. He seemed to be pressing forward, anticipating what was to come, exhilarated by the prospect of the night's certain danger, convinced that before the night was over they would both look death in the face.

"I can't believe everything that has happened since I left your house this afternoon," David said when they were out on River Road and he could feel Glenn waiting for him to begin. "No, I'll start with last night, I mean Wednesday night, after all of you left Parsons." David told him about seeing the phantom—Frony, or whatever it was—on the widow's walk and not understanding or believing what he had seen. "At the time there was no connection with what I had seen—thought I had seen—and my wanting to go to Huntington—that's where I went after I left your house. I just had the impulse to go."

He told it as quickly as he could—exploring the old house, finding Son's lair on the second floor with Frony's suitcase in it, discovering the secret tunnel to the bottom of the dry well and to the river on the other side. Glenn didn't stop him until he told about finding Dick's grave.

Glenn slammed the steering wheel with the palm of his hand.

"That raving goddamn maniac! He got Dick McKenna, too! I thought Dick was far enough away to be safe. How many of us does that make? I don't mean Cornell and the Marshall kid. And

Howard doesn't count because he was killed at Anzio. D and Frony and Dick. And you say he hasn't been dead more than a couple of days. Then Gil yesterday. That's three within the last seventy-two hours." He paused to count. "That's four altogether. There are only three of us left."

"Four. I'm afraid for Grace."

I shall be with you on your wedding night.

And David knew now that, if they survived, he would marry Grace.

Glenn turned to look at him quickly, taking his eyes off the road just long enough to register his surprise. "Why Grace? She's not one of us—I mean, she wasn't with us when we made Son hate us. Her name wasn't even mentioned in that letter."

"I don't think that means anything to Son now. Maybe it never did. He has killed two innocent people—Cornell and the Marshall boy—for other reasons. His mind seems to swing wildly from his obsession with revenge to the character he's playing from *Frankenstein*. He's killed D, Gil, and Dick purely for revenge—they have no counterpart in the Frankenstein story. I don't really know about Frony. Maybe in Son's mind she really was the mate created for the monster and then destroyed." David would not mention that of those left, the next in line would be the counterpart of Victor Frankenstein's friend, Henry Clerval—who was, of course, Fleming's friend, Glenn Walker. Instead, he asked, "Glenn, do you remember the last person Frankenstein's monster killed?"

"Well, he didn't actually kill Victor Frankenstein. It was Elizabeth, wasn't it, on the night of their wedding?"

"Yes, Frankenstein's bride, and she was innocent, as all the others had been innocent." David thought for a few moments of how to tell Glenn about his fears for Grace. They would be at Huntington in ten or fifteen minutes. If he were going to tell him all of it, he'd have to hurry. "I know you know about Grace and me. So does Son. This is hard as hell to explain, Glenn, but he blames me for Frony's inability to be the mate he has searched for all these years, and he knows—somehow—that I will marry Grace. So Grace is my Elizabeth to him, and he intends to act out part of the book. He'll try to kill her on our wedding night! That's the last thing he said before he choked me into unconsciousness."

David finished telling what had happened, rushing to get it all said, and Glenn listened silently as the bizarre details—from Frony's reappearance on the widow's walk to Son's hurling her over the cliff—shocked him into rigid-faced disbelief.

"Incredible! Goddamned incredible! And the last thing he said to you was '*I shall be with you on your wedding night*'?"

"Yes. That's why I'm so afraid for Grace. I hope you can understand this, Glenn, but Grace was my gift from Frony. She knew about us, too, and she was happy about it. Grace was her release, and mine, from all the years of torment we had caused each other."

The headlights picked up the pillars of the gate to Huntington, and David told Glenn to slow down. When they turned off the road, David could see that the aluminum gate was open. Son was inviting them in.

There was still enough moonlight for Glenn to drive without lights, so he turned off the switch as they started up the driveway. David was sure it didn't make any difference; Son would know they were coming. But if Glenn hadn't turned off the lights, David would have told him to. They were hunters now, and could feel muscles and brain cells adjusting to the part, blocking out the fear. Stealth. Caution. Step lightly. Speak softly. Be ready and don't tremble.

David directed Glenn to the spot by the first outbuilding where he had parked less than twelve hours before. As Glenn cut the engine, David lit a cigarette and handed it to him and then lit one for himself. There were some things they needed to talk about before they left the sanctuary of the car.

"You handed that to me like it might be the last one I'd ever have," Glenn said with just enough lightness in his voice to take the edge off the gravity of the words.

"It just might be, old friend." David took a deep drag and began talking while he was still exhaling the smoke. "It could be very important for you to know as much as I can give you in a couple of minutes about the physical layout of this place. We'll go in the back door because there's enough glass to see what's ahead of us until we get to the center hallway."

David described the grounds, the tunnel, the room layout on the first floor, and the locations of the stairway and bedroom Son used on the second floor. The last thing he drew in his verbal picture was the entrance to the tunnel on the left side of the study fireplace.

"There's no way to predict where he'll be waiting for us. There's not a light on in the house. So let's take it room by room downstairs before we go up. And for Christ's sake, Glenn, let's stay together. Take it slow and stay together." David picked up Glenn's pistol by the barrel and handed it to him butt first. "Do you think you'll have any trouble using this?"

"I don't think I'll have any choice. Do you?"

"No. Son's done all the talking he's going to do. What I'm saying is that you'll have to shoot him on sight. No conversation. No hesitation. Just kill the bastard. Empty the gun into him if you have to. Can you do that?"

"Yes. Can you?"

"You bet your ass." David picked up the flashlight from the car seat and Glenn retrieved his from the glove compartment. "There's one more thing. I'm ninety-nine percent sure he won't have a gun. He wants us the same way as the others—by the throat. Don't let that bother you—him not having a gun. He never gave anyone else a chance." They both thought of Gil.

Glenn reached over and took David's hand. He gripped it hard for a few seconds.

"Let's go get the fucker," Glenn said and opened the car door.

The back door to Huntington was closed but not locked. A quick circuit of the flashlight beam through the window David had entered earlier showed the back foyer to be empty, but a film of dust on both sides of the glass in the French doors prevented the light from penetrating into the center hall. For a moment they hesitated.

"He's been in the dark until his eyes are dilated," David whispered to Glenn as he shoved the flashlight into his right armpit and grasped the doorknob with his left hand. "The door opens out this way. If he's on the other side when I jerk it open, get that light into his face and aim for his chest. Stand back a little bit. Okay. Now!''

The hall was empty, a dark cavern with walls that pressed in on the searchers. They walked lightly, sliding their feet softly in the motes of dust, but their footfalls seemed to echo thunderously through the house. The doors to all the main rooms on the first floor that had been open in the afternoon were closed. Son had anticipated the way they would search for him. He had provided, with his maniac's mind, the agony of opening all those doors. David touched Glenn's arm and he turned with him to face the blank mahogany of the morning-room doors. Wordlessly, they repeated their act—doors jerked open by David, Glenn's flashlight held chest high for a giant, guns held rigidly in both hands for two or three counts, deliberate steps forward into the room, light beams played into every empty corner—for every room on the first floor. Son waited somewhere else.

So side by side they climbed the stairs, catching their breath when the treads groaned under their weight.

He would be waiting in the bedroom, of course, standing beside Frony's still naked and broken body on the vulgar bier of his iron-framed bed, David thought.

In front of the bedroom door they paused, tensing themselves, getting ready to kill. It would be easier now, while the adrenaline was still flowing.

David turned the knob slowly, feeling for the release of the catch, waiting for one breathless moment before he slammed the door open with his foot. Glenn crouched beside him, his arms rigidly outstretched to point the gun and flashlight into the horrible rectangle of darkness. David went in low, two steps obliquely to the right and then one step backward to get his back against the wall: Glenn followed on the other side and pressed against the open door.

Could I have been wrong? The question screamed in David's brain. Is this the wrong room?

There was no giant rushing toward them with strangling hands. There was no bed with Frony's mangled corpse—no bed at all. No blue suitcase on the floor. No clothes hanging in the closet. No chairs, or tables with kerosene lamps. Nothing. The room was completely empty.

But this was the same room. The door that opened to the porch over the back portico was open, and David could feel Glenn's puzzled eyes following him as he walked over to stare through it toward the river. He went out on the porch, and Glenn came to stand beside him at the rail. A faint glint of the river could be seen through the trees where the land fell away to the east.

"Dave—"

"This is the room, Glenn. I don't know when he had time to move the stuff out, but this is the room. I was out for over an hour when you found me in the field. He could have done it then—and when we were looking for Frony—but everything I told you about was in this room yesterday afternoon."

"Why should he clean the place out? From what you said it was just a bunch of junk."

Yes. Why would he? Except for the clothes, there wasn't two hundred dollars' worth of furniture in the room—real Salvation Army stuff.

"Glenn, has it occurred to you that nobody but me has seen Son, really seen him to know who he is?"

"Well—no. I hadn't thought about it, but that's true. The rest has all been conjecture, speculation. What are you getting at?"

"I don't know what kind of records Gil kept downtown—in the police department. I know he said the homicide lieutenant, Jack Evans, was supposed to know what was going on. Some of them knew they were looking for a big guy, the one in the apartment over the Sea Room. But what else did they know? His name, maybe."

"There have to be copies of the transcription from the tape Gil made when we told him about our trip to Whitfield," Glenn reminded him. "They'll have all that background."

"Do you remember how hard it was for Gil to accept what we told him? And he was directly involved, he was one of us. It will just sound like a wild-assed theory to anybody else. The only hard evidence they'll have is the letter Son left on my desk."

"For God's sake, Dave! We'll have three corpses when we find Gil and Frony. You saw him throw her off the cliff. You're an eyewitness to murder. And I found you nearly strangled to death out in the field. You've still got the mark of that goddamn chain on your throat. The story we'll tell the police is so bizarre they'll have to believe it. And Son's not going to just take off. The only chance he's got is to kill us, including Madelyn and Grace."

Glenn was right. David wasn't thinking straight. Son had committed himself and the only chance he had was to kill him and Glenn and go back for Madelyn and Grace, and he had to do it before the police started looking for Gil. He had to do it tonight.

"That son-of-a-bitch is smarter than I thought he was," David said slowly. "He cleaned out the bedroom so there couldn't be any connection between Huntington and the big man in the apartment on Grove Street. Nobody would ever know he was here. All that furniture is in the river. The heavy stuff is on the bottom and the rest of it will float so far away nobody would ever connect it with Huntington."

"So, he's still here," Glenn said grimly.

"Yes. He's here."

"There's no need to search the other rooms, is there?"

"No."

They both knew where Son was waiting. They could feel the presence of his great bulk, sense his impatient prowling of the dark corridors—waiting. The oppressive stink of that black pit was already strong in David's nostrils.

The panel beside the library fireplace was closed flush with the rest of the wall, and it took them four or five minutes of muted cursing and digging at the panel seams before they found the release. It was a cleverly concealed piece of molding at the top of the baseboard. Glenn discovered it with one of a series of frustrated kicks after they had gone over every square inch of the ornately milled mantel. The door popped open on its groaning hinges, and they stood for a few moments looking at the vertical slit of blackness it created.

"I'll go first," David said to Glenn as he hooked the end of his flashlight into the crack and swung the door fully open. "There are about twenty steps and at the bottom the tunnel goes off to the right. Stay about two steps in back of me in case I stop suddenly."

"How long is the tunnel—before we get to the well?"

"About fifty yards. It's too narrow for us to walk side by side. I'm going very slowly, Glenn. The floor is brick and it's damp and slippery. Oh, yes. There's a small room before we get to the well. If he's there, he'll see our lights long before we get to the opening on the tunnel side. He'll expect us to stop and try to check out the inside corners before we go on. I don't intend to do that. As soon as I can pick up the opposite wall and see that it's clear, I'm going to turn off my flashlight and hit that opening on a dead run. When my light goes out, that will be your signal. Turn yours out, too, count to five, and turn it on again. I'll be against the wall on the other side. If he's in there he'll be between us. And, Glenn, if I start shooting, you come in and empty that forty-four."

The twenty downward steps seemed interminable. An overwhelming dread came over David, to such an extent that he paused halfway down to control his trembling legs. He felt Glenn's firm hand on his shoulder.

"Steady, Dave. We've only got fifteen more minutes of this—one way or another."

A strange transformation came over David. The palsied trembling stopped. The hand of courage on his shoulder transfused him with the resolution that had somehow drained away. What was it Son had said? *I am fearless, and therefore powerful.* So am I, you ugly bastard, so am I, David proclaimed to himself.

Before he continued down the steps, another of the monster's threats came to him. *"I will glut the maw of death, until it be satisfied with the blood of your remaining friends."* Like hell you will! David thought fiercely.

Their unsynchronized footsteps echoed faintly from the tunnel walls. Twice David stopped to listen, and Glenn in imitation held his breath, both straining to hear some rustling movement or to feel the wind of suspiration from Son's mighty chest. Their ears rang with the silence.

Fifteen or so feet from the opening to the anteroom David held up his hand for Glenn to stop. He moved from one side of the tunnel to the other, getting as much angle as he could for the flashlight beam through the doorway. The far walls and corners of the room were clear. For a long moment David stood forming a mental picture of the space he would have to cover in the dark before he got to the well on the opposite side of the room. He turned to face Glenn and waved his flashlight to indicate that he was ready. Glenn nodded and stepped to within a pace of where he was standing. David breathed deeply twice and then snapped off his flashlight. Glenn's light went off almost simultaneously with the searing white explosion of pain that hit David's face as he charged through the opening.

The sensations came to David one by one. His eyes opened to complete darkness. His whole face burned with the pain of split lips and broken teeth. He couldn't breathe through his nose, and the taste of blood was in his mouth. He was lying on his left side and something hard was digging into his ribs. Rolling over onto his back almost caused him to strangle as blood and tooth fragments settled into his throat. Sputtering, coughing, he sat up and spat the choking mess onto the anteroom floor. His hand brushed the flashlight that had been under him when he fell. It rolled away, and he searched blindly, running his hands over the damp bricks until he found it.

Glenn wasn't more than three feet away, lying on his back, his lifeless eyes staring at the vaulted ceiling. Glenn, his closest friend, was dead. The monster had killed his Clerval. David's anguished roar of outrage reverberated from all the subterranean surfaces.

"Son, you fucking son of a bitch!" he bellowed. "You cocksucking bastard!"

His gun was in the corner. The arrogant maniac hadn't bothered to take it. Nor had he taken Glenn's forty-four caliber cannon. It was lying at the tunnel's entrance where it had fallen from his dead fingers.

He is still here! I can feel it, David thought. He wants to know that I have looked into Glenn's dead eyes, wants to hear me say it. All right, goddamn you, Son! I will say it!

"Clerval is dead, Monster!" David shouted into the doorway of the well. "But he is the last you will kill!"

Did David hear him laugh as the echoes of his own voice died away? Was there the soft sound of receding footsteps out in the well or in the tunnel on the other side? He listened for a moment and then shook his head and listened again. There was only his own rasping breath.

David leaned down and picked up Glenn's pistol. The thirty-two was more comfortable in his hand, so he shoved the heavier gun under his waistband and tightened the belt over it. If it took twelve bullets to stop him, the six small ones would go in first.

Without hesitation he walked from the anteroom onto the floor of the well, half expecting to meet him in that circular arena for the last struggle one of them would ever have. But the flashlight beam showed only the bare bricks of the cylindrical walls. He entered the anteroom on the other side more cautiously, ducking as he went in. He didn't need another fist in the face. Nothing hit him and he stood in the middle of the empty room sucking air in through his mouth. He spat blood from his lacerated gums and lips onto the floor and ran his tongue over the broken teeth.

There were no concealing corners on the other side of the entrance to the riverside tunnel. The flashlight beam broadened to i!luminate the entire surface of the heavy wooden door a hundred feet down the passageway. Another closed door! David had left it halfway open, as he had found it, a half-dozen hours before.

He was there, behind that door. He had to be. Suddenly David knew why. The river was his sanctuary, his escape route. The tunnel's sharp downward slope on the other side of the door took it completely below river level so that water intruded into the completely closed south end. Son had to swim only fifty feet under water and he would be at the tunnel opening beneath the river's surface. How many times had he come and gone that way?

David pulled Glenn's gun from under his belt and replaced it with his own. Thirty seconds of long breaths. Then he ran as quickly as he could over the slippery bricks until he was no more than fifteen feet in front of the door. He clamped the flashlight under his left arm and, using both hands to steady the big pistol, began squeezing the trigger. One deafening explosion, two, three, four. The holes in the door were from belly to chest high for someone seven feet tall.

When the door began to open, David turned and retreated five steps, whirled, and fired the fifth round before he had steadied the pistol—a miss that whined off the tunnel wall and plocked into the wood of the doorframe. The sixth round caught Son in the left shoulder above another red blossom that stained his shirt just below his rib cage. Two hits out of six and he was still coming, filling the tunnel with his hugeness, rage bellowing from his twisted mouth.

In one motion David dropped Glenn's pistol and jerked his own from his belt. The first shot went in under Son's right collarbone and the second missed because Son snapped over into a crouch, spun, and dove back through the doorway. As he went through his foot caught the door's edge and it swung three quarters closed. By the time David got the door open he was halfway to the water's edge, running so bent over his hands almost touched the floor. Three steps past the doorway David stopped, braced himself, and fired. The bullet hit him in the right hip, and David could see he was going down. But his momentum took him splashing past the water's edge twenty yards ahead of David. He went facedown into the water, then came up to his knees as if he had bounced from the surface. He straightened and for an instant his broad back presented itself over the sight at the end of the pistol. The hole the next bullet made in his shirt was high between his shoulder blades just to the right of center. He plunged forward into the water so quickly David couldn't get off another shot. It took only four or five seconds to get to the water's edge, and David went in up to his knees and fired the last two rounds into the boil of water where Son should have been. He went farther in, up to his waist, feeling around for the trunk of Son's body against his legs.

Five bullet holes in you, mother-killer, maybe seven, and you'll probably drown before you bleed to death! But you're dead, Frony-killer, you're dead!

How many more steps into the water would it have taken to find him? Two steps more, maybe three, to feel that great corpse and pull it up on the tunnel floor and look into its dead face. But David retched and gagged and vomited the only thing in his stomach, blood from his own shattered mouth.

Somebody else can haul you out, cocksucker, and I hope you bloat before they do, David swore silently. Tears from his nausea, and from everything else, wet David's cheeks as he turned and stumbled out of the water. His yellow summer slacks were streaked with the bright red blood of Simple Son.

Chapter Eighteen

David thought the young policeman who opened the Walkers' front door was going to blow his head off before Madelyn came up behind him and cried, "My God! David!" The policeman lowered the pistol and watched with open-mouthed amazement as this man with the mangled face pushed past him into the living room. Grace gasped when she saw him, hesitated for a second or so, and then came to take his arm to guide him into the bathroom. Looking briefly over his shoulder, David found Madelyn was still standing at the open door, waiting for Glenn.

No wonder I scared the hell out of the policeman, David observed as he examined himself in the mirror over the lavatory. Eyes swollen almost shut—lips split and protruding an inch past the red pulp of his cheeks—nose skewed to the left with blood-clotted nostrils—rust-colored stains on his white shirt that came from his own drippings and matched Son's darkening blood on his slacks.

Grace stood helplessly beside him with a damp washcloth in her hand, unable to bring herself to raise it to his face. He took it from her, turned her around, and pushed her out the door. He ran the basin full of warm water and lowered his face into it. As gently as he could, he exhaled through his nose until he dislodged the clotted blood. He changed the water in the basin to cold and soaked his face until the trickle of new blood from his nose stopped. When he looked into the mirror again, his appearance wasn't much improved, but he felt a hell of a lot better. Glenn's bathrobe was hanging from a hook on the door, and he stripped off his clothes, including his shoes and socks, and put it on.

For a full minute David stood with his hand on the doorknob, thinking about what he was going to say to Madelyn. How do you tell a woman that the other half of her is dead? The only way you can—quickly—and have the courage to look into her eyes and watch the light in her soul go out.

Madelyn was sitting on the sofa, staring unblinkingly at the door to the hall when he came through it. He didn't want the policeman in the room when he told her, so he walked directly to the overstuffed chair where the detective was sitting.

"Come in the kitchen with me, please," David said, walking back into the hall before any objection could be registered. He led the way into the kitchen and closed the door. The policeman started to speak, but David held up his hand and stopped him. "I don't have time right now to explain. I want you to call the next man in line to Gil Thomas in the homicide unit—that's Lieutenant Evans, I believe—and tell him to get his ass over here. I don't care where the fuck he is. If he's in bed, get him up. Tell him whatever you have to to get him over here in the next thirty minutes. Do you understand me?"

The young policeman was smart enough to realize that this wasn't the time to argue.

"Yes, sir," he said and waited, because he could tell that David wasn't through instructing him.

"Now, I've got something very difficult to tell those two women in there, and I want to tell it to them alone. I'll come get you when I'm ready for you to come in." The color of offended dignity came into the policeman's youthful cheeks, but he didn't speak his protest. David turned and left him.

David told Madelyn as quickly and as kindly as he could, sitting knee to knee with her and holding both her hands. Her eyes never wavered from his face, even when they glazed with tears. Her nails dug into his palms while the internal battle of acceptance and rejection of Glenn's death raged inside her. She had been sitting rigidly erect, tense in every fiber, as she listened to David's horrible words. When acceptance came, she closed her eyes and slumped against the sofa cushion.

Grace, who had sat and watched them silently from the other end of the sofa, sobbed and got up and left the room. Several minutes passed as Madelyn controlled the rage inside her.

"Is he still down there—in that tunnel?" she finally asked. Her voice was level, except for an almost imperceptible shudder.

David could see in her face what she saw in her mind's eye—the loneliness of Glenn's death in that dark and damp cavern.

"Yes, he is, Madelyn. I couldn't move him. I didn't have the strength. And the police—"

"And Son—you killed him?"

"Yes, he's dead."

"There's more to tell, isn't there, David?"

She must have read it in his face, the dread of having to tell Grace about Frony, of having to tell them both about Gil—and Dick McKenna.

Grace came back with three glasses a quarter filled with brandy.

"Joe Fant, the policeman in the kitchen, said to tell you Lieutenant Evans is on the way over here," she said as she handed them the glasses.

He had fifteen minutes, maybe twenty, to finish it. The brandy set his whole mouth on fire, but he gulped it down and gently pulled at Grace's arm until she was sitting close to Madelyn on the couch. Grace looked at him apprehensively as he sat facing them, holding both her hand and Madelyn's in his.

"I don't have much time to tell you everything that's happened," he began. As unemotionally as he could he told them what had taken place since he had left them the afternoon before. Grace's eyes widened and she leaned forward when he told her about Frony and Son on the widow's walk.

"Mother was there with that Son Hammond? I mean, she was there willingly? The way you tell it, she wasn't tied up or anything. She was just—"

"Wait, Grace! Wait a minute." The command came sharply through his swollen lips to stop the rising wail of hysteria that had begun in her voice.

The three of them sat in momentary silence while he tried to think of how to go on. So far he had done a very bad job, telling too much or too little of the detail. He certainly couldn't describe the grotesque sexual ritual between Frony and Son. No, not just between them—among the three of them, because he was involved, too, as Frony's sexual partner in the twenty-year-old fantasy that had made an enraged surrogate of Simple Son.

So he went on quickly, almost brutally, and pulled Grace into his arms when he told of Frony being hurled from the cliff. When Grace's trembling had stopped, after she had looked into David's face with hopeless eyes—and Madelyn had raised her head from her hands and hissed, "That bastard! That fucking bastard!"—he finished telling all he thought they could bear, including brief, softened accounts of the deaths of Gil and Dick McKenna.

The shock of it paralyzed the two women's minds. They sat stunned, unable to think through the horror of so much death, so much senseless killing. And when Grace could begin to think, when a semblance of reason returned, she still couldn't erase the mental picture of her mother being flung into the abyss.

So it was Madelyn who recovered enough, after long moments in her own private hell, to ask, "Did you find Gil's body?"

"No, but he's there, Madelyn. There's another new grave at Huntington, somewhere."

"We're all that are left—out of all of us—just you and I." There was heartbreaking sadness in her voice.

"We have Grace." David squeezed Grace's shoulder. "Frony has left us Grace."

The knock of the door was like a rifle shot, and they all jumped convulsively into attitudes of rigid defense.

"Joe," David called so that the young detective in the kitchen could hear, "come open the door for Lieutenant Evans."

David spent the rest of the night talking to two incredulous homicide detectives in a small room at police headquarters. Joe Fant spent the rest of the night fidgeting in the Walkers' living room. Grace and Madelyn had enough brandy to put them to sleep in each other's comforting arms in Glenn and Madelyn's king-size bed.

Son's body wasn't in the water inside the riverward leg of the tunnel. Divers in scuba gear searched later in the morning, traversing the submerged passageway again and again.

"I don't know how he did it with five bullet holes in him, but he must have made it to the river," Lieutenant Evans said as he stood on the riverbank with his hat dangling from his hand, scratching his scalp through thinning blond hair. "We'll have to drag the goddamn thing."

It was almost noon when David arrived at Huntington, driven there in an unmarked police car by a talkative homicide detective whose name he never did get.

"You look a hell of a lot better than you did when I first saw you this morning," the detective offered when David got into the car.

"What?" So far as David knew this was the first time the driver had seen him.

"I saw you in Jack Evans's office before you took your little nap." David had collapsed for three hours on a cot in a small windowless annex to Gil Thomas's office. "You looked like shit."

They rode in silence for several minutes.

"I was the one went over to your place and got you some clothes." He seemed to take considerable pride in the errand. "It's a good thing those blood tests turned out the way they did, or you'd be wearing blue denim over at the jailhouse."

"Blood tests?"

"Yeah. Evans was really pissed when they found Captain Thomas like you said they would. Found him about eight o'clock this morning. The blood on your pants wasn't his, though. Proved there was somebody else down in that tunnel beside you and your friend who got killed. Same blood was in the water down there—a hell of a lot of it."

The detective was just showing off. David knew he had never really been a suspect, as the man implied. The blood tests were routine, performed in an attempt to place all the players in this horrible melodrama. Jack Evans knew what was going on, knew about Son and the threats he had made. He just didn't know what had happened since he last saw Gil Thomas alive.

"Where did they find Gil Thomas?" David asked.

"Down by the river, close to the drop-off down to the water. The grave was real shallow. The guy hardly covered him up. Must have been in a hell of a hurry."

"How was he killed? Strangled?"

"Yeah, I'd say so. There wasn't any sign of blood."

"What about the big guy, the man I shot? Did they get his body out of the water down in the tunnel?"

"Nah, not by the time I left. The divers had been working over an hour, and I left about ten. They could have found him after that. Probably did. He's got to be in there, with all that blood. We'll know pretty soon."

Lieutenant Evans clapped his hat back on his head in disgust.

"I've never pulled a body out of the river with a hook, all the times I've tried. The way the current's running, the son-of-a-bitch could be halfway to the coast." He turned to look at David. "Don't worry. He'll pop up one of these days, if we don't fish him out today or tomorrow. If you hit him where you said you did, he's a dead mackerel. I'm just surprised he could make it to the end of that tunnel. He lost more blood than most men have in them."

He turned and walked toward his car. David followed and listened while he used the radio to order the crew and equipment necessary to drag the river.

"Lieutenant," David said when he'd got back out of the car. "I know you searched the grounds until you found Gil Thomas. The woman I told you about, Frony—Margaret—Bennett, did you . . ."

"No. We didn't find her. We'll go over this place inch by inch, but I don't think we'll find her. She's probably in there"—he pointed toward the river—"a couple of miles farther downstream than your crazy old buddy."

Lieutenant Evans's pessimism about the likelihood of dragging Son's body out of the river was justified. David watched the grappling hooks splash into the river until almost dark. The only thing they brought up was the iron bedframe and one of the kerosene lamps he had seen in the upstairs bedroom at Huntington. The talkative policeman drove him back to Parsons, and he crawled into bed and slept for twelve hours with his mouth open because he still couldn't breathe through his nose.

The next day David went to the hospital and had one of the residents straighten his nose as best he could. Then he spent an uncomfortable hour with Grace and Madelyn—they were all polite and evasive with one another, careful not to start another emotional binge—before he drove back to Huntington.

By four o'clock in the afternoon the boats had worked five hundred yards downstream without bringing up anything but ordinary river debris. Evans called off the search and sent everybody back into town.

"Mr. Fleming," Evans said as David was about to get in his car and leave, "I don't understand all I know about this case. Gil Thomas filled me in on some of the details, but he was pretty much handling it himself. I can understand that—I know he was on that crazy bastard's hit list with the rest of you. But I don't know what I'll find in his records. You obviously know as much as anybody about what's happened here. I want to know everything you know—everything—starting tomorrow morning at nine o'clock. Bring everything you've got to my office, and plan to spend some time with us, Mr. Fleming."

"Tomorrow's Sunday," David protested. He had something else to do.

"We work on Sunday," Evans said pointedly.

"Make it ten o'clock. I have to make arrangements for a funeral."

Evans looked at him through narrowed eyes for five long seconds.

"Okay, I'll see you at ten."

Glenn was buried Monday morning—Gil in the afternoon. Some of the people who came to the funerals didn't even know them, and they whispered to each other, surreptitiously pointing to

Madelyn, or Grace, or David. They had become principals in a drama that had drawn national attention. Accounts in the media had been inadequate, and for the most part inaccurate. But a policeman had been killed, and a college professor, and another man practically nobody remembered. An innocent woman and a madman were presumed dead. There was a beautiful surviving wife and a beautiful sorrowing orphan girl. And that writer who owned Parsons, that spooky old place out on River Road, was somehow involved. The town was agog with it, came to stare and be part of it.

David sat between Madelyn and Grace in two churches and stood between them at two gravesides while they stared dry-eyed at the closed coffins. It was a grim day of constant struggle to insulate themselves from the emotional pain.

The thirty-seven-year-old widow and the twenty-year-old orphan prepared dinner, and the three of them drank enough of what was left in the Walkers' liquor cabinet to let them talk about it. They talked until two o'clock in the morning, and David went to sleep on the living-room sofa. Over and over again in his dreams he heard the question Grace had asked him repeatedly, like a litany—*They won't find Mother, will they, David?*

By the end of the week he had spent over thirty hours with Evans, going over the details of what had happened since he first found the note from Son on his desk. There weren't any surprises in Gil Thomas's records. All the notes he had made of the events as he interpreted them agreed almost completely with what David told Evans. They physically retraced the steps that had taken David to Whitfield (where Evans talked at great length with Dr. Betchel), to the apartment on Grove Street, and to the room on the second floor of Huntington. Evans came to Parsons and walked the floor of the widow's walk. He sat beside David in a lawn chair under the tulip tree and looked at the spot on the ground where Son and Frony had acted out the carnal prelude to her death. He stood on the edge of the cliff and peered into the rock-banked stream below. They returned again to Huntington and went into the tunnels, where David acted out the final minutes of the previous Saturday morning's horror. As he entered the antechamber he could feel again the explosion of that brute fist in his face and could see Glenn's dead eyes staring up from the damp brick floor. In the south tunnel David pointed his finger and put five bullet holes in Son, crouching as he had crouched, trembling with the same rage and fear, seeing the blood blossoms on Son's shirt, feeling the same nausea when he had finished.

That was the end of it. They came back up into the sunlight, got into the detective's car, and drove away from Huntington.

"Okay," Evans said as he stopped his car in the driveway at Parsons. "I've got everything I need. You and Mrs. Walker and Miss Bennett will have to sign depositions. I'll bring them out to the Walker house Monday, about three in the afternoon."

He had been very considerate of Madelyn and Grace, coming to sit in the Walkers' living room for three or four hours of gentle questioning rather than have them go in to police headquarters. They learned that Gil had been his closest friend, and they could see how Lieutenant Jack Evans, a hard, lean man not given to emotion, grieved for him. They all came to like him immensely.

"There will be an inquest toward the end of next week," he said out of the window of the car as David began to move toward the porch steps. David could tell he was reluctant to mention it. "Probably Thursday or Friday. We'll need the three of you there." He hesitated for a moment. "It shouldn't take too long. Will you tell the ladies for me?"

Neither Son's nor Frony's body had been found by the time of the inquest, so the findings of the grand jury had a rather tentative tone. No indictment was brought, because the person accused of three definite and one probable (Frony was assumed deceased) homicides, one Ralph Edward Hammond, was also assumed deceased. The jury did most of its work without the witnesses present, and Madelyn, Grace, and David were required only to swear to the accuracy of the depositions they had signed. It took less than twenty minutes.

Lieutenant Evans walked with them out of the courthouse.

"Is that it?" David asked when they were standing on the curb beside his car.

"That's it."

"You don't need us for anything else? This ends it?"

"Well, yes, I think so. Unless of course—there's the possibility . . ."

"Of your finding my mother?" Grace asked.

Evans hesitated. "Yes. There would be some formalities."

"You've been very kind and patient, Lieutenant Evans," Madelyn said, taking his hand in both of hers. It wasn't a handshake, more a gesture of gratitude. "We've all lost someone very dear to us. We just want to get away from here and start getting our lives back together."

"Yes, I understand. If there's anything I can do . . ." He looked at the three of them in turn and then walked away.

David spent the next two weeks getting his teeth capped and helping Madelyn and Grace work out the details of their financial futures. Glenn had carried a surprising amount of life insurance, enough to last Madelyn for years with frugal management. "Of course, I'll get a job of some kind," she said. "I'll need it for more than just money." Mortgage insurance paid off the remaining debt on the Walkers' house. Madelyn was financially secure, at least for the time being.

Grace's situation was something else again. Frony had less than two thousand dollars left of the settlement from D's parents. The house was paid for, but Grace couldn't sell it because of the legal complications of Frony's not being declared officially dead. The three of them decided Grace should rent it and move in with Madelyn. They needed each other. David and the two women worked out all the details like the three surviving members of the same family—all the details except one.

David intended to marry Grace—they had even discussed it obliquely on several occasions—but he felt no sense of urgency about it. She didn't, either, really. She knew that first they had to get back into living patterns that would give some normality to their lives. She knew it would take time.

But there were two areas in which David knew he was going to have trouble with Grace. The first was the reaction he predicted she would have to a decision he had made: He was going away. In some ways he had been even more emotionally scarred than either Madelyn or Grace. They had all lost people they loved; parts of them had been brutally torn away. But he had killed a man, and no matter how he justified it to himself, the fact of it was still indelibly imprinted in his mind. So David had decided to leave Parsons. He was going to Europe to finish writing his book—and reorder his life.

The second problem with Grace was getting her to return to school. She didn't think the world needed another English major, but that was only a minor part of her argument.

"I'm not going to school," she declared heatedly as the two of them sat in David's study at Parsons. "I'm not going to be a goddamn charity case. If Madelyn can go to work, so can I."

"Who said anything about charity?" David argued. "You can work in the summertime, and the rent from the house will take care of most of your other expenses. You'll be living off campus, and you won't have dormitory expenses."

"Okay. Say I'm going back to school. What about tuition?"

"You've got enough for next year."

"I'm only a junior next year."

"We'll worry about it one year at a time."

"You're thinking I'll be able to sell the house by the time I'm a senior, aren't you?"

"Yes."

The implication of her being able to sell the house stopped her for a moment. She shook off the melancholy thoughts that had begun to form in her mind.

"Then, why did you set up the account in my name?" she asked suspiciously. "That's your money, and if what you say is true, I won't need it."

"It's just some money you should have available in case of an emergency."

"What kind of an emergency? If anything comes up that Madelyn and I can't handle, you'll be here."

The time had come to tell her.

"No, Grace. I won't be here."

His statement had the effect he had anticipated. There was anguish in the surprise on her face.

"Why? What do you mean you won't be here? You work here."

"I'm taking a leave of absence, for a year."

"A year? You're leaving for a year?"

"Yes."

"Where are you going?"

"To Europe."

Grace's mouth fell open in dismay.

"Europe? You're going to Europe for a year? For Christ's sake, what for?"

David told her, as best he could, why he had to leave. He told her why he wanted her to finish college and become part of the ordinary world they would both live in when he came back. He talked to her until she understood, as best she could, that it was not yet their turn. But she still asked, "You've absolutely made up your mind?"

"Yes."

"When are you leaving?"

"Monday morning."

She stared at him in hurt disbelief. It was too soon.

"That's day after tomorrow."

"Yes, Grace. We have two days." He took her in his arms. "I want you to stay here with me until I leave."

She began to cry.

Chapter Nineteen

The cottage the leasing agent got for David was fifteen miles from the Mediterranean in the hills north of Cannes. He moved in with three suitcases, four boxes of books, a typewriter, and a motherly housekeeper who could speak enough English for them to communicate with each other.

At first, working was extremely difficult. For two weeks he tried to get himself back into the discipline of sitting at the typewriter until the breaks came in the endless string of impasses his book was presenting to him. It took that long for him to realize—it came to him while he was on one of his long daily walks—that he shouldn't have been working on the book at all. He wasn't ready for it because he hadn't finished something that had to be done first—the journal he had begun sitting in the field under the tulip tree.

The book was what had brought him to France; his immersion in the writing of it would be his emotional therapy. He knew that. But the journal was the mental purgative that was necessary before he could start that therapy. The book would have to wait.

He worked on the journal for two months, finishing it in the reportorial style he had used when he started. He then rewrote it in narrative style so he could recapture the terrible emotions he had felt.

Five bullet holes in you, mother-killer . . . You're dead, Frony-killer, you're dead.

That's the only way the catharsis would work. He had to go over it again and put it on paper—the way it had happened. And when he had finished, when the purge was almost complete, only rarely then did his dreams hold Glenn's lifeless eyes shining in the flashlight's beam at the bottom of the pit, or Frony's arched and naked body falling into the void at the edge of the world, or Son's twisted mouth in his grotesque face bellowing his rage in the echo chamber of a slimy subterranean tunnel. Gone from his mind's wakeful conjuring were the bloated faces of D and Gil and Dick McKenna; and fading and ephemeral were the visions of the broken bodies of a little boy and a guiltless doctor. When the time came that David no longer visioned a crumpled ghostly figure in a white nightgown, the journal was finished.

The book began to flow. The thoughts came and expanded and grew and the book became bigger than he had thought it would. He had over a thousand pages of manuscript before he typed "The End" on the last page. As the dimensions of the book changed, so did David's plans for returning home. Time and again he had to explain the extensions of his absence in his letters to Grace and Madelyn. Both women stopped asking when he planned to come back to Parsons. While David was writing they were weaving the strands of their lives back together. Madelyn's salvation was a job in the college's admissions office. Grace became a second-semester senior while he was writing his last chapters.

David finished the book thirteen months after he'd finished the journal, rewrote and edited it in sixty days, and had a girl from the American Express office in Cannes type the final draft.

He received the publisher's acceptance and the letter from Madelyn on the same day.

Dear David,

I've begun to think you may never come home again. How long has it been now? Two years in July, and it's almost March. I think Dean Johnson is beginning to wonder, too. I saw him the other day, and he was asking about you. He said your place is still open on the faculty, but I get the impression he's getting a little impatient to hear what you plan to do. He probably considers himself quite generous to have given you the second year's leave of absence. I guess he was, at that. At any rate, I suggest you drop him a line and let him know your plans. Not just incidentally, I'd like to know what they are myself. So would Grace.

That brings me to the real reason I am writing so soon after my last letter. I received yours only yesterday and there was no mention of your coming home for Grace's graduation. It's none of my business if you want to expatriate yourself; I know you love France. But now that your book is finished, couldn't you come home for commencement? She's worked her butt off for that degree, and we're the only thing she has resembling a family. I'm not nagging. I know you've been very good about writing to her—to both of us—and you've been very generous with the money you put in the account for her. She just needs more than that now.

I'm going to say one other thing that's none of my business. Grace is still desperately in love with you, David. That's the main reason you should come home—to straighten things out with her, so she can go and do whatever she's going to do with her life.

God! That's enough of that! I *am* nagging!

Things are going very well with me. You know I loved every minute of being Glenn's housemarm, playing the part of faculty wife, but I think I've found another dimension to myself, now that I'm a working woman. You probably got tired of my whining in the letters I wrote during the months just after Glenn's death. I hope you notice I don't do that anymore. This job is the best thing that could have happened to me. I thought you'd like to know that, because you keep asking me about it in your letters. I was frightened to death at first, but now I love it. I've learned that I can cope, David. I can hack it by myself. I never knew that before. It's a goddamned good thing to learn on the eve of my fortieth birthday.

There's still nothing to report on Frony and Son. Jack Evans doesn't think they'll ever be found, not after all this time. He says it's not all that unusual, especially in the river.

There are so many submerged trees that they could get caught under. I hate to write about it; it's so macabre. I won't anymore, unless something happens.

Jack has been very good with Grace. He has been out a number of times to talk to her, and he has almost convinced her that it will be better if Frony isn't found. Grace may never accept it completely, poor kid. I wish she could. I can imagine what kind of nightmares she has when she thinks about how both her parents died.

I can't remember whether I wrote you that Jack has been promoted to captain. He has Gil's old job as head of the homicide unit. He's an unusual man, all stern and leathery on the outside, but very gentle on the inside.

There is really not any more news to report. I go to Parsons every several weeks to check on old man Varnell. He seems to be taking care of the place very well. He's not much of a gardener and the grounds are getting to look a little ragged. Let me know if you'd like to have me get a landscape crew to come give the yard a going over.

You told me you plan to go to Monte Carlo the first week of March and lose some of the money you're going to earn on the new book. I hope you have a good time. That's about the same time as spring break for Grace. Maybe we'll take off for a few days, maybe go up to the mountains. It would do us both good to get away for a while.

Give some thought to what I said about coming home, David, and let me know what you decide.

Love,

Madelyn

David read the letter twice before putting it aside. He thought about the things Madelyn had written in the order he considered most important.

First, there was Grace. He sat on his small terrace in the sun looking at the southern hills that sloped down toward the sea, cursing himself for the fool he was. Of course he was going home for her graduation. He had planned it long ago, as a surprise! He hadn't even told Madelyn. Now he rued his stupidity. A surprise! Who needed it? What Grace needed was the comfort of knowing that the fool she was in love with would be with her on this very important day in her life. She didn't need some egomaniac showing up at the eleventh hour just so he could see the glow of gratitude on her face. Well, he could fix that. As soon as he worked out his timetable for the next couple of months, he would write Madelyn—no, Grace—and tell her when he would be home. He wanted to read the galleys of the book before he left France, but they should be ready before the first of May. He could read them in a couple of weeks. That would be plenty of time; commencement was on the fifth of June. He would have everything arranged before he left for Monte Carlo.

David was feeling very pleased with himself, with his show of decisiveness, until he realized he had been indecisive about the most important thing of all. He had neglected to arrange his future—with Grace. There was no question about his still being in love with her. No girl from the beach at Cannes had been able to replace her, except for brief moments in his bed. Jealousy raged in him when he thought of being similarly replaced by some strutting campus hero. God, how he wanted her! It was time for him to go back home.

Neither Frony nor Son had been found. Madelyn always reported this negative news, and he was always glad to hear it. How he dreaded the letter that would announce the discovery of Frony's battered corpse. He dreamed of Son's hideous face slowly emerging from the murky river water. Jack Evans was right. It would be much better if they were never found.

Jack Evans. Jack, Madelyn had called him. "*Jack has been very good with Grace . . . very gentle on the inside.*" He wondered—not about Grace, but about Madelyn herself. "*He has been out a number of times to talk to Grace.*" I'll bet! He smiled when he thought of Madelyn being courted by the stern and leathery policeman. Why not? It had been long enough. Madelyn was a very sexy lady, and Jack Evans could be a very lucky man.

The day David left for Monte Carlo he mailed the two letters, one to Grace and one to Madelyn. Expect me on the twenty-sixth of May, he told them both, and he asked Madelyn to get the landscape people and house-cleaning crew out to Parsons to spruce up the place. The baron of River Road was coming home—for good.

It was after six o'clock when he checked into his hotel in Monte Carlo. He showered, changed clothes, and came back downstairs to the bar to buy himself the first really celebratory drink he had had since he sold his book: Not that he hadn't lifted a few when he first got the news, but drinking alone on his terrace in those silent hills wasn't the same as hunkering down on a barstool and finding his smiling, self-satisfied face among the others reflected in the smoky, flower-patterned mirror behind the bar.

David sipped the second Scotch slowly and used the mirror to survey the dimly lit cocktail lounge in back of him. The people at the occupied tables were lost in conversations that were animated and punctuated with laughter, or excited, with stabbing gestures of pointed fingers, or intimate, with caressing eyes and softly touching hands. A few people sat at tables alone, waiting. In a semicircular booth at the back of the bar a woman in a white dress sat alone in the darkness, her back to the far wall—waiting. David's eyes were repeatedly drawn to the indistinct face, as pale as a cameo, framed in dark hair, hauntingly familiar. Was she watching him? Her expression was unchanged as she slowly spun her stemmed wineglass on the polished surface of the table. He couldn't break his eyes from her dim reflection, and as he watched, she rose and walked toward the bar, toward him. Before her face became distinct he could only make out the white chiffon dress and the high-heeled white sandals.

My God! My God!

He wheeled on the barstool to face her as she came up behind him.

"Hello, David. I've been waiting for you."

"Grace! For Christ's sake! You—I thought you—"

"Oh, David! I didn't mean for you to think that. You do look like you've just seen a ghost. Did I look that much like her?"

He was still sitting on the high barstool with his feet spread on the floor for balance. She stepped between them, put her hands on his shoulders, and looked down into his still-startled face, waiting for him to answer.

"Yes, you looked that much like her," he said as he stood up. Her hands fell from his shoulders, and he caught and held them for a moment before turning her and guiding her back to the booth where she had been sitting. Neither spoke again until they had ordered drinks from the waitress who had followed them to the table with David's bar check.

"Will you kiss me, David, before you ask me a lot of questions?" She leaned toward him.

He took her face in his hands and kissed her slightly parted lips.

"Do you realize you almost gave me a heart attack, showing up like that?" There was no amusement, only reprimand, in his voice. The sternness was more than he had intended. He dropped his hands from her face and sat back to look at her. In the dim light she *was* Frony. Her appearance had shocked him so severely because he had feared that the apparition in the white dress was mind-invented, a haunting memory that had come to him countless times before. As he shook his head to dispel the illusion, another disturbing thought came. How could Grace dress the way her mother had that last night on the widow's walk, the night she died? Then he remembered he had never told Grace about Frony's appearance that night and how she had undressed for Son in the yard.

Grace followed his eyes.

"I shouldn't have worn this dress," she said solemnly. "I bought it, and the shoes, because I remember how you—I mean, on your trip with Mother—Christ! I didn't mean to shake you up like that. I feel like such a fool."

She sat with downcast eyes, her hands twisting miserably in her lap. This hadn't been the joyous reunion she had expected after their long separation. David knew he was acting like a displeased uncle—certainly not like the passionate lover she remembered. He was being a colossal disappointment, and he knew it. He put his hands on hers to stop the twisting.

"Grace, I'm glad you're here," he said and waited for her to raise her eyes to meet his. "Let's start over with that, and how lovely you look. You're absolutely sensational in that dress. I'm glad you wore it."

"Are you, David? You're not just saying that to keep me from feeling stupid?"

The waitress brought their drinks before David could answer. Grace had ordered wine and she slowly twirled the glass as she had when David observed her in the mirror. She waited for him to speak.

"Grace, I'm over my shock, and I can't imagine you sitting with me in this bar in Monte Carlo wearing anything but that white dress." David paused long enough to take a sip from his drink. "Now, I have about two dozen questions to ask you, but I have to have an answer to one right away."

"What's that, David?" She was apprehensive because he had spoken so seriously.

"Do you still love me?"

The trouble left her face, replaced by a broad smile. "Do I? God! Do I!" she cried and flung her arms around his neck. "And me, David?" she demanded. "Do you still love me?"

"More than I'll ever be able to tell you, my darling," David whispered into her ear.

The drinkers at several adjacent tables turned to look at them briefly. Neither really cared, but David pushed her gently away. It was time to talk. There were quite a few things he wanted to know about this little surprise party she had arranged for him.

"How did you know I'd be here?" he asked after she'd settled back down beside him in the booth and contented herself with hand-holding.

"You gave all the details in the last letter you wrote Madelyn. The name of the hotel and the day you were coming, everything except the time you'd get here. I just took my chances you'd be thirsty. You generally are."

David smiled at the pendulum swing in Grace's mood. Moments before she had been hand-wringingly miserable because of his less-than-enthusiastic welcome. Now she was comfortable enough to venture the wisecrack about his drinking habits. He thanked God for her emotional flexibility.

"I can see that two more years of higher education haven't taught you any more respect for your elders." The good humor in his voice was consistent with Grace's bantering tone. "You're still a smart-ass."

"If I weren't a smart-ass, you wouldn't be insanely in love with me." She ran her free hand up and down his arm. "I just don't want you to get drunk. Not tonight."

"I gather you have something in mind."

"I've had this in mind for almost two years, David." She took his hand and pressed it against the inside of her thigh.

"Before or after we eat?"

"Before. Now."

"Are you checked into this hotel?"

"No. I told the man at the desk I was waiting for my husband to show up. I was going to surprise him. I don't think he believed me." She giggled.

"Where's your luggage?"

"In the checkroom."

"Give me your passport. I've got to check you in and change rooms. My room has twin beds."

The desk clerk examined Grace's brand-new passport and smiled thinly when he reregistered them as Mr. and Mrs. David Fleming.

Their first coupling was wild and quick. The excitement that mounted in David reminded him of his adolescence. He had been celibate for over six weeks—no girls from the beach in Cannes; it had been too cold. Grace seemed sex-starved enough for him almost to believe her claim that he had been the last man to enter her.

They made love a second, less frantic time, after David ordered food sent to the room. They had eaten the food and drunk the wine, sitting naked at the serving cart, leering at each other, touching, fondling, whetting their sexual appetites as they ate. This bout in the bed was better, more satisfying, because it lasted longer. They did things with their hands and their mouths that they hadn't taken time for before.

"When did you decide to come to France, Grace?" David

asked. She had lain down beside him, and his lips moved in the hair at her temple.

"A month ago."

"I assume Madelyn knows you're here."

"She bought me the airline tickets."

"Will you not misunderstand if I ask you why you came? It's a pretty outrageous thing to do, you know."

"No. I understand. I've been waiting for you to ask me." She looked away for a moment and ran her hand over his chest while she thought of what she was going to say. "I wanted to find out about you and me, David. I kept telling myself you still loved me and that you were coming home and that—well, you never said anything in your letters about your plans—I mean, about me. I didn't even know whether you were coming home for my graduation, but even if you were, I didn't want to wait that long. If I'm going to be part of your future, I want to know it now."

Her face had grown serious and all the levity had left her voice as she talked. She was giving it to him straight.

"I just mailed a letter to you, Grace, about my coming home for your graduation. It didn't say much about the future, but I'll tell you now. You *are* my future." Her sharp intake of breath—almost a gasp—indicated the effect his words had had on her. He turned and kissed her before she could respond. "We've got some time to think about the future. Let's think about what we're going to do *now*. How long have you got?"

"Six days," Grace said exultantly. "That's how long I've got. It's just going to be you and me for six long goddamn days. This trip is your graduation present to me, David. You're paying for it, so I hope you enjoy it. I used what was left in the account you set up for me."

"God, I'm glad you're here," David said for the second time as he pulled her to him. "I'm glad you spent the money that way. But that's not your graduation present. There'll be something else. What would you really like to have?"

"I'd like to plan the next six days," she answered quickly. "I've thought about this ever since I decided to come."

"Okay. What do you want to do?"

"I want you to take me to the Casino tomorrow night so I can see all those jaded men and women you wrote about in your book."

"Do you want to go tearing-ass out of the Casino to catch the train to Rome?" The idea appealed to him. He had caught some of her excitement.

"No, not Rome. Florence. I checked the train schedule. We can make it if we leave by twelve thirty. I want to fuck on the train, in one of those little compartments, with the outside shade up. I want you to buy me an opal ring on the Ponte Vecchio. I've got enough money with me to pay my share of everything but the ring. The ring is the extra thing I want as a graduation present."

At Monte Carlo Grace glowed. Her raven hair shone; it cascaded to her bare shoulders and bounced with the energy of her restless movements. The excitement was in her lovely, flawless face. Her mouth was never completely closed; sheer joy parted her lips. She was glorious in the white dress and she turned men's heads. She leaned over the gambling tables so that they could see her nipples. Jealous women glowered at their gaping, inattentive husbands and lovers.

For the second time David had brought the loveliest of all. And for the second time he ran down the Casino steps to catch a midnight train.

As the train rolled out of the station, they drank red wine and ate French bread and cheese with the lights on. One hour later and fifty miles across the Italian border, they turned out the lights and made love on the hard bunk of the train compartment, with the outside shades up.

The opal David bought Grace on the Ponte Vecchio was oval, bigger than a dime, bigger than any he had bought Frony. Wherever they were, she would turn her hand so that the ring could catch the light, and the fire would flash from the stone. They spent two days and two nights in Florence, submerged more in themselves than in the art, languishing till midmorning in bed in their Renaissance room in the Hotel Berchielli on the west bank of the Arno, strolling the streets, fighting for seats in the Ristorante Il Latini, where enormous hams hung from the ceiling.

When they returned to Monaco, they stayed in the casino till dawn, ate omelettes and French doughnuts before they went to bed, and slept until early afternoon. As they lay in bed on the second such afternoon, Grace made an observation.

"You don't really like to gamble, do you?"

David thought for a minute and realized she was right.

"No, not really," he admitted, "but I'd like to know what brought you to that conclusion."

"The way you bet when you're at the tables. You won't bet enough to win much or lose much. You're probably not a hundred bucks one way or the other."

"Are you saying I'm a chicken-shit gambler?"

"No. I'm saying you go to the casino for a different reason. You gamble just enough to keep up appearances. You really go to watch the people."

She was right about that, too. He admitted it.

"Yes, I do go mostly to look at the people. It fascinates me to see that kind of elegance, all those jeweled women and super-sophisticated men. I get tired of it after a few days."

"Are you tired of it now?"

He propped himself up in bed and looked down at her. They had both been lying on their backs, talking up to the ceiling.

"I have a feeling you're working up to something."

"I am, so answer me. Have you had enough of the casino?"

"Yes, I guess I have."

"Then, let's go to your place. I've got two more nights, and I want to play house." She turned on her side and looked up at him expectantly. "What do you say, lover? Want to?"

"Yeah, I want to," he said and sat up abruptly. "Get up and pack. We can make it in time to buy stuff to cook our dinner tonight."

As the time grew closer for Grace to leave, she became quieter. Often David would catch her staring at him, her face serious, contemplative. They were seldom apart, even for a few minutes, but if he was in another part of the house, momentarily away from her, she would come looking for him, not using any pretext of having something to tell him or to ask him. She would slip her arms around his waist and raise her face to be kissed.

The morning of the day she was to leave—it was Saturday and her flight was at three o'clock in the afternoon—they had breakfast on the terrace. She took her coffee cup and made a slow circuit of the terrace, pausing occasionally to look at the hills that were lightly shrouded in the morning mist.

"I don't want to leave, David." She was standing with her back to him, leaning on her elbows over the terrace's low stone wall.

David got up and went over to stand beside her. They both looked down the slope of the hill that fell sharply away from the side of the house. In the valley five hundred feet below several cottagers worked in garden patches.

"You like it here, don't you?" he asked.

"Here?" The question in her voice surprised him. "Oh, yes. I like it well enough here. It's beautiful. I understand now why you wanted to work here. But that's not what I meant. I don't want to leave *you*. I'm afraid you won't come back."

"I told you I was coming back, Grace," he reminded her. "It will only be a little over two months."

"But are you coming home for good, David?" She turned to face him, leaning on one elbow, her hip against the stone wall. "You said a week ago we'd think about the future—that *I* was your future—but we haven't really talked about it."

"Okay. Let's talk about it. There are a lot of things we need to—"

"How rich are you, David?"

The question startled him. Grace had never seemed to be that interested in money.

"I'm not rich, Grace. Not yet. Why do you ask?"

"But you don't really have to work. I mean, go back to the university, do you?"

"No, I don't have to, not for a while anyway."

"Are you going back? Madelyn said Dr. Johnson will have to know early in the summer."

Grace was dissembling, scouting around the edges of what she really wanted to talk about, afraid to be too direct. She didn't give a damn about the money, or whether he was going back to the university. She wanted to ask him how she could be part of his future if he didn't know what it was. She wanted to tell him that the time had come for some stability in his life and that she wanted to be the stabilizer. She wanted him to do something about *her*—for God's sake!

David knew it; her intent wasn't lost on him. The time had come for his commitment.

"I'll decide when I come home. What I do depends a great deal on you."

"On me? You know I want you to stay home. You belong at Parsons no matter—"

"And you belong at Parsons with me," he interrupted. He had continued to look into the valley as they talked. Now he turned to look into her wide gray eyes. "I want you to marry me, Grace, because I love you more than life. Will you marry me, my darling, and come to Parsons and be my bride?"

She had caught her breath when she realized what he was asking her. Now she exhaled explosively.

"Yes. Oh, God! Yes. Yes. I'll marry you."

She threw her arms around his neck and kissed him wildly. When she broke away, she held his face in her hands.

"When, David? When can we get married?"

"Whenever you say."

"Now. Today. Let's get married today."

He chuckled and took her hands from his face and held them. "No. Not today. We're in France, my impetuous sweetheart. It takes a little time over here. And you've got to go back and do what's necessary for me to watch my fiancée graduate from college."

"The day after commencement, then." Her eyes danced, waiting for him to say yes.

"Okay, June sixth. Go home and buy yourself a wedding dress."

Grace turned, picked up the coffee cup, and threw it down the hill, the equivalent, for her, of breaking a wineglass in the fireplace. Then she held out her hand to him.

"Come inside. I want to give you something to think about until the sixth of June."

At the airport they sat talking quietly, holding hands, waiting for her boarding call. When it came, they stood up and kissed quickly, and she turned away, only to stop after a few steps.

"Don't fuck any more of those beach girls before you come home," she said loudly enough for a number of hurrying passengers to hear and look up at them. David's face burned in embarrassment as she was lost in the stream of people going through the gate. He stood there wondering how she knew about the girls from the beach.

Chapter Twenty

The landscapers had done a good job at Parsons. The grounds had been manicured and had a late-spring lushness when David got home at the end of May. The inside of the house sparkled. Madelyn had overseen the housecleaning crew. She told him in exquisite detail about the mess old man Varnell had left behind for her to clean up.

Grace wouldn't let him sleep with her. There wasn't any sudden moral fastidiousness in her denial. "I told you in France I wanted you to think about it until the sixth of June," she had reminded him. "Anyway, it's not even two weeks. You can wait that long." So he went to bed early every night after she and Madelyn put him into a semicoma talking about the wedding.

"I've decided I want to get married in the living room at Parsons," Grace announced the first night he was home.

"Well, I—" he began before Madelyn agreed with Grace.

"Yes, David. That's the best solution. None of us goes to church, unless you reformed while you were in France, so a home wedding will solve the problem."

"What problem?" he asked.

"Of picking out a church," Grace said a little impatiently.

"I don't even know a preacher," David admitted. "Does either of you?"

"I asked Reverend Simmons," Grace said.

He had to think for a few moments to place him. "The guy up at the chapel on campus?"

"Yes," Grace confirmed. "He's sort of nondenominational. He seemed like a logical choice."

"He'll be fine," David said, "but isn't it a little funny to have a wedding in the groom's house?"

"Since when have you worried about that kind of etiquette?" Madelyn asked a little testily. "It'll give the people around here something to talk about. Let's get on with it. You'll have to give me a guest list tonight. The invitations are printed and I've got to get them in the mail tomorrow."

For the first time David realized that he didn't really know anybody in his hometown well enough to invite to his wedding. All his old friends were either gone or dead—thanks largely to Son.

"Well, let's see," he said as he tried to think of whom he could invite. "There are a few people at school, maybe a half dozen."

"That's enough, if they bring their wives," Madelyn said practically. She sat with her pencil poised over her writing pad. "Who are they?"

He could only think of five. "Maybe I should ask Dean Johnson," he said speculatively.

Madelyn looked up at him from her pad. "Does that mean you've decided to go back on faculty in the fall?"

"It means I'm thinking about it. Inviting him to the wedding won't be any kind of commitment. I just want to be on his good side in case I decide to go back."

Grace looked pleased. She reached over and squeezed his hand.

"Who's going to stand up with you, David?" Madelyn asked.

"What? Oh, you mean best man. My God! I hadn't thought about that." He was having enough trouble just thinking of people to invite. Who in the hell could he ask to be best man? A friend of his who worked on the paper in New York would come if he could get away. "Maybe I could get Bill Petrie to come down."

"You better call him first thing in the morning and find out," Madelyn instructed. "What will you do if he can't come?"

"Well, I don't know."

"Couldn't you ask Mr. Evans?" Grace offered.

David looked at her in dismay. "You mean the policeman, Lieutenant Evans?"

"Captain Evans," Madelyn corrected, color coming into her face. "I wrote you that he had been promoted to Gil's job."

Madelyn's reaction convinced David his speculations about her and Evans had been correct.

"Well, I've only met Jack Evans a couple of times, but he seems like as good a candidate as anybody else around here." He felt a little foolish admitting that he was prepared to ask someone he hardly knew to play the role that should be filled by a lifelong friend. But he could tell that Madelyn was pleased. What the hell! It really didn't make any difference to him. So if it made Madelyn happy, why not?

Petrie couldn't come, but David postponed talking to Jack Evans until Madelyn couldn't stand it any longer and invited him to dinner. As David drove to Madelyn's house, already late, he crept along, worrying about how he was going to ask a man he still called "Mister" to be best man in his wedding. As it turned out, it was remarkably easy. He hadn't counted on Madelyn's cunning or the comfort of Jack Evans's personality. When he thought about it later, he realized that Madelyn had probably prepared Evans to be asked, maybe even practiced with him the way she would manipulate the conversation to the point where it would have been awkward if David hadn't asked. His acceptance was natural and gracious. Of course, they were Jack and David to each other by then, and had been since early in the evening. David liked the man enormously, admired his quiet strength, his obvious intelligence, his unmistakable devotion to Madelyn. David hoped he was sleeping with her.

The two men left the house together and walked to their cars at the curb. There was a special warmth to their handshake as they were saying good night.

"I'd like to thank you, Jack," David said a little hesitantly as he was about to open his door. "This all must seem a little—uh—peculiar, my asking you to do such a personal thing."

"Not at all. I know I'm doing what you would have asked Glenn Walker to do. It's what I would have asked Gil Thomas to do. The sad thing is that we both need substitutes. If the shoe were on the other foot, I would probably ask you. Madelyn would see to that."

The implication of what Evans had said wasn't lost on David, and he was tired of wondering, so he asked, "Jack, I won't say it's none of my business, because it is. Madelyn is the closest thing to family I have. If I said I thought you were in love with her, that you were in love with each other, would I be right?"

"Is it that obvious?"

"Like high school sophomores are obvious."

He laughed with David. "God! I thought I was being so cool about it. Madelyn wanted to try me out on you, see how we got along, before she told you. I guess I screwed it up for her; she wanted to tell you herself. Look, we better go. They're both probably looking out the window wondering what the hell we're talking about. Can we get together in the next day or so? There are some things a little less romantic I want to go over with you."

"That sounds ominous." David had so far successfully avoided any detailed recounting of the horror he had experienced two years before. He and Madelyn and Grace had skirted its edges, carefully avoiding any full entry into that painful territory. Now he was apprehensive. "Has anything turned up—"

"No. No, nothing like that. Just a few details to clear up before you and Grace take off on your honeymoon."

"Do you want me to come downtown to your office?"

"Not necessarily. Why don't you invite me over to Parsons for a couple of drinks and a tour of the place? The circumstances were—not very pleasant when I saw it a couple of years ago."

"Okay. How about tomorrow night?"

"Hmm. No, I've got to—well, not tomorrow. How about the day after, about six thirty?"

"Fine. That will give me time to lay in some supplies. I'll grill you a steak." David paused, then asked, "We don't want the women around, do we?"

"I think not. Good night, David."

Jack Evans arrived before David had everything set up in the field, so he helped carry stuff from the kitchen and the storage room at the back of the house. He was wearing slacks and a sport shirt open at the throat, and the look of the austere policeman had vanished with the coat and tie David had never seen him without. He sat down, stretched his long legs out straight in front of him, and accepted the drink he was offered.

"Thank you, David," he said with a sigh of anticipation. "I'm going to enjoy this."

"Did you work today?" It was Sunday, and David remembered another time when Jack had said, "We work on Sunday."

"Yes, I generally do. You wouldn't believe what people do to each other on Saturday night."

"I believe," David said, remembering what one man had done on a Saturday morning. "Well, you've had enough of it for one day. Let's talk about you and Madelyn before we get into the other things you wanted to go over. Mind filling me in?"

"No. I don't mind, but I thought she would have told you by now."

"She really hasn't had a chance. Seems she's been busy planning a wedding and asking me every five minutes if I plan to stay here or take Grace off to live in Europe."

"I hope you decide to live here, for everybody's sake. I know it's what Grace wants, and Madelyn, too. She's very fond of you, David. Wants you and Grace around. She'd be very lonely if both of you were gone."

"I've told Madelyn I'm home for good. She's just skeptical. Anyway, I had the idea you would keep her from getting very lonely."

Evans laughed. "It's not the same thing, David. I'm just in love with her; I'm not part of her family, at least not yet." He paused long enough to notice the raised-eyebrow look of inquiry David gave him. "Oh, I very definitely want to marry Madelyn. We've talked about it, and I think she wants to get married. I honestly believe she's waiting for you to tell her it's okay. You were Glenn's best friend, David, and I think Madelyn thinks you're the only one who has a right to criticize what she does. She wants you to say it's all right for her to love somebody else, that it's not disloyal to Glenn."

"That's pretty ridiculous, Jack. I've never known a woman more independent than Madelyn. If I told her I didn't think she ought to get married, she'd tell me to go jump."

"I hope so, but for some reason I don't think so. As you say, she is one hell of an independent woman, but I think she's still got emotional problems about Glenn. She's told me how it was with them, and I'm glad she did. At first she wouldn't talk about it, but when she finally did, when she cried on my shoulder and let me share the grief, I think she allowed herself to start loving me. It's hard for me to make her understand that I expect her to grieve, even after we're married. I don't want her to forget Glenn. That would take too much of her life away from her."

David sat and looked at Jack Evans's strong face. What he had just said was the most emotionally mature thing David had ever heard. Madelyn was fortunate indeed to be loved by this intelligent and gentle man.

"What do you want me to do, Jack?"

"I want you to tell her that it's all right to be in love with me, or anybody else she wants to be in love with. She desperately needs somebody she respects to tell her that. And if you approve of our getting married, tell her that, too." Suddenly Evans leaned toward David in his chair. "My God! I've just asked you to approve of your lifelong friend marrying someone who's almost a total stranger. I apologize for that. Let's let it drop until Madelyn can tell you how she feels and we can get to know each other better. I'll appreciate it if you don't mention to her what I've said."

"Of course not. I'll let her tell me all about it. But if it will make you sleep better tonight, I'll tell you that I don't consider you a stranger." David studied Evans for another moment. "As a matter of fact, I don't think I'm going to get to know you much better. Now, let me fix you another drink."

The flood of relief on the policeman's face was the only response he made.

They carried their drinks with them as David conducted the promised tour of Parsons. They went through the house and then walked the grounds, coming to stand at the escarpment's edge.

David was sure the same thoughts were running through both their minds.

"I'd better go light the charcoal or it will be too dark to eat outside," David said, and they both turned away from the threatening ledge. "While the fire's getting ready you can start with the stuff we've avoided talking about."

Evans helped himself to another drink and mixed one for David as he prepared the fire. The detective sat down in the lawn chair and waited for his host to join him.

"Has Grace said anything about wanting to sell the house?" Evans asked when David turned away from the grill and picked up his drink.

"No, she hasn't. Does she want to sell it?"

"She talked about it before she went over to see you in France. She hasn't mentioned it, that I know of, since she came back."

"I guess she thought she'd need the money," David reflected. "I don't see any reason for her to sell it, unless it's a nuisance. Is that what you wanted to talk about?"

"Part of it. I've discouraged Grace from pursuing the sale of the house, at least for the time being. I really haven't explained to her what's involved. She'd have to go to court and have Frony declared legally dead. It can be done—has been done to settle estates—but it's not easy after just a couple of years. You'd have to give testimony because you're the only one who has firsthand knowledge of the presumed cause of death."

"What do you mean 'presumed'? The court will have the deposition I signed at the time of the inquest. I spelled it all out in vivid detail. I saw her thrown off that cliff back there. Nobody could have survived that fall. Most of the grand jurors came out here to see for themselves. I don't see why I would even have to testify."

"It would just be a court procedure. There wouldn't be a jury; the judge would make a ruling. You have to realize the difference in the legal actions involved. Your deposition was accepted by a grand jury, not a court with a sitting judge. But the grand jury didn't take any action. Do you know exactly how a grand jury functions?"

"Well, no, I guess I don't," David admitted.

"In this state, most states for that matter, twelve people are selected from a panel of about twenty candidates for a ninety-day term. Their job is to examine evidence presented by the district attorney's office to see whether someone has committed an indictable offense. There are three options open to the jury: They can vote an indictment; they can vote for dismissal, which is called a 'no bill'; or they can just do nothing, that is, not take any action at all. That's not exactly correct, but I'll get back to that in a minute. In this case there wasn't anybody to indict. At the time of the hearing there was such strong evidence that the perpetrator of homicide, Son, was also deceased that there wasn't any pressure for 'indictment in absentia,' which sometimes happens. There wasn't any case against anybody else, so there wasn't much sense in voting a 'no bill.' The net result is that they just didn't do anything."

"You said that wasn't exactly right," David reminded him. "What did you mean by that?"

Evans sat for a while twirling his glass in his hands, considering, David assumed, what he was going to say.

"The grand jury can, in effect, keep the case open by recommending that the next grand jury review the case records as a sort of continuing investigation. That's what happened in this case, David." He paused and took a long swallow from his drink. "This is the seventh grand jury to examine the records upon recommendation from the preceding one. Not one goddamned new piece of evidence has been turned up, and won't be, but they won't close the case. They're fascinated with it. It's the most bizarre multiple homicide in the state's history, and they just won't let it go."

David sat and stared at Jack Evans, not really understanding the significance of what he had been told. He got up and put the meat on the fire while he formulated the question he wanted to ask. He took the glasses and mixed them both half a drink when Evans held his thumb and forefinger together to indicate he wanted a "little" one.

"You mean that only the morbid interest these juries have in this case, and not any other real reason, has kept it from being closed?"

"Yes, I guess that's about it."

"And that's the reason it's not a good idea to try to settle the thing with the house? I mean, it wouldn't be all that easy to go to court and get Frony declared dead while they're still passing the thing along?"

"That's right. I'd advise Grace to wait if I were you. She's probably not worried about it now, anyway. You can see what this jury does. They only have about a month left on their term."

David got up and turned the steaks.

"How do you like yours?" he asked.

"Rare."

"Okay. About two more minutes. Want to put the salad in those two bowls?"

They ate steak, salad, and rolls on individual folding picnic tables. Once they'd finished, they carried a load back to the kitchen and returned with mugs of coffee to go with their after-dinner cigarettes.

"Jack, doesn't the grand jury accept the recommendation of the district attorney's office in cases like this?" David asked after they had been sitting silently for a few minutes.

"I don't quite follow you, David."

"Well, they've been rehashing this thing every three months for almost two years. Doesn't the district attorney's office think that's a tremendous waste of time? Wouldn't they close the case if the district attorney's office asked them to?"

"I don't know—they might. They wouldn't have to."

David sat and looked at Jack Evans in the fading twilight. There was an almost imperceptible note of evasiveness in his voice. David was getting into something he sensed the policeman didn't want to talk about.

"Then the district attorney has never asked them to close the case, has he?" David asked, knowing the answer from what Evans had said before.

"No, he hasn't." There was resignation in the way he said it.

"Why not, Jack?"

"We never found Son, David. In two years we should have—"

"You told Madelyn you didn't think you'd ever find him. You said that wasn't unusual when it came to recovering bodies from the river. You told me yourself you had never pulled one out of the river with a hook."

"I didn't say we never found them, eventually."

"What about what you told Madelyn?"

"What did you want me to tell her, David?" He leaned forward with his forearms on his thighs and looked questioningly into David's challenging face.

David couldn't believe what Evans was implying. The thought was staggering, and he had to be sure.

"You mean the district attorney doesn't believe—you don't believe—Son is dead?"

"Look, David, it's not as simple as what I believe or the DA believes. The initial presumption of death was based on the description of where you put the holes in Son and the tremendous loss of blood that was apparent when we went down into the tunnel. At the time, the coroner agreed that the possibility of survival was so remote that the presumption of death was completely justifiable. But when we couldn't turn up Son's body after a couple of months, the coroner reexamined your statement. You said the first two bullets, the forty-fours, went in below the rib cage on the left side and high on the left shoulder. The thirty-twos hit him just under the right collarbone, in the right hip, and high between his shoulder blades a little to right of center. You didn't know whether the last two shots, the ones you fired into the water, hit him at all." Evans got up, walked a few paces, dug a cigarette lighter out of his pants pocket, and sat back down. He lit a cigarette before he continued. "As I said, the coroner got curious when Son hadn't come out of the river after a couple of months. He began to think in terms of vital organs the bullets would have hit. He went over and over it, reviewing anatomical diagrams, moving the points of bullet entry an inch or so one way or the other to compensate for any possible inaccuracy in what you remembered. He concluded that no absolutely vital organ had to have been hit. In his final analysis there was no justification for unequivocal presumption of death; the gunshots were not necessarily lethal. That's what he told the original grand jury before their term expired. In his opinion, Son actually could have survived."

Jack Evans flipped his cigarette into the grass and sat back, looking into David's rigid face. He hadn't wanted to say all this, but he had been pressed. It occurred to David that maybe the pressing had enabled Evans to unload something that obviously was bothering him—the thing he really wanted to talk about but didn't know how to approach. Why else had he really come to Parsons? David asked himself. Certainly not just to ask him to be his advocate with Madelyn or to tell him Grace shouldn't go through the court procedure necessary to sell the house. That was only the prologue. David hated the question he had to ask now. He felt the rush of that two-year-old horror.

"Jack, do you believe Son is still alive?"

"I don't know, David." He seemed to have anticipated the question. "It's not reasonable that he could be, but I just don't know."

But David had to know what Jack Evans really thought.

"If you were a betting man, would you bet he was dead?"

Just a flicker of hesitation showed before he answered, a reluctance in his eyes that David could just barely see in the gathering darkness. "No, David, I wouldn't."

And now the final question. A shiver of dread ran up David's back before he asked it.

"Frony, Jack, what about Frony? You don't think she's dead, either, do you?"

"No, David, I don't."

They talked about it. David argued what he had seen, what he had done, and Jack Evans quietly agreed. David was probably right, he said. It was a policeman's job to be skeptical, he said. There were plenty of cases where bodies had never been found, he concurred. But by the time David walked with him to his car in the pale light of the rising moon, his conviction had weakened and the unformed specters of calamity had begun to build in his mind.

Premonition brought him back into the field to sit and smoke and wait, not for the lantern face to appear in the dark of the woods, but for her ghost, the flutter of white on the widow's walk. When it came an hour later—materializing slowly from the back of the platform until the outline was sharp, whiter, more pronounced against the rail than before—all the terror that had come to occupy David's mind was gone. He walked slowly across the field, watching the whiteness fade into gray, to the final subliminal fluttering on the empty widow's walk.

There was no urgency in his steps as David climbed the three flights of stairs. There would be no waiting beast, no resurrected lost love in white chiffon, no clue left behind on the bare platform floor. For five minutes he stood at the rail and looked south toward the river. The light murmur of it seemed to come to him on the gentle wind, and with it the vision of moon-brightened sand and a lovely girl with outstretched arms. He closed his eyes to obliterate the agony of memory and turned to start the slow descent of the stairs, the deliberate reenactment of the ritual. He entered the study and stared down at the note in the center of his desk—the horrible threat in the single line of disciplined lettering.

"I shall be with you on your wedding night."

THE NURSERY

by David Lippincott

Harriet and Henry Griggs just loved little girls. Hadn't they come to Maryland, built Blossom House because they understood so well? They knew that—even on her wedding day—a rebellious little girl like Jennifer Delafield had to be snatched from the arms of the young man who would surely harm her. They knew that little girls had to be watched, protected, taught to obey—and kept from harm forever in THE NURSERY.   A DELL BOOK   16474-5 $3.50

Stranger in the House

by Patricia J. Macdonald

After ten years, no one believed her, but Anna knew her missing child was still alive. And now her faith was rewarded: Paul had been found! He was coming home. But Anna would never forget that day fear walked in the door—and a danger that threatened her family, her marriage and life itself. Someone had a secret. Someone still wanted her son. Someone who would not give up until Paul was dead and gone—forever.

A DELL BOOK   18455-X $3.50